黑暗传

胡崇峻 搜集整理

张立玉 臧军娜 英译

[美] H.W. Lan 审校

"十三五"国家重点图书
中国南方民间文学典籍英译丛书
丛书主编 张立玉

THE LEGEND OF DARKNESS

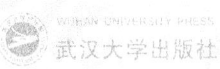
武汉大学出版社

·汉英对照·

图书在版编目(CIP)数据

黑暗传:汉英对照/胡崇峻搜集整理;张立玉,臧军娜英译.—武汉:武汉大学出版社,2019.9(2025.8重印)
中国南方民间文学典籍英译丛书/张立玉主编
"十三五"国家重点图书
ISBN 978-7-307-21033-2

Ⅰ.黑… Ⅱ.①胡… ②张… ③臧… Ⅲ.史诗—中国—汉、英 Ⅳ.I227.3

中国版本图书馆 CIP 数据核字(2019)第 138238 号

责任编辑:罗晓华　　责任校对:汪欣怡　　版式设计:韩闻锦

出版发行:**武汉大学出版社**　　(430072　武昌　珞珈山)
（电子邮箱:cbs22@whu.edu.cn　网址:www.wdp.whu.edu.cn）
印刷:湖北云景数字印刷有限公司
开本:720×1000　1/16　印张:25.25　字数:303千字
版次:2019年9月第1版　2025年8月第4次印刷
ISBN 978-7-307-21033-2　　定价:78.00元

版权所有,不得翻印;凡购我社的图书,如有质量问题,请与当地图书销售部门联系调换。

丛书编委会

学术顾问

王宏印　李正栓

主编

张立玉

副主编

起国庆

编委会成员（按姓氏笔画排列）

邓之宇	王向松	艾　芳	石定乐	龙江莉	刘　纯
陈兰芳	汤　茜	李克忠	杨　柳	杨筱奕	张立玉
张扬扬	张　瑛	和六花	依旺的	保俊萍	起国庆
陶开祥	鲁　钒	蔡　蔚	臧军娜		

序

近年来，民族典籍英译捷报频传，硕果累累。韩家全教授等人的壮族系列经典翻译陆续出版，王宏印教授等人的系列民族典籍英译研究著作已经问世，李正栓教授等人的藏族格言诗英译著作不断在国内外出版，王维波教授等人的东北民族典籍英译著作纷纷付梓，李昌银教授等人的"云南少数民族经典作品英译文库"于2018年年底出版，其他民族典籍英译作品也在接踵而至。

近日，中南民族大学张立玉教授传来佳音：他们要出版"十三五"国家重点图书——"中国南方民间文学典籍英译丛书"。虽叫民间文学，其实基本上都是民族典籍。这一系列包括十本书，它们是：《黑暗传》《哭嫁歌》《哈尼阿培聪坡坡》《彝族民间故事》《南方民间创世神话选集》《查姆》《召树屯》《娥并与桑洛》《金笛》《梅葛》。其中，好几本是云南少数民族的。只有一本是汉族典籍，即《黑暗传》。很有意思的是，这些典籍展示了不同民族的创世史诗或诸如此类的东西。

《黑暗传》以民间歌谣唱本形象地描述了盘古开天辟地结束混沌黑暗，人类起源及社会发展的历程，融合了混沌、盘古、女娲、伏羲、炎帝神农氏、黄帝轩辕氏等众多英雄人物在洪荒时代艰难创世的一系列神话传说。它被称为汉族首部创世史诗。《哈尼阿培聪坡坡》是一部完整地记载哈尼族历史沿革的长篇史诗，堪称哈尼族的"史记"，长5000余行，以现实主义手法记叙了哈尼族祖先在各个历史时期的迁徙情况，并对其迁徙各地的原因、路线、途程，各个迁居地的社会生活、生产、风习、宗教，以及与毗邻民族的关系等，均作了详细而生动的辑录，因而该作品不仅具有文学价值，而且具有重大的历史学、社会学及宗教学价值。《南方民间创世神话选集》包括一些创世神话，主要是关于世界起源和人类起源的神话。本书所列包括生活在广泛地域的民族，如门巴族、珞巴族、怒族、基诺族、普米族、拉祜族、傈僳族、毛南族、德昂族、景颇族、阿昌族、布朗族、佤族、独龙族、水族、仡佬族、布依族、仫佬族、高山族和侗族等。这些神话不仅讲述了世界的起源，也讲述了人类的始祖，以及人类对世界的改造。《梅葛》是彝族的一部长篇史诗，流传在云南省楚雄州的姚安、大姚等彝族地区。"梅葛"本为一种彝族歌调的名称，由于人们采用这种调子来唱彝族的创世史，因而创世史诗被称为"梅葛"。《查姆》是一部彝族史诗，是彝族人民唱天地、日月、人类、种子、风雨、树木等起源的长篇史诗，被彝族人民当作本民族的历史来看待。

其余几本书展示了一些少数民族的风俗习惯、恋爱故事、斗争故事等。《哭嫁歌》是土家族文化典籍。"哭嫁"是土家族姑娘在出嫁时进行的一种用歌声来诉说自己在封建买办婚姻制度下不幸命运的活动，是指土家族姑娘的抒情歌谣，富有诗韵和乐感，融哀、怨、喜和乐为一体，以婉转的曲调向世人展示土家人独特的"哭"文化。《彝族民间故事》是一部以流传于云南楚雄彝族自治州彝族人民中间的民间故事为主体，同时覆盖全省包括小凉山等彝族地区的民间故事集。这些故事丰富多彩，从中能看到民族民间故事的各种形态和生动、奇妙而颇具彝族民族特色的文化特征。《召树屯》是傣族民间长篇叙事诗，叙述了傣族佛教世俗典籍《贝叶经·召树屯》中一个古老的传说故事。这部叙事诗一直为傣族人民所传唱，历久不衰。《娥并与桑洛》是一部优美生动的叙事诗，一个凄美的爱情悲剧。《金笛》是一部苗族长篇叙事诗，富于变幻性和传奇性，尽情铺叙扎董丕冉与蒙诗彩奏的悲欢离合，热情赞颂他们在与魔虎的激烈斗争中所表现出来的坚贞不屈、英勇顽强的精神，许多情节含有浓郁的民族特色。

这些故事都很引人入胜，都很符合国家文化发展需求，向世人讲述中国故事，传播中华文化，并且讲述的是民族故事，充分体现了党和国家对各民族的关怀。

民族典籍英译是传播中国文化、文学和文明的重要途径，是中华文化"走出去"的重要组成部分，是国家战略，是提高文化"软实力"的重要方式，在文化交流和文明建设中起着不可或缺的作用，对提升中国国际话语权和构建中国对外话语体系以及对建设世界文学都有积极意义。

中国民族典籍使世界文化更加丰富多彩、绚丽多姿。我国各民族典籍中折射出的文化多样性极大地丰富了世界多元、特色鲜明的文化。人们对多样性形成全新的认识角度和思维方式，有助于开阔视野，丰富思考问题的角度，挖掘这些经典中的教育价值和文化价值，对世界其他民族都有指导和借鉴意义，并且有助于建设我国的文化自信。

民族典籍翻译与研究事业关乎国家的稳定统一，关乎民族关系的和谐发展，关乎世界多元文化的实现。在中国，民族典籍资源极为丰富，有待进一步挖掘、翻译，仍有许多少数民族典籍亟待拯救，民族典籍翻译与研究工作任重而道远，民族典籍翻译事业大有可为。

李正栓[①]

2019 年 7 月 19 日

[①] 李正栓，中国英汉语比较研究会典籍英译专业委员会常务副会长兼秘书长；中国中医药研究促进会传统文化翻译与国际传播专业委员会常务主任委员。

前　言

　　《黑暗传》是一部汉族民间神话历史叙事长诗，被称为"汉民族首部创世史诗"。著名神话学者袁珂认为它是"汉民族广义神话史诗"。《黑暗传》是明清以来广泛流传于神农架及周边地区的"孝歌""丧鼓歌"，以七言韵文为主体，在丧葬仪式中由大歌师以隆重形式演唱。

　　《黑暗传》主要内容从宇宙生成、天地开辟、洪水泡天、人类再造一直唱到人祖创世，时空背景广阔，叙事结构宏大，内容古朴神奇。它承担了丧葬仪典中的一部分娱神功能和教化功能，用孝歌形式宣扬对父母及先祖要尽忠尽孝，对民族历史要寻根求源，蕴涵了中华民族以"忠孝爱国"为核心的民族精神。《黑暗传》在思想文化内涵上还展现了儒家的入世精神、伦理要求，佛教的因果轮回、历劫成佛观念及道教的丹药修行、隐逸山林的精神追求。总之，其中蕴涵的"文化精华"是深厚的中华古文化积淀。

　　本次翻译的原文选自胡崇峻先生搜集整理的《黑暗传》版本，由长江文艺出版社于2002年4月出版发行。分为开场歌、歌头、歌尾及天地玄黄、黑暗混沌、日月合明与人祖创世四部分内容。

　　译者除了潜心对《黑暗传》进行大量的文本研究外，还曾数次奔赴神农架及周边地区，对《黑暗传》起源地进行实地调查。通过田野调查，译者对《黑暗传》的传承语境及研究现状有了更清晰和具体的认识。在此基础上，译者采用综合性的翻译模式,在翻译过程中尽量展现《黑暗传》这一汉民族神话长诗的语言诗性特征、文化表征特征和口头表征特征。

在全面深化改革开放的新时代,翻译"汉民族神话史诗"——《黑暗传》,表达了我们对中华传统文化、思想的认同和尊崇。我们希望在中华文化二次传播过程中,通过英译《黑暗传》,能更加增强我们的文化自信,增强民族自信力与自豪感,增强中华民族的凝聚力,从而推进中华民族伟大复兴崇高使命的进程。

张立玉　臧军娜

2019年5月于南湖书斋

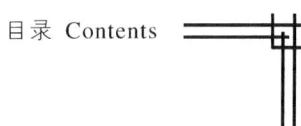

目　　录

开场歌 ………………………………………………… 2
歌头 …………………………………………………… 30
一、天地玄黄 ………………………………………… 34
二、黑暗混沌 ………………………………………… 116
三、日月合明 ………………………………………… 162
四、人祖创世 ………………………………………… 204
歌尾 …………………………………………………… 388

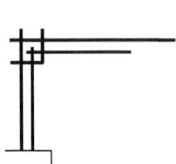

黑暗传　The Legend of Darkness

Contents

The Opening Song ·· 3
The Beginning of the Song ·· 31
I. Before Creation ··· 35
II. Darkness and Chaos ·· 117
III. The Sun and the Moon Illuminating Together ············ 163
IV. Human Ancestors' Inventions ································ 205
Coda ··· 389

开 场 歌①

东边一朵红云起，
西边一朵紫云开。
谁个孝家开歌场？
引得四方歌师来。

开歌路，歌路开，
起歌楼，搭歌台，
千山万水聚拢来。
脚踏山来山也动，
脚踏水，浪花翻。
脚踏龙，龙抬头，
老虎豹子齐逃散，
不顾生死往前赶。

---

① 开场歌，又叫开歌路、起歌头、歌头等。采用了10种孝歌歌头仪式歌谣综合而成。开场歌头是由歌师在门外十字路口开始，直到孝家门前，正好进孝堂转丧的歌调。歌头有长有短，根据情况灵活掌握，长的歌头能唱三个多小时，从盘古到三十六朝，人称"小黑暗传"。

开场歌　The Opening Song

The Opening Song[1]

A red cloud is flowering in the east,
and a purple cloud is blooming in the west.
Which pious family's opening song,
is bringing forth masters of songs from everywhere?

With their trailblazing songs ringing, the roads are open,
the Song Tower is raised, the stage is formed,
and all the hills and streams are cheering.
Treading forward, the masters shake the hills,
stir up the waves,
and raise the dragon's head.
Tigers and leopards are fleeing,
on seeing the determined masters.

---

[1]　The Opening Song is also called Song-Beginning Road, Beginning Song, and The Song Beginning. It is combined with ten sorts of beginning of rite ceremony. The beginning of the opening song is a kind of melody sung by the master singer from the outdoor crossing through the mourning door to the mourning hall. There are long and short opening songs, varying in response to the situation. And the long opening songs can last more than three hours, from Pangu to thirty-six dynasties, which are called "Mini Legend of Darkness".

日吉时良，天地开张，
歌鼓二人来开歌场。
开，开，开，盘古老祖下山来，
一开天地阴阳，二开日月三光，
三开五方五地，四开闪电娘娘，
五开风婆雨师，暂且退让！
六开古老前人，先祖先王。
七开金龙凤凰，青狮白象，
八开魑魅魍魉，不可阻挡！
九开天地人三界，人间天堂。
十开一条条大道，直达歌场。

歌场开得长，水路八百，旱路千里，
歌场开得大，歌场开得宽。
奉请千军万马，八路神仙。
歌场比武，擂台摆上。
唱个短的太少，唱个长的太长，
不长不短到天光。

开场歌　The Opening Song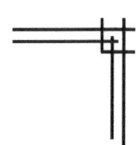

On an auspicious day, with the blessings of heaven and earth,
a singer and a drummer founded and opened the Song House.
Oh, it was the ancestral Pangu who came down from the mountains,
to create the first Yin and Yang, then the sun, the moon, and the stars,
then the five directions and parts of the earth, then Goddess Lightning,
then Old Woman Wind and Maiden Rain, and let them be!
Pangu's sixth creation was the ancestors and former emperors.
The gold dragons and phoenixes were the seventh creation,
with green lions and white elephants,
and the eighth creation was irresistible demons and monsters!
The ninth creation was heaven, earth, humans, and the paradise on earth.
The tenth was all the roads, all leading to the Song House.

The Song House is on a piece of long-stretched land,
with eight-hundred *li*'s① of waterways and thousands of *li*'s of roads,
and the area is spread far and wide.
Thousands upon thousands of horses and soldiers are invited,
so are the eight immortals.
For the marshal arts contest at the Song House, a drum-beating platform is set up.
The short song is too short while the long one, too long,
so the one neither too long nor too short,
is just right to be sung till daylight.

---

① A Chinese *li* is about 0.31 miles.

一二三四五，擂动三阵鼓，
未曾开口汗长流。
讲起鼓来根古长。
鼓儿圆圆檀香木，
昆仑山上长，昆仑山上出，
月亮照见它出土。
露水将它哺成树，
鲁班把树来砍倒，
剃了枝柯拖出林，
锯一节空心檀香木。
刨子刨来锛子锛，
鼓梆八块分八卦，
上为阳来下为阴。
内含五形分四象，
春夏秋冬分八音。
锣儿本是黄铜打，
暗合太阴与太阳。
锣槌一个，鼓槌一双，
让我歌鼓二人早进歌场。

开场歌　The Opening Song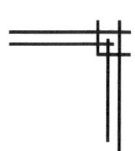

Three times the drum is hit one, two, three, four, five,
sweat streaming before even the singing of the songs.
About the drums, they have a long history.
The round drum is made of sandalwood,
which came from Mount Kunlun.
The moon shined upon sapling as it broke out of the ground,
and the dew watered it as it grew into a tree.
Lu Ban came to chop it down,
shaved all its branches, hauled it out of the forest,
and selected a hollow section of the sandalwood tree.
Polishing with a plane and shaping with an adze,
Lu Ban made eight drum clappers according to the Eight Diagrams,
with Yang on the top and Yin at the bottom.
Inside the drum are the Five Elements within the Four Images,
and spring, summer, autumn and winter that are divided into eight notes.
The gong is made of bronze,
coinciding with Taiyin and Taiyang, two of the four images.
With one gang stick and a pair of drumsticks,
let us sing and drum our way into the Song House without delay.

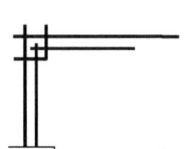

头顶天，脚踏地，
来到孝家大门前。
孝家门前搭高楼，
搭的走马转角楼。
四道高门在四方，
一道中门在高堂。
打开东门好跑马。
打开西门好耍枪，
打开北门招歌郎。

歌台搭在楼中央，
上盖青色玻璃瓦，
下铺玉石方砖，
八根全梁玉柱。
置下梭罗门两扇。
早晨开门金鸡叫，
晚上关门凤凰鸣。

歌鼓堂前好光景，
好比天堂玉殿形，
锦幛上面绣海马，
海马上下绣乾坤，
乾坤之上绣日月，
日月旁边绣彩云。
彩云旁边绣花朵，
花朵旁边绣鹌鹑。

开场歌 The Opening Song

With the heads touching the sky and feet on the ground,
the masters arrive at the gate of the pious family.
A high tower is in front of the gate,
and the masters and their horses must go around the tower.
Four high gates stand in four directions,
with a middle gate to the main hall.
When the east gate is open, there is space for a horse race.
When the west gate is open, there is room for a sword contest,
and when the north gate is open, enter the singers.

The stage is in the middle of the tower,
with a green ceramic tiled roof,
the white-jade tiled floor,
and eight golden beams and marble columns.
There are two shuttle-net doors.
They open in the morning with the crowing of a gold rooster,
and close at night with the singing of a phoenix.

The stage hall is a stunning spectacle,
as splendid as the palace in heaven.
On the brocade silk scroll was embroidered sea horses,
above and under sea horses embroidered heaven and earth,
above heaven and earth embroidered the sun and earth,
beside the sun and earth embroidered bright clouds.
by the colourful clouds are embroidered flowers, and
by the flowers, embroidered quails.

打开歌楼一重门，
一重门里不见人。
只见一对怪兽把守，
一个含绣球，一个戴铜铃，
这是青狮白象，守在两旁。
叫一声青狮白象，
请你站在一边，闪在一旁，
让我歌鼓二人，早进歌场。

孝家一副好棺木，
说起棺木根古长。
昆仑山上一棵树，
此树名叫长生木。
上面枝叶四季青，
上有一枝朝北斗，
下有一根穿泉壤。

左边枝头凤做窝，
右边根上老龙洞，
只有盘古神通大。
手执一把开山斧，
先天元年砍一斧。
先天二年砍半边，
先天三年才砍倒。
先天四年落凡间，
鲁班先师一句话，
先造死，后造生。
生生死死根连根，
万古千秋到如今。

开场歌　The Opening Song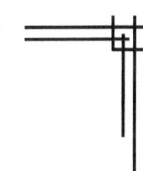

Opening the first door of the tower,
the masters see nobody there,
but a pair of monsters guarding,
one holding a silky ball in its mouth, the other wearing a copper bell.
They are Green Lion and White Elephant, each guarding on one side.
Green Lion and While Elephant,
please stand aside and let us through, so that we the singer and the drummer,
can enter the Song House as soon as possible.

The pious family has a good coffin,
and it, too, has a long story.
On Mount Kunlun, there was a tree,
with the name Immortal Wood.
Its leaves were green in all seasons,
with one branch above facing the Big Dipper,
one root connected to the underground spring.

Having a phoenix nest on its left branch,
and a dragon cave on its right root,
the tree surrendered itself only to the marvelous Pangu.
With a mountain-splitting axe,
Pangu struck one strike the first year of the first era.
He then struck off half of the tree the next year,
and finally struck the tree down the year after.
In the fourth year, the tree was brought down to the earth,
and Master Lu Ban said,
one's life is predetermined by the karma of one's previous lives.
The living and the dead are intertwined,
through all ages.

哪一个，白头不老得长生？
哪一个，神仙不是做古人？
想昔日，神农皇帝尝百草，
中毒而亡无药医。
想昔日，老君不死今何在？
想昔日，八百寿命一彭祖，
到头来，骨化形销一堆土。
黄金若能买活命，
皇王要活万万秋。

昔日螳螂来扑蛾，
岂知黄雀在后啄，
黄雀又被金弹打，
打弹之人被虎拖，
老虎掉在深坑里，
坑内又被黄土梭，
黄土上面长青草，
青草又被镰刀割。
镰刀又被铁匠打，
铁匠又被无常捉。
自古一报还一报，
劝人行善莫做恶！

开场歌　The Opening Song

Who lived forever and never died?
Which immortal didn't become one of the ancients in the end?
Remember, Emperor Shennong tasted hundreds of herbs,
but was poisoned to death with no herbal medicine to his rescue.
Remember, if the daoist ancestor Laojun were an immortal,
why is he nowhere to be found?
Remember, Pengzu lived long but only for eight hundred years and
in the end, flesh and bones became a pile of dust.
If gold could buy life,
emperors would have lived forever.

In the old days, a mantis was stalking a moth,
not knowing that itself was being stalked by an oriole at the same time,
but the oriole ended up being shot by a sling-shooter,
who was dragged away by a tiger,
who ended up falling into a deep pit,
which was filled with the loess,
on which grew green grass,
which was cut by a sickle.
The sickle ended up being hammered by a blacksmith,
who was tortured by capricious destiny.
Since ancient time, what goes around comes around,
so goes the advice to do good, not evil!

歌场来了两个客,
孝子施礼忙迎接。
一个童子五尺高,
一个老者貌堂堂。
打开歌楼二重门,
二重门里不见人。
只见一对金鸡把守,
头戴金冠,尾开宝扇。
这不是金鸡,是凤凰,
请你站在一边,闪在一旁,
让歌鼓二人,早进歌场。

打开歌楼三重门,
三重门里不见人,
只见两个红黑二将。
原来是两位门神,
叫声门神,请站在一边,闪在一旁,
让歌鼓二人,早进歌场。

开场歌　The Opening Song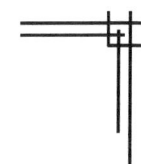

Two guests arrive at the Song House,
and the pious son hurries forward to welcome them with a salute.
One guest is a boy, five *chi*① tall,
the other an old man in splendid apparel.
The second door to the tower is open,
but still no one is in sight.
There is only a pair of golden roosters guarding the door,
with the golden crown and gemstone-like tail spreading out like a fan.
Not a golden rooster but a phoenix,
please stand aside and let the singer and the drummer enter the Song House as soon as possible.

The third door to the tower is open,
yet still no one,
but two generals were in sight, one with a red face and the other black.
Ah, door-gods,
please stand aside and let the singer and the drummer enter the Song House as soon as possible.

---

①　A Chinese *chi* is slightly short of a foot, and so is a Chinese *cun*, of an inch.

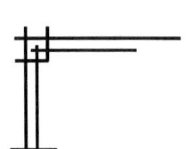

打开歌楼四重门，
四重门里不见人。
只见两个女子，站在两旁。
一个短来一个长，
原是长三娘，矮三娘，
她们所生五个儿郎。
各个饱读诗书，做得文章。
只是五郎年纪小，
专爱打鼓闹夜。
唱些山歌野腔，
只见他早已进了歌场。

打开歌楼五重门，
五重门里两个神。
手拿刀斧刨锯，
原是鲁班两个弟子，
张郎与李郎，木匠与漆匠，
做得一口好棺木，
刨得平，漆得光，
棺木原是一棵桑。
长在昆仑山顶上。
四块长的在四方，
两块短的在中央，
鲁班造下一口仓，
专殓亡者上天堂。

开场歌　The Opening Song

The fourth door to the tower is open,
but still,
only two women are in sight, standing on the two sides.
One is short, the other tall,
the Tall Aunt and Short Aunt,
who have five sons.
Everyone of them is well-educated and good at writing.
But Wulang, the youngest one,
likes to drum for fun all night long.
He sings folk songs with a crude tone, and
he has entered the Song House a while ago.

The fifth door to the tower is open,
and inside were two immortals,
with the knife, the axe, the plane and the saw in their hands.
They were two of Lu Ban's disciples,
Mr. Zhang and Mr. Li, a carpenter and a painter.
They were good at making coffins,
planing them smooth and finishing them with a sheen.
The coffin was once a mulberry tree,
which had grown on the top of Mount Kunlun.
With four long pieces of wood as the four sides,
and two short ones in the center,
the special storage Lu Ban made,
for the deceased to go up to heaven.

请问你是哪里来的歌郎？
人又生得聪，气宇轩昂。
歌又唱得好，声音洪亮。

答曰：不是远道而来的宾客，
而是打鼓闹祖的歌郎。

旱路水路，五湖四海访歌友，
学得一些稀奇文章。
打开他小小行囊，
一个小小的笼箱，
拿一套歌本，满篇诗行，
龙行虎步，走进歌场。

问曰：歌本有几千几百本？
歌有几千几万零？

答曰：歌本有三千七百本，
歌有十万有余零。

问曰：哪年哪月歌出世？
哪年哪月歌出生？
歌是前朝什么人作？
什么人传歌到如今？

开场歌　The Opening Song

Would you tell us where you came from, singer?
You are smart with an impressive appearance.
You also sing well with a pure and sonorous voice.

Answer: I am not a guest from afar,
but a drummer and singer at ancestral festivals.

He has visited singer friends by dry and water ways,
and read some articles on fantastic happenings.
He opens his little travelling bag,
a small cage,
and holding a set of songbooks, full of poems,
he enters the Song House, with a majestic gait.

Question: How many songbooks do you have?
How many songs are there?

Answer: There are three thousand and seven hundred books,
and more than a hundred thousand songs.

Question: When were the songs known?
When did they become known?
Who were the composers?
Who helped to pass the songs on till today?

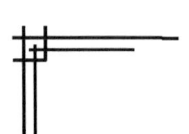

答曰：起初年间歌出世，
起初年间歌出生。
歌是前朝古人作，
代代相传到如今。

问曰：什么年间天开眼？
什么人布下满天星？
什么人看见地翻身？
什么人出世擂战鼓？
什么人出世会弹琴？
什么人取火烧自身？
歌师一一来说清，
才算歌场老师尊。

答曰：盘古出世天开眼，
斗母布下满天星，
地母看见地翻身，
雷公天上擂战鼓，
女娲出世会弹琴。
闪电娘娘取火种。
取得火种烧自身。

开场歌　The Opening Song

Answer: The songs were known in ancient years.
They were composed in ancient years.
The former ancients wrote the songs,
generation after generation of people have helped to pass them till today.

Question: When did the sky open its eyes?
Who cast the stars in the sky?
Who saw the earth turning over?
Who was born beating the war drums?
Who could play the zither at birth?
Who fetched the fire and burned themselves?
Please explain one by one clearly,
so as to deserve the title of Respectable Master Singer in the Song House.

Answer: Pangu's birth made the sky open its eyes.
Mother Dou cast stars in the sky.
Mother Earth witnessed the earth turning over.
The God of Thunder beat the drum in the sky.
Nvwa could play the banjo at birth.
Goddess Lightning fetched the first fire.
and burned herself after that.

问曰：讲天由，讲天由，
天河岸上几条沟？
几条沟里出桃子？
几条沟里出铁牛？
什么人放？什么人收？
什么人置下铁笼头？
铁牛闯下什么祸？
铁牛又被何人收？

答曰：天河岸上九条沟，
九条沟里出铁牛，
老君放，老君收，
老君置下铁笼头。
吃了昆仑山上草不长，
喝了黄河水不流。
撞塌天宫三万三千琉璃瓦，
撞倒王母娘娘三千三万金柱头。
玉皇大帝生了气，
贬到人间作家畜。
牧童放，农夫收，
耕田耙地老黄牛。

开场歌　The Opening Song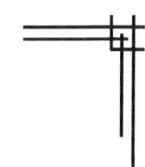

Question: Let's talk about heaven next.
How many ditches were there on the bank of the Milky Way?
How many ditches were there that grew peaches?
How many were there that raise iron cattle?
Who herded the cattle? Who took care of them?
Who made the bridles?
What kind of mistakes did the iron cattle make?
Who adopted the iron cattle later?

Answer: There were nine ditches on the bank of the Milky Way,
and nine ditches where the iron cattle lived.
Lao Zi herded them, cared for them,
and fastened bridles onto them.
Grazing the grass on Mount Kunlun, they stopped the grass from growing;
Drinking from the Yellow River, they stopped its water from flowing.
They collapsed thirty-three thousand glazed bricks in the Heavenly Palace,
and crashed the Queen Mother's thirty-three thousand gold columns.
The Jade Emperor was angry,
and expelled them from heaven to be domestic animals on earth.
Herded by cowboys, cared for by farmers,
they became old cattle plowing and harrowing the fields.

水有源，歌有头，
句句丧歌有根由。
歌师知得天根由，
请你给我讲清楚。
要讲清，说不完，
天地奥妙玄又玄。
下至泉壤上九天，
问混沌，说黑暗。
或问日月怎团圆？
黑暗混沌多少年？
才有人苗出世间。
玄黄老祖传混沌，
混沌传盘古，
九番洪水三开天，
才有日月星光现。
伏羲女娲传人烟，
千秋万代往后传。

谈天上，顺天游，
谈地上，江湖走。
身骑一只梅花鹿，
上走黄河九十九道弯，
下走长江青龙偃月滩。
三山五岳任我走，
看景致，访歌友，
歌鼓场上乐悠悠。
我问青山何时老？
青山问我几时闲？
我问流水翻什么浪？
流水问我白什么头？
叹得人生多忙碌，
难比山常青来水长流。

开场歌 The Opening Song

As water has its origin and songs have their beginning,
each sentence of the funeral song also has its roots.
Since the master singer knows the root,
please tell me clearly.
To explain clearly, one won't be able to stop,
because the origin of heaven and earth is a mystery.
From the springs under to the ninth heaven above,
one must inquire into the chaos and speak of darkness,
or ask how the sun and the earth reunited with each other.
How many years of chaos and darkness elapsed,
before human beings were born?
The story from Ancestor Xuanhuang to Chaos,
and to Pangu is that,
nine floods separated heaven from earth three times,
before the sun, the moon and the stars appeared.
Fu Xi and Nvwa made human beings, and from then on,
the human race has continued from generation to generation.

Speaking of heaven, I travel in the sky.
Speaking of earth, I journey by rivers and lakes.
Riding a sika deer,
I have passed by ninety nine bays of the Yellow River,
and the Qinglong Yanyue shoal of the Yangtze River.
Roaming through the mountains,
I relish the scenery, visit with singer friends,
and delight in going to Song Houses everywhere.
I ask the green mountains when they will become old,
while they ask me when I will take a break.
I ask the flowing water why its waves roll up,
and it asks me why my hair turned gray.
It's a pity our life is so busy,
unlike the green mountains and flowing rivers.

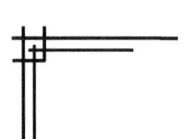

我在这里高拱手,
歌师、歌兄、歌弟、歌朋友,
一场山歌唱出头,
好比江河向东流。
未曾唱歌请歌师,
要请歌师起歌头。

这时请来一位老者,
腰儿弯弯,背儿驼驼。
长长的胡须,高高的额头,
肩挑一担,手提一笼。

问曰:哪里来的歌师?
哪里来的高手?

答曰:扬州的歌者,
柳州来的鼓手。

问曰:肩挑一担是什么?
手提一笼是何物?

答曰:肩上一担是阳雀,
手提一笼是画眉。

问曰:阳雀怎么叫?
画眉怎么啼?

开场歌　The Opening Song

Here I am saluting with jointed hands raised high to,
the master singers, senior-brother singers, junior-brother singers,
and all singer friends.
To sing the beginning of a mountain song,
is like the rivers flow toward the east.
I invite a master singer before I sing,
to start the song.

Presently a senior man was invited,
with his waist bending, back hunching,
beard long, forehead high,
and with a pole on the shoulder, a cage in the hand.

Ask: Where is this master singer from?
Where is this expert from?

Answer: The master singer is from Yangzhou,
and the drummer is from Liuzhou.

Ask: What are you carrying with the shoulder-pole?
What is it in the cage?

Answer: Sparrows are what I am carrying,
and thrushes are in the cage.

Ask: How does the sparrow sing?
How does the thrush sing?

答曰：阳雀叫的咕溜扯，扯咕溜，
画眉闹林度春秋。
一声歌儿唱出来，
好比泉水出洞口，
船儿弯在浪沙洲，
一阵顺风调了头。

开场歌 The Opening Song

Answer: The sparrow chirps chattering and chattering,
and the thrush sings in the forest all year long.
Once they sing,
the song is like a spring flowing out of a cave.
Even the boat on the beach,
turns around with the help of a burst of favourable wind.

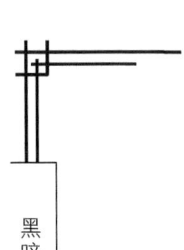

歌　头

打扫堂前起歌头，
哪位歌师先开口？
香烟袅袅纱悠悠，
敲起龙凤鼓，
打起青铜锣，
一拜师来二访友。

开了歌头莫住声，
要唱古往与来今。
或唱天文与地理，
或唱日月并五星。
或唱昆仑与五岳，
或唱开天辟地人。
或唱稀奇并古怪，
或唱黑暗与混沌。
或唱青山并水秀，
或唱走兽与飞禽。
歌朋歌友显才能，
一夜唱到大天明。
歌场好比野山藤，
将藤割回搓根绳，
将绳拴住歌场人。

歌头 The Beginning of the Song

The Beginning of the Song

Clean the singing hall and start the festivity.
Who will sing first?
With the smoke of incense rising in volutes,
the dragon- and phoenix-drum beating,
the bronze gongs playing,
we learn from the masters while also visiting with friends.

Don't keep silent once the song begins.
The song is about ancient times and the present moment:
about astronomy and geography,
about the sun, the moon and the five stars,
about Mount Kunlun and the Five Mountains,
about the creator of the world,
about oddities and fantasies,
about darkness and Chaos,
about green mountains and clear waters,
or about animals and birds.
All singers demonstrate their talents,
singing till the dawn of the next day.
The Song House is like a wild rattan rope,
that keeps everyone inside.

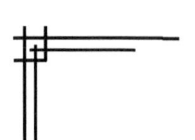

万国九州有贤师,
五湖四海出能人。
高拱手来低作揖,
为弟去此讲书文。
师出题目我做文。
题目出在哪本书?
我将题目问先生。

十年难逢金满斗,
五年难遇腊庚申①,
今日相逢有缘分,
众星捧月到天明。
唱歌要唱本头歌,
大树不倒盘根深。
追根求源有学问,
脚穿草鞋慢追寻。

提起四游并八传,
考倒多少假好汉。
任你提起哪几游哪几传,
四游八传哪一段,
玄黄、混沌和黑暗,
说尽天地也不难,
生铁补锅显手段,
龙凤鼓上试试看——

---

① 金满斗、腊庚申:均为吉祥的日子。

歌头 The Beginning of the Song

There are many virtuous teachers from all over the world,
talented people from different places.
Saluting with hands folded high, bowing with hands folded low,
I, as the younger brother, begin to tell stories.
I will speak according to the subject the Master selects.
From which book does the subject come?
I ask the Master.

It's rare to have an auspicious day in ten years,
and hard to have a lucky one in five.
We must be meant to meet today,
and must be like the stars grouped around the moon till morning.
When singing, we'd better sing foundation songs,
like the deep roots that make the big tree stable.
The true knowledge goes deep, so,
let's take our time and pursue it in our straw sandals.

The four Travelling Journeys and eight Legends,
exposed numerous boasting men.
No matter which story you ask about,
no matter which episode of the stories you ask about,
whether it is about Xuanhuang, Chaos or Darkness,
it is no problem for me to talk about any of them.
As it can showcase one's skill if the pig iron is used to mend the pot,
let me showcase mine by using the drum—

一、天地玄黄①

天上日月星斗寒，
天地故事甚非凡。
天有多大，有多高？
地有多厚，有多深？
东南西北有多远？
几多名称在里边？
歌师如果记得全，
真正算得歌神仙。

---

① "天地玄黄"标题为整理者所加，内容包括三个抄本：一是松柏镇堂房村农民曾启明（1999年病故，时年76岁）本。他曾于1946年在房县西蒿坪背铁矿石，在打麻沟一私塾先生处烤干粮时，发现私塾先生正在抄《黑暗传》，他趁机把已抄好的4页纸顺手带走，计13段歌词。收集时间为1984年5月。二是在林区新华乡派出所特派员黄成彦处收集到《玄黄》《昊天》两个抄本（残缺）。《玄黄》为同治七年甘儒朝抄本，《昊天》为光绪十四年李德樊抄本。以上编入1986年湖北省民间文艺家协会出版的《神农架〈黑暗传〉原始版本汇编》一书。三是2001年1月8日，在保康县店垭镇收集到一本有书名的《玄黄全传》的清代抄本，收集者杨宜明为该镇干部。

一、天地玄黄 I.Before Creation

I. Before Creation[①]

The sun, the moon, and the stars are high in the cold sky,

so the stories of them are extraordinary.

How vast is the sky and how high is it?

How thick is the earth and how deep is it?

How far do the east, south, west and north go?

How many names go with those directions?

If the master singer remembers them all,

you will be a true singer fairy.

---

① The title "Before Creation" is added by people who sorted. There were three transcripts: one was hand-copied by Zeng Qiming (died of an illness in 1999 at the age of 76), a farmer in Tangfang Village, Songbo Town. When he was toasting solid food at a private tutor in Dama Village on the way carrying iron ore in 1946, he found the tutor transcribing *Legend of Darkness*, so he seized the chance to take the four pages that had been transcribed, totaling 13 paragraphs of lyrics. It was then collected in May, 1984. The second was what Huang Chengyan, a commissioner at Xin Hua local police station in a forest region, collected from *Xuanhuang*, *Haotian* (incomplete). *Xuanhuang* was Gan Ruchao's manuscript in 1868, while *Haotian* was Li Defan's manuscript in 1888. Both of them were assembled in *The Compile of Original Edition of Legend of Darkness in Shennongjia*. The third one named *Complete Biography of Xuanhuang* in Qing Dynasty, which was collected in Dianya Town, Baokang County, on January 8th, 2001. The collector was Yang Yiming, who was a cadre leader in the town.

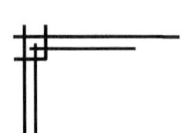

黑暗传 The Legend of Darkness

问我记得熟不熟？
天地自然有根由。
天河泥沙此化出，
从小到大有生于无。
无极太极有两仪，
混沌之时无宰主。
善变故掌天地枢，
昆仑之山产万物。
昆仑之山分东西，
东西南北极乐府。
洪水之时妖魔现，
四十八祖动刀斧。
山崩地裂洪水后，
重整江山分九州。

一声闪电沙泥动，
霹雳交加雷轰轰，
分开混沌黑暗重。
哪有黑暗根基深，
哪位歌师他知情？
要盘根来就盘根，
天地自然有根痕，
才产天精与地灵。

一、天地玄黄 I.Before Creation

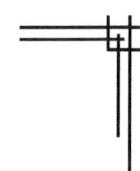

How clearly do I remember?
Nature and the world have their beginning.
The Milky Way, the mud and the sand transformed,
from small to big and from nothing to things.
From Wuji came Taichi, which was twofold;
there was not a ruler during Chaos.
Adeptness at change was the way of heaven and earth,
the reason for the abundant products from Mount Kunlun.
Mount Kunlun, divided into the east part and west part,
was Pure Land in all directions.
When demons appeared during the flood,
the forty-eight ancestors fought with knives and axes.
After the mountains fell, the earth was split and flooded,
the world was rearranged and divided into nine parts.

A lightning shook the sandy mud,
was followed by clapping thunderbolts and rumbling thunders,
and then separated Chaos.
Which master singer knows,
where the darkest was?
Let's find it out.
Heaven, earth and nature took their roots first,
and then there were all the spirits of heaven and earth.

黑暗传 The Legend of Darkness

先从天河来讲起，
化得混沌有父母，
化得黑暗无母生，
黑暗出世有混沌，
混沌之后黑暗明，
才把两仪化成形。
两仪之后有四象，
四象之中天地分，
然后才有日月星。
说天星，讲天星，
讲起天河一段根，
不知哪年生一虫，
此虫大得无比伦。
渴了喝的天河水，
饿了忙把砂石吞。
吞了吐，吐了吞，
不知吞吐几万春。
砂石磨得亮晶晶，
好比珠宝放光明。

此虫吞食渐长大，
生甲长角一龙形。
一日来把砂石吞，
一口喷出满天星。
此龙追赶忙飞腾，
五色祥云来包住，
结成一团出混沌。

一、天地玄黄 I. Before Creation

Let' begin with the Milky Way.
Chaos came from its parents,
but Darkness was born without its mother.
After Darkness was Chaos,
but after Chaos Darkness turned into light,
and the twofold Taiji appeared.
The twofold Taiji was followed by the Four Images,
within which heaven and earth were separated,
and then the sun, the earth and the stars came into existence.
Speaking of stars, talking about stars,
I must trace their beginning.
A worm was born in the year which was unknown,
and it was of an incomparable size.
It drank from the Milky Way when thirsty,
and swallowed the sandstone when hungry.
It swallowed and then spit it out, spit it out and then swallowed,
for an unknown number of thousands of years.
In the end, the sandstone was ground bright,
as a glittering pearl.

As the worm grew up by swallowing the stone,
it developed scales and horns of a dragon.
One day after it swallowed the sandstone,
stars came out of it spreading all over the sky.
When the dragon hurriedly chased after them,
it was enclosed by some auspicious clouds in five colors.
and Chaos came into being from the clouds.

砂石包龙龙追石，
砂石把龙包中心。
日月星斗包在内，
将来万物从此生。
砂石飞出天河外，
日后此龙化昆仑。

万物包在山中心，
砂石日后多变化。

哪位歌师讲得真？
油波滇汜消沸化，
口张吐水放金霞，
当时有个潚渌①祖，
潚渌生浦湜，
浦湜就是混沌父，
潚渌就是混沌母，
母子成婚配，
生出一元物，
包罗万象在里头，
好像鸡蛋未孵出。

---

① 潚渌（音"幽泉"）

一、天地玄黄 I.Before Creation

Surrounded by the sandstone, the dragon chased the sandstone,
at the very center of the sandstone.
Within the sandstone were generated the sun, the moon, and the stars,
that were to give birth to everything else.
Then the sandstone flew out of the Milky Way,
and the dragon later formed Mount Kunlun.

The mountain contained myriads of things,
and the sandstone was to weather great changes.

Which master singer can tell the truth about this?
With waves and creeks of wondrous changes,
flowed out a splendid light from the dragon's mouth.
At the time there was the ancestor Youquan,
who gave birth to Pushi.
Pushi was Chaos' father,
and Youquan, Chaos' mother.
It was the marriage of the mother and the son,
that produced the original object,
the all-embracing object,
like an egg that had not been hatched.

当时黑暗生黑蛋,
黑蛋生出众神祖。
五条黑龙往外钻,
九大名山包在内,
包罗万象天地产。
混沌出世劈两半,
众位老祖才出生,
混沌里面生黑水,
放出黑水放光明。
汗清又出世,潲潦变滇汝,
混沌从前十六路。

一路生潲潦,潲潦生浦湜,
浦湜生滇汝。二路生江泡,
三路生玄真,四路生泥沽,
五路生汗水,六路生提沸,
七路生雍泉,八路生泗流,
九路生红雨,十路生清气,

十一生菩提,十二生重汗,
十三生浬沤①,十四生汦浬②,
十五生洞汻③,十六生江沽④,
江沽出世才造水土。

---

① 浬沤(音"里五")
② 汦浬(音"丘里")
③ 洞汻(音"洞六")
④ 江沽造水土资料来源于兴山县古夫镇马檀园村的清代抄本,因故摘抄了江沽造水土等部分内容。

一、天地玄黄 I. Before Creation

Darkness also laid an egg, Dark Egg,
which gave birth to all immortal ancestors,
of which five black dragons bored their way out,
with nine famous mountains within them,
which contained everything in nature.
When Chaos was born, he hacked it all in two halves,
and all ancestors were thus born.
Chaos had within it Dark Water,
which, when let out, gave off light.
Then Hanqing was born, and Dianru followed Youquan.
From there Chaos had sixteen ova.

The first gave birth to Youquan, who gave birth to Pushi, who then gave birth to Dianru. The second gave birth to Jiangpao.
The third was Xuanzhen, and the fourth Nigu.
Hanshui was the fifth, and Tifei, the sixth.
The seventh was Yongquan, and the eighth was Siliu.
The ninth as Red Rain, and the tenth was Clear Air.

The eleventh was Bodhi, and the twelfth was Chonghan.
The thirteenth was Liwu, and the fourteenth was Qiuli.
The fifteenth was Dongliu, and the last was Jianggu①,
who was the one making water and soil.

---

① The material about Jianggu's making water originated from a manuscript at Ma Tanyuan Village, Gufu Town, Xingshan County in Qing Dynasty, therefore, the part of content about Jianggu's making water was extracted.

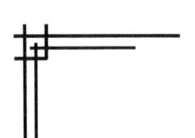

说江沽，有根古。
江沽出世水干枯，
尸骨化水成泥土。
青华山下有水池，
潲潦池中有家谱。
潲潦来把卵珠吐，
生出浦湜一个神，
这才传出混沌根。
提起十六卵珠子，
传卵圆物里边孕。
江沽出世一鱼形，
广吸元气长成精。
渐渐长大无比伦，
一口喝干天池水，
天干地枯无水分。

江沽找水四方寻，
千里万里多艰辛。
闻听北溟是大海，
一日千里往前行。
北溟万里冰雪海，
有一尊祖号北溟。
北溟海中有黑谷，
黑谷之中有洞府。
洞中住的北溟祖。
要见北溟取玄冰，
要取玄冰做水母。

一、天地玄黄 I.Before Creation

As for Jianggu, here is his origin.
When he was born, all water was dried-up,
and only the decayed corpses turned soil into mud.
There used to be a pool at the foot of Mount Qinghua,
where Youquan started his family tree.
It was here Youquan produced his first heir,
Pushi, an immortal.
This was the origin of Chaos.
Now the sixteenth pearl-like ovum,
was impregnated.
Jianggu was born the shape of a fish and,
grew into a spirit by inhaling vigour from everywhere.
Eventually, he grew into an incomparable size.
He drank up all the water in the heavenly pool in one gulp,
leaving heaven and earth in a great drought.

Jianggu went everywhere to search for water,
thousands and thousands of *li* away, hard and far.
When he heard about Beiming, a big sea,
he traveled there, traveling thousands of *li* every day.
The Beiming Sea, covered with tens of thousands of ice and snow,
got its name from an honorable ancestor Beiming.
In a black valley in the Beiming Sea,
there was a cave,
where lived ancestor Beiming.
Ancestor Beiming must be visited for the mystery black ice,
which must be fetched to produce water.

江沽来到北溟中，
来到大海水中游，
不知洞府在何处。
一日游到冰山中，
只见光亮照虚空。
江沽沿着光亮找，
果然亮处一洞府。
此洞好比水晶宫，
光分五彩一明珠。

北溟老祖洞中坐，
口含明珠放光明。
生得一条白龙样，
见了江沽怒眼睁。
江沽连忙把话云：
乞求老祖赐玄冰。
北溟来相问，哪里来的大鱼精？
江沽答曰：出身中土地，
溚溹是母亲，
只因喝干天池水，
天干地也枯，天干水也枯，
难以活性命，才到此处游。

一、天地玄黄 I.Before Creation

When Jianggu came to the Beiming Sea,
he jumped in and started swimming,
but did not know where the cave was.
One day when swimming among the ice mountains,
he happened to see a single ray of light.
He followed the light,
and indeed the light led him to a cave.
This cave was like a crystal palace,
a pearl glowing with colorful lights.

Ancestor Beiming was sitting in the cave,
with a pearl in the mouth, shining.
He had the shape of a white dragon,
and he opened his angry eyes to look at Jianggu.
Jianggu immediately pleaded:
I beg your eldership to give me the mystery ice.
Beiming demanded: where are you from, the big fish kid?
Jianggu replied: I was born in the middle of the land,
Youquan being my mother.
I drank up the water in the heavenly pool,
causing the drought in heaven and earth, without a drop of water now.
Lives could no longer survive, and that's why I came here.

天地干枯难保生,
特请溟祖赐玄冰,
玄冰化水救生灵。
唯有玄冰是真净水,
才是万物救生根。
北溟一听开言道,
玄冰原是水之精。
玄冰非是容易化,
需得玄光一宝珍。

北溟之北有一神,
名叫玄关坐昆仑。
玄关口中含玄珠,
玄珠才能化玄冰。

北去昆仑千万里,
问你江沽如何行?
江沽一听泪水淋,
北溟老祖心怜悯。
拿出九个泥团子,
乃是泥精来做成。
叫声江沽来吞下,
力大无穷有精神。
北溟开口来相问,
愿不愿意来化身?
要化大鹏金翅鸟,
要去昆仑一时辰。

一、天地玄黄 I.Before Creation

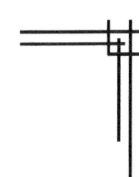

The life will be no more without water,

so please, Ancestor Ming, grant me the mystery ice,

which when melts into water can save lives.

Only the mystery ice is pure water,

the hope for the life of everything.

After hearing this, Beiming said:

Mystery ice is the water fairy,

and it does not melt easily,

without the precious mystery light of a pearl.

To the north of the Beiming Sea is an immortal,

whose name is Xuanguan and who is sitting in Mount Kunlun.

He has a mystery pearl in his mouth,

the pearl that can melt the mystery ice.

Mount Kunlun being tens and thousands of *li* north of here,

how can you get there?

On hearing this Jianggu had tears falling like rain.

Ancestor Beiming took pity on him,

and brought out nine clay balls,

made of clay spirits.

He asked Jianggu to swallow them,

to become infinitely powerful and energetic.

Beiming asked:

Would you like to transform yourself,

into a roc with gold wings,

so that you can fly to Mount Kunlun in an hour?

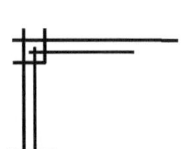

江沽听了心欢喜，
取来珠宝见师尊。
霎时江沽变了样，
脱了鱼皮化鸟形。
展开翅膀腾空起，
一翅飞起到昆仑。
昆仑山中一洞府，
洞府中有老仙神。

行过礼后忙开言，
尊声玄关老仙神，
万里迢迢借玄珠，
不知尊神肯不肯？
玄关一听心了然，
定是北溟把话传。
点化他来借玄珠，
取了玄珠天黑暗，
玄冰化了洪水淹。

玄关老祖心默算，
也是江沽有劫难。
天生他要造水土，
玄关这时一声叹，
玄珠乃是火中精，
看你如何取回还？

一、天地玄黄 I.Before Creation

Jianggu was happy to hear this,
and fetched some jewels for his master.
Instantly Jianggu transformed,
shedding the fish skin and turning into a bird.
Flapping his wings, he soared into the sky,
and arrived at Mount Kunlun immediately.
In a cave in Mount Kunlun,
lived the old immortal.

After he saluted to the immortal, he spoke right away,
respectfully addressing Xuanguan as the "Senior Immortal",
I came from tens of thousands of *li* away to borrow your mystery pearl.
Would you mind lending it to me?
On hearing this, Xuanguan knew immediately,
that it was Beiming who told him about the pearl,
and taught him how to come to get it.
Yet once the mystery pearl was taken away, the sky would turn dark,
and the mystery ice would turn into floods.

Xuanguan thought to himself:
it must be Jianggu's ill-fated life,
to be born to make water and soil,
so Xuanguan sighed and then asked:
The mystery pearl being the fairy among all fires,
how would you manage to fetch it?

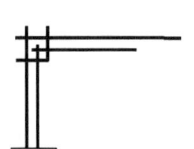

江沽回言不要紧，
含在口中往回转。
江沽飞到北溟地，
口中玄珠如火炭。
刚要落在洞府口，
口中玄珠落下来，
万丈光焰腾空起。
洞中玄冰来融化，
顿时波涛千万里。

只见空中起黑云，
黑水已经漫天眼，
天摇地动好惊人。
听得哗啦一声响，
黑水淹到黑天外，
狂涛巨浪盖天顶。
天盖呼啦塌下来，
把地扣得紧沉沉，
后出盘古天地分。
玄黄老祖收黑水，
来把黑水四下分，
这时天地重新创，
又出多少稀奇文。

一、天地玄黄 I.Before Creation

Jianggu answered: it is not a problem.
I will return with it in my mouth.
Jianggu flew back to Beiming,
with the mystery pearl like the burning charcoal in his mouth.
But right before he landed in front of the cave,
the mystery pearl fell,
and flames shot up tens and thousands of *zhang*① high into the sky.
The mystery ice began to melt,
and at once waves gushed from the cave to tens and thousands of *li* away.

Meanwhile, the black clouds gathered in the sky,
with the black water rising up to it:
it was astonishing with the sky shaking and earth quaking.
With a loud clashing noise,
the black water flooded outside the black sky.
and the roaring waves covered the sky's roof.
The roof collapsed with a deafening boom,
flopping itself flat onto the earth heavily,
the reason Pangu later had to separate heaven and earth.
Ancestor Xuanhuang, too, had to recall the black water,
and divided it into four parts.
This was when heaven and earth had to be recreated,
an event that brought forth once more numerous fantastic stories.

---

① A *zhang* is ten *chi*. A *chi* is almost but not quite a foot.

上有赤气降了地,
内有包罗吐清气,
生出一个叫元湜。
唯有元湜有一子,
一子更名叫沙泥,
沙泥传沙滇,沙滇传沙沸,
沙沸传红雨,红雨传化极,
化极传苗青,苗青传石玉。
千变万化有根基,
谁人知得那玄秘?

当时有个混沌祖,
天地自然有根古。
内中他还有一物,
名曰包罗生水土,
土生金,金生火,
水上之浮为天主,
刺凿其额为江沽,
三爻五爻为乾象,
飞龙化出羽毛长,
才有恶鸟横空出。
无天无日无星斗,
糊里糊涂说出口,
哪个知得这根古?

一、天地玄黄 I.Before Creation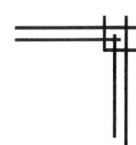

From up in the sky the red air came to land on the earth.
Inside the air was Baoluo, which spat fresh air,
and gave birth to someone whose name was Yuanshi.
Yuanshi had a son,
who was named Shani.
Shani passed it all to Shadian, and Shadian to Shafei,
Shafei to Red Rain, and Red Rain to Huaji,
Huaji to Miaoqing, and Miaoqing to Shiyu.
Vicissitudes of changes all have their origins,
but who knew the most mysterious of the secrets?

There was an ancestor Chaos at that time,
and that was the origin of the world.
Inside him, he had one thing,
named Baoluo, which brought forth water and soil,
Soil gave rise to gold, and gold to fire.
What floated on the water was natural,
Jianggu was the one who had his forehead tattooed.
The third and the fifth line in the Eight Diagrams made the Qian Gua.
Only when the flying dragon grew long feathers,
did the evil birds come into being.
There was no daylight, no sun and no stars,
and all talks were but confused,
so who could know the origin of these?

五条黑龙往外钻，
挤破黑蛋生黑烟。
黑烟放出生黑水，
黑水漫漫又滔天。
黑水流出来观看，
凸凸凹凹万重山。
几处凸来几处凹，
昆仑出世有根源。
黑水之中生灵气，
黑蛋落在水中间。
不知过了多少年，
黑蛋炸开玄又玄。
黑水流出黑龙先，
五条黑龙闹翻天。

黑水之中长座山，
名叫青龙有根源。
山顶好似莲花开，
里边现出一毫光，
滚出一块青石来，
下面好似莲蓬样，
上面青石生五孔，
五股青烟冒出来。
结朵祥云生五彩，
五彩云霞一散开。
掉下一个圆物件，
露出一个小人来。
随风长大多奇怪，
胸前自带头像来。
半边黄来半边黑，
玄玄二字现出来。

一、天地玄黄 I.Before Creation

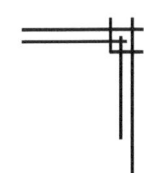

When the five black dragons bored their way out,
the black egg cracked and let out black smoke.
When the black smoke came out, black water emerged,
which flowed and surged towards the sky.
When the black water rushed out, behold,
the tens and thousands of undulating mountains.
Rising and falling,
they were the origin of Mount Kunlun.
Now the black water developed its inner energy,
and the black egg fell into the black water.
No one knew how many years had passed,
before the black egg burst open mysteriously.
Ancestor black dragons flowed out of the black water,
five of them who wreaked havoc.

Rising from the black water was a mountain,
named Green Dragon, which had its own stories.
Its top was like a blooming lotus flower.
Inside it a ray of light appeared,
and then a green stone rolled out of it.
The bottom of the stone resembled the lotus,
and the top of the stone had five apertures,
from which five columns of blue smoke came out.
They formed five auspicious colorful clouds,
and then the colorful clouds dispersed.
From the dispersed clouds fell out a round thing,
and a tiny person showed up from it.
Amazingly, the person grew with the wind,
and a self-portrait appeared on his chest.
The portrait was half yellow and half black,
eventually emerging were the two characters—Xuanxuan.

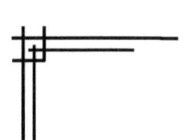

黑暗传　The Legend of Darkness

玄玄出世有根苗，
出世更比玄黄早。
青龙昆仑高又高，
暗通阴阳生根苗。
玄玄出世小又小，
全身不满二尺高，
见风成长高万丈，
地眼灵气结成胎。

他与玄黄来争斗，
般般武艺使出来。
玄黄斗赢玄玄输，
口称玄黄把师拜，
玄黄收他为弟子，
昆仑山中坐灵台。

谁个出世是混沌？
混沌之时出玄黄，
玄黄出世天地生。
玄黄出世玄又玄，
无有日月共九天，
无山无水无星斗，
更无火来又无风，
也无人苗和万物。

一、天地玄黄 I. Before Creation

There was a history of Xuanxuan's birth,
which was even earlier than Xuanhuang's.
The Qinglong and Kunlun Mountains were very high,
quietly embracing Yin and Yang to bear life.
At birth, Xuanxuan was quite tiny,
less than two *chi* tall,
but when exposed to the wind he became tens and thousands of *zhang* tall,
because his entire fetal development was nourished by Yin-Yang spirits.

When he first fought with Xuanhuang,
he did use all his fighting skills.
Xuanghuang won, and Xuanxuan lost,
so he asked that Xuanghuang be his master,
and Xuanghuang, accepting him as an apprentice,
sat him down by the spiritual terrace of Mount Kunlun.

Who was born during the time of Chaos?
During the time of Chaos, Xuanhuang was born,
and Xuanhuang's birth brought forth heaven and earth.
Xuanhuang's birth was the mystery of all mysteries.
For nine days there were not the sun, the moon,
the mountains, the water, the stars,
not to mention the fire and the wind,
or the humans and myriads of things.

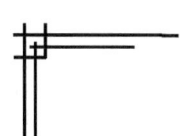

讲起玄黄他的根,
公山昆仑母青龙,
两山相连合拢来,
一声霹雳又分开,
地眼开口好古怪。
冒出青气化一人,
青龙山上化一怪,
冒出黄气化一神,
玄黄老祖结灵胎。
要知二人这根古,
听我从头唱出来。

玄黄怎么出的世?
什么地方又冒烟?
什么地气化神仙?
化身之后么情景?
又出什么众神仙?
歌师如果说得全。
也会成为歌神仙。

一、天地玄黄 I.Before Creation

About the origin of Xuanhuang,
the male Kunlun Mountain and the female Qinglong Mountain,
first came together,
but then separated with the sound of a thunderclap,
and then the earth opened its eyes and strange things happened.
With the blue smoke emerged a person;
on top of Mount Qinglong emerged a monster;
with the yellow smoke an immortal emerged;
then Xuanhuang's fetus came into existence.
If you want to know the story of these two,
listen to me to tell you from the beginning.

How was Xuanhunag born?
Where did the smoke rise again?
Where did he change into an immortal?
What happened after he became an immortal?
What other immortals came to be afterwards?
If a master singer can tell us the complete story,
he will also become a singer fairy.

未分天地有一山，
它为众山之根源。
山川社稷从此起，
天地阴阳万事全。
山高三百六十丈，
山峰五万并九千。
八万四千里为方圆，
生有八万四千根毫毛，
三百六十根龙骨节。
五气朝元接五行，
乃通九窍接九千。
山有三峰并两凹，
远看如似笔架山。
此山名为"玄黄山"，
高大宽广为祖山。

内隐胎息并神育，
变化无穷万象全。
一胎育山山育气，
有胎有气是活山。
孕者气藏融合聚，
凝结土宫在深山。
气之藏聚方为孕，
四处发脉悠悠然。

一、天地玄黄 I.Before Creation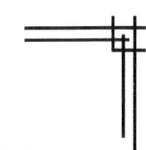

Before the separation of heaven and earth, there was a mountain,
which was the origin of all mountains.
All mountains and human affairs started from there,
which contained Yin-Yang and everything else.
This mountain was three hundred and sixty *zhang* high,
with fifty-nine thousand peaks.
It extended as far as eighty-four thousand *li*,
with eighty-four thousand body hairs,
and three hundred and sixty dragon-bone joints.
Its Five Qi were connected to the Five Elements,
and so its nine orifices were connected to nine thousands of others.
Three of the mountain peaks formed two valleys,
making it look like a pen-rack mountain when seen from afar.
It was named the "Xuanhuang Mountain",
an ancestral mountain with its height and width.

Carrying the fetus inside and nourishing it with the spirits,
the mountain changed endlessly and contained everything it needed.
While the fetus nurturing the mountain which produced the energy—Qi,
the mountain was alive with both the fetus and the Qi.
The pregnant mountain collected all the Qi and spirits,
in the clay palace deep in the mountain.
All the Qi collected was best for the pregnancy,
as seen in the mountain range, extending everywhere leisurely.

一支山脉左边去，
结成一座青龙山。
又生一脉左边去，
长成一座昆仑山。
青龙、昆仑山二座，
名为玄黄耳手山。
二山相对互环绕，
龙虎威武巍巍然。

玄黄山如笔架形，
生在西域圣地境，
又无生物和人烟。
昆仑一脉到塞外，
东土东胜名神州。
外生一座峈峊①山，
发脉又到太荒山。
太荒山又发支脉，
长出五座好神山。

第一瀛洲二方壶，
第三峤山四岱舆。
第五蓬莱五太岳。
旸谷、扶桑在东海，
具是昆仑三脉端。
又发二脉离方去，
南澹部州砢碣②山。

---

① 峈峊（音"洛至"）
② 砢碣（音"罗贺"）

一、天地玄黄 I.Before Creation

One mountain ridge reached to the left,
and turned into Mount Qinglong.
Another ridge developed to its left,
and became Mount Kunlun.
Qinglong and Kunlun were the two mountains,
that together were named Mount Xuanhuang Ershou.
Facing each other,
they were mighty and magnificent like a tiger and a dragon.

Mount Xuanhuang, in the shape of a pen rack,
stood in the sacred land of the western regions,
with no lives or traces of human beings.
One ridge of Mount Kunlun spread beyond what's now the Great Wall,
with the soil in the east being called the Divine Land.
Splitting from it was Mount Luozhi,
which stretched to Mount Taihuang.
From Mount Taihuang grew its own,
five more sacred mountains.

The first was Yingzhou, and the second, Fanghu.
The third was Qiaoshan, and the fourth, Daiyu.
The fifth was Penglai, altogether five high mountains.
In the east sea were Yanggu and Fusang,
both were at the ends of the three Kunlun mountain ridges.
In the other directions, the mountain range stretched towards Lifang,
and there Mount Luohe was formed in Nandan.

西牛贺州在兑方,
又生一座砎砘①山。
四支山脉坎方去,
又在卢州长成山。
结成硝硌②山一座,
俱是乾方西北延。
四大名山把脉连,
生出千山并万山。
气之变化玄黄山,
即是无极包万象。
两仪四象在其间。

诸物万象生变化,
水火金木土育孕全。
变化青赤黑白黄,
五形五色化石泥。
万物由此才发源。

左山玄黄右青龙,
阳气赤气冲虚空。
玄黄山中黑气起,
后山青气如云烟。
黄气青气一齐绕,
五色云彩结成团。
霎时之间结一物,
五色圆物空中现。

---

① 砎砘（音"加托"）
② 硝硌（音"肖各"）

一、天地玄黄 I. Before Creation

Xiniu Hezhou was in Duifang,
where Mount Jiatuo took shape.
When the four-ridge mountain range extended toward Kanfang,
another mountain came into being in Luzhou.
Its name was Xiaoge,
and it extended towards the northwest.
And all the four famous mountains were linked,
breeding tens and thousands of small mountains.
The Qi that moved constantly in Mount Xuanhuang,
comprised all manifestations of nature,
including the Yin-Yang Taiji and the four images.

When myriads of images changed,
Water, Fire, Metal, Wood and Earth were born.
Green, Red, Black, White and Yellow,
became the five colors of the stone and mud.
Myriads of things were then originated.

With Xuanhuang to the left and Qinglong to the right,
the Yang-Qi and Red-Qi circled in the void between them.
The black smoke rose from Mount Xuanhuang,
and the blue smoke rose from the back mountain.
With the yellow and blue spiral up together,
a five-color cloud was formed.
Suddenly something took shape,
a five-colored round thing hanging in the sky.

空中咚咚一声响，
一下落在玄黄山。
山顶之上滚五转，
一阵清风云烟散。
忽然化成人一个，
身高十丈巍巍然。
头上青发白色面，
两足赤红似火焰。
站在玄黄山顶上，
极目连连四下观，
四周黑暗如墨团。

见一赤气光闪耀，
走进赤光过细观，
原是一个大地眼。
一团圆物在眼中，
冒着热气团团转，
又见前边山顶上，
一股白气光闪闪。
走近白气闪耀处，
也是一个圆窟眼。
又一圆物在其中，
一道霞光来冲起，
白雾青黄并紫烟。
此人朝着霞光走，
一块黄石光如玉。
黄石高有九丈零，
十二丈宽形四正，
此人就往石上坐，
化为九色宝莲台。

一、天地玄黄 I. Before Creation

With a loud clamor in the air,
the thing fell onto Mount Xuanhuang.
It rolled five times on the top of the mountain,
and it then dissipated like smoke with a gust of wind.
A person suddenly appeared,
with the height of an imposing ten *zhang* tall.
With black hair and a white complexion,
he had two feet as red as fire.
Standing on the top of Mount Xuanhuang,
he strained his eyes to look in all directions,
and in all directions it was as dark as an ink ball.

Then he saw a glittering red light,
so he walked up to it to take a closer look:
it was an eye of the earth.
Something round was inside the eye,
spitting hot air while turning around.
Next he saw on the top of the mountain in front of him,
a whiff of white smoke shining.
As he moved closer to the shining white smoke,
he found another round eye.
There was again something round inside it,
but here a ray of rosy light rushed up,
with the white mist and then the green, yellow and purple smoke.
He walked up toward the light,
and saw a yellow stone as smooth as polished jade.
The stone was more than nine *zhang* tall,
twelve *zhang* wide on all four sides.
He went and sat on the stone,
which changed into a magic lotus platform with nice colors.

诗曰：黄石一块九丈高，
十二丈围玄黄苗。
变为九色莲花瓣，
蕊现霞光透九霄。

此人坐在宝台上，
心中暗想甚原因。
一只阴眼一只阳，
天地玄黄此时生，
自己取名叫玄黄。

诗曰：未生天地吾在前，
一名真一又玄元，
有影无形常自在，
巍巍躯体在先天。
黑暗未有星和斗，
浑浑瑗碟无人烟。
身借五色祥云化，
无神无仙吾占先。

一、天地玄黄 I. Before Creation

The Poem says: A yellow stone, nine *zhang* in height,
surrounded the young Xuanhuang with its twelve *zhang* circumference.
It changed into a lotus petal in nine colors,
the stamens shining the rosy light that penetrated the sky.

Sitting on the magic platform,
he thought to himself about all the happenings.
With two eyes, a Yin one and a Yang one,
heaven, earth and Xuanhuang were born then and there,
and he named himself Xuanhuang.

The Poem says: I was born before heaven and earth,
having one name True and the other Mystery,
roaming freely with a shadow but with not a shape,
my mighty and impressive body preceding heaven and earth.
It was dark yet without the stars,
chaos everywhere without human beings.
The five colorful auspicious clouds became my body,
so I was born before all immortals.

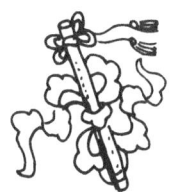

再说天眼和地目，
二目圆睁天地眼。
以后不断来变化，
多少稀奇在里边。
玄黄坐在黄石上，
青龙山顶白气冒，
冲上虚空云一团。
又见昆仑山顶上，
一道赤气红光闪。
赤气白气来合拢，
结一圆物落下边。
落在玄黄山顶上，
顿时化成一个人。
身长九丈粗五围，
黄色头发白色面。
此人抬头来观看，
四边都是黑暗暗。
独有一山霞光现，
一朵莲花多耀眼。
五彩祥云拥金莲，
中间坐了一个人，
不知何人在此间。
此人慢慢来走近，
见一神人好威严。

一、天地玄黄 I. Before Creation

Let's return now to the eyes of heaven and earth,
those two wide-open round eyes.
They were to change ceaselessly,
and many a wondrous story they kept to themselves.
When Xuanhuang was sitting on the yellow stone,
the white smoke rose from the top of Mount Qinglong,
curling up into a cluster of cloud.
Seen also on top of Mount Kunlun,
was the red smoke with a ray of red light sparkling.
When the white and red smoke gathered together,
They formed something round that fell down from the mix.
It landed on the top of Mount Xuanhuang,
and right away turned into a person,
nine *zhang* tall and five *zhang* around his waist,
with yellow hair and a white complexion.
He raised his head to look around,
but there was nothing but darkness,
except one mountain with some rosy light shining,
with a dazzling gold lotus flower.
The five colorful auspicious clouds surrounded a gold lotus flower,
with a man sitting in the middle,
a man he didn't know.
He slowly walked up,
finding a stately immortal.

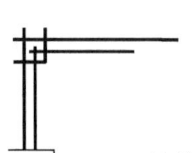

连忙来把老者唤,
老者闻听睁开眼。
看见此人把话问,
你是何人把我见?
姓什名谁哪里来?
有何事情快开言。
此人连忙来回答,
无名无姓生地眼。
玄黄忙把名字取,
奇妙之名号玄元。

玄黄收他为弟子,
结伴前行山中玩。
师徒游玩一山顶,
山上一个大洞门。
石洞宽敞如洞府,
一重门来二重门。
一重门里有瑞气,
照得里面甚通明。
二重门面鲜花开,
鲜花谢了结鲜果,
吃了不老万寿春。
三重门里香扑鼻,
上垂璎珞下铺锦,
玉石床和玉石凳,
真是神仙之妙境。
与之一一取个名。
取名就叫鸿濛洞,
石上刻字传后人。

一、天地玄黄 I.Before Creation

He hurriedly greeted the immortal,
who opened his eyes on being greeted.
The immortal asked,
Who are you that came to see me?
What is your name and where are you from?
Tell me quickly what brought you here.
The man replied quickly,
I was born from the earth's eye without a name.
Xuanhuang named him at once,
Qimiao with the assumed name Xuanyuan.

Xuanhuang accepted him as a disciple,
as a companion to enjoy the mountain together.
Once when they strolled in the mountain,
they found a gate to a big cave.
The cave was spacious as a palace,
with one layer of gate after another.
Behind the first gate was the celestial air,
that illuminated every corner inside.
Behind the second gate were fresh blooming flowers,
that, after withering away, bore fresh fruits,
which would make one immortal and forever young.
Behind the third gate was the intoxicating aroma,
with various jade and pearls hanging above and brocade spreading under,
with beds and stools made of jade,
a fairyland for the immortals indeed.
They named each thing respectively.
They named Cave Hongmeng,
engraved it on the stone to hand down to their offspring.

一日师徒出洞门,
来叫玄黄山上行。
又见地眼赤气出,
山上天眼青气出。
忽听轰然一声响,
二气氤氲结一团,
落在山中滚三转,
顷刻又冲半天中。
又落玄黄山顶上,
山顶之上放祥光。

诗曰: 天地参差落滑塘,
内安日月并星光。
中藏五形并四象,
分开阴阳是玄黄。
滑塘池中一圆物,
滚去滚来放豪光。

玄黄吩咐奇妙子,
取来圆物我观赏。
奇妙来到滑塘池,
一池清水起波浪。
圆物好似一珠宝,
伸手取宝喜非常。

一、天地玄黄 I.Before Creation

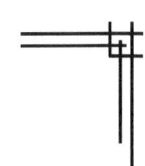

One day the master and the apprentice left the cave,
to visit Mount Xuanhuang.
Again, the red smoke came out of the earth's eye,
and the blue smoke, from the sky's eye on the mountain.
Suddenly with a loud crash,
the two kinds of the enshrouding smoke became one ball,
fell onto the mountain, rolled around three times,
and then at once roared up midair.
It then dropped on the top of the mountain,
which shone with auspicious light.

The Poem says: Heaven and earth were positioned within Huatang Pool,
within which were the sun, the moon and the stars.
Insider were the five colors and four images,
and Xuanhuang embodied Yin and Yang.
There was something round in the middle of Huatang Pool,
rolling here and there shining with bright light.

Xuanhuang instructed Qimiao,
go fetch the round object for me to take a close look at.
When Qimiao came to the pool,
the wave of the clear water started rolling.
The round object was like a piece of jewelry,
and he was delighted to go fetch it.

空中掉下人一个,
此人身高五丈长。
奇妙连忙问姓名,
那人口称"浪荡子",
要与奇妙夺宝珍。
两人争夺不相让,
拉拉扯扯争输赢。
浪荡一口来吞下,
奇妙连忙见师尊。
玄黄叫来浪荡子,
为何吞了我珍宝?
快快吐出不理论。

你是哪里的浪荡子?
你在哪里来出生?
浪荡答曰根基深,
荷叶老祖一门生。
自古长在池塘内,
长出荷叶莲花开。
荷叶上有水珠子,
随风滚去又滚来。
久而久之得灵气,
化出吾身浪荡名。

一、天地玄黄 I.Before Creation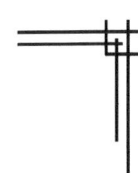

A man dropped from the sky,
who was five *zhang* tall.
When Qimiao asked for his name,
he called himself "Loafer",
and said he was here to compete with Qimiao for the jewel.
They fought with each,
neither willing to give up.
Then Loafer swallowed the jewel,
and Qimiao hurriedly went to his master.
Xuanhuang ordered Loafer to see him.
Why did you swallow my treasure?
Spit it out quickly with no excuses!

Where did you come from, Loafer?
Where were you born?
Loafer said that it was a long story,
going all the way back to the time when he was a pupil of Ancestor Lotus.
I have lived in the pool ever since birth,
where the lotus flowers blossom.
The drops of water on the lotus leaves,
rock back and forth with the wind.
After a while I developed the spirit within myself,
and transformed into who I am today—Loafer.

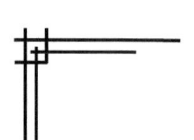

那颗珠宝已吞下，
看你如何来理论？
奇妙震怒吼一声，
飞来一只开天剑，
空中旋转飞下来。
就把浪荡来斩了，
身分五块五下横。
宝剑依然飞腾去，
空中飘飘荡荡行。

诗曰：吾已知此剑，不是炉中炼，
自成亿斯年，原是五气变。
快快落下地，莫在空中旋。
宝剑一听落下地，
落在奇妙子面前。
突然落地已不见，
落剑之处开金莲。
金莲花中有物象，
物象一现就杳然。
飞剑已斩浪荡子，
身分五块血流出，
鲜血流出如红水，
腹中蹦出那宝珠，
宝珠落地滚溜溜。

一、天地玄黄 I.Before Creation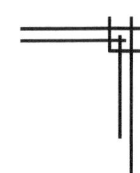

I have swallowed that jewel.
What can you do about me?
Qimiao roared with a rage,
with which a sky-openning sword,
swirled down from the sky.
It cut up Loafer,
into five parts.
Then the sword flew back up,
poised gracefully in the sky.

The Poem says: I know this sword, which was not refined in a stove,
but was born billions of years ago and transformed from Five Elements.
Stop rotating in the sky, and come down quickly!
On hearing this, the sword came down,
landing in front of Qimiao.
Yet it had disappeared by the time it landed,
And a gold lotus flower appeared in its place.
There was the image of something inside the flower,
but it, too, disappeared as soon as it appeared.
The flying sword had killed Loafer,
but as blood flowed from his five parts,
the blood that was running like the red water,
the pearl jumped out of his belly,
and rolled around on the ground.

玄黄叫声奇妙子，
你将珠宝来劈开，
一半黄来一半青，
青上浮来黄下沉。
只听咔嚓一声响，
逢中劈开一般匀。
青赤二气两分开，
玄黄山下产育精。

虚空混合盘旋转，
结成元物似蛋形。
青的半边化青气，
黄的半边在地平。
霎时天青地又黄，
不断扩大无边境。
青的为天又为云，
黄的为浊往下沉。
从此天地初出世，
黑暗之中现光明。

玄黄又叫奇妙子，
拿个葫芦你且去，
滑塘池中取壶水，
快去快来莫迟疑。
这时奇妙到滑塘，
五色祥云忽飘起。
滑塘之中有池水，
不知多深往上溢。
放下葫芦来打水，
池水全进葫芦里。

一、天地玄黄 I.Before Creation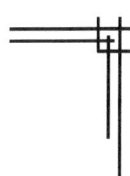

Xuanhuang asked Qimiao,
to split the pearl into two,
half yellow and half blue,
the floating blue and the sinking yellow.
Then with a click,
the pearl was split up evenly.
The blue and the red smoke-Qi now separated,
they could procreate at the foot of Mount Xuanhuang.

Some mixture was swirling,
and then formed an object in the shape of an egg.
The blue half rose up as the blue vapor,
while the yellow half came down to the ground.
Suddenly, the sky was blue and the earth, yellow,
expanding ceaselessly and limitlessly.
The blue became both the sky and the clouds,
while the yellow became earthy and heavy.
From then on heaven and earth were born,
and there was light in the darkness.

Xuanhuang asked Qimiao again,
take with you the gourd for water,
and fetch a gourd of water,
as quickly as possible.
When Qimiao came to Huatang,
the five-color auspicious clouds instantly floated up.
There was a pool in Huatang,
but, with its water gurgling up, it was hard to tell its depth.
As he put down the gourd to get water,
the entire pool of water went into the gourd.

诗曰：小小葫芦三寸高，
玄黄山上长根苗，
却能装尽天下水，
不满葫芦半中腰。
玄黄接过葫芦水，
五块尸体五下淋，
口中连忙吹口气，
叫声快快来化身。

诗曰：吾乃非凡神，一气变化身，
吾吹一口气，借气化五行。
五行化五神，去到五方行。

一块尸体化一人，
身高数丈有威灵。
面分青黄赤白黑，
此是五方五行神。
五人个个来下拜，
叫声玄黄为师尊。
玄黄一见心中喜，
五人个个取下名。
各管东西南北中，
各有职责在其身。
自然生成有妙用，
分开阴阳配五行。

一、天地玄黄 I.Before Creation

The Poem says: The little guard was but three *cun* tall,
having spent all its time in Mount Xuanhuang,
but could hold all the water in the world within itself,
with only half of the gourd.
When Xuanhuang received the gourd,
he sprinkled the water from the gourd onto the five pieces of the corpse,
taking a breath and then blowing the air hurriedly,
he commanded: change quickly.

The Poem says: I am not some commoner but can change lives with a breath.
Blowing the air, I borrow the energy from the Five Elements.
The Five Elements can turn into five immortals that go in five directions.

Each piece of the corpse became one immortal,
everyone being several *zhang* tall and very stately looking.
Their faces were of the green, yellow, red, white and black colors, respectively,
and they became the five immortals of the five directions.
They each came to show respect,
addressing Xuanhuang as their honorable Master.
Xuanhuang was pleased,
and named each one of them.
Each one was in charge of the east, west, south, north and middle, respectively,
with individual responsibilities.
The natural processes had their own use,
with Yin and Yang and the Five elements working together.

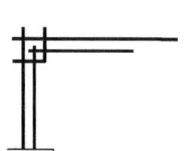

玄黄山右青龙山，
山上有处大老林。
老林之中长奇树，
有的花叶成人形。
阴阳交媾二气化，
才使万物来赋形。
但见青龙山顶上，
五棵古树自成林，
五色花朵满树开，
枝叶茂密树皮青。

原是七珍七宝树，
波罗苍树、菩提名，
还有檀香梭罗树，
棵棵宝树都有名。
有的结果小人样，
有的叶子现图形。
树枝盘曲如龙蛇，
阵阵花香扑鼻根。
突然花果落下地，
顿时化成人一群。
见了玄黄忙迎接，
个个前来叫师尊。
突然一阵狂风起，
树叶落地化九人。
九叶原是灵叶变，
又拜玄黄为师尊。
九人一一取了名。
师徒十人一大群，
跟着玄黄到昆仑。

一、天地玄黄 I. Before Creation

To the right of Mount Xuanhuang was Mount Qinlong,
where there was a large and old forest.
In the old forest grew strange trees.
and even flowers with leaves in the human shape.
It is because Yin and Yang wed and transform each other that,
myriads of things take on their shapes.
Therefore it was seen on the top of Mount Qinlong,
five ancient trees formed a forest themselves,
with blooming flowers in five colors,
with flourishing leaves and swarthy tree barks.

They turned out to be the seven-treasure trees,
and Boluo, Cangshu, Bodhi,
Sandalwood and Suoluo,
were the names of the treasure trees.
Some bore man-shape fruits,
but others had leaves with different patterns.
Their branches slithered like dragons and snakes,
and the aroma of the flowers was intoxicating.
Suddenly the flowers and fruits fell from the tree,
and instantly they transformed into a crowd of people.
On seeing Xuanhuang, they greeted him immediately,
and everyone addressed him as the honorable master.
Then came a gale of wind,
that blew the leaves off the trees and turned them into nine immortals.
The leaves were magic ones,
and all the nine of them bowed to Xuanhuang and addressed him as their master.
Xuanhuang named each of them.
Master and apprentices made a big group of ten now,
and following Xuanhuang, the apprentices went to Mount Kunlun.

山上有一清泉洞，
一池清泉为水根。
昆仑山为名山祖，
分支通脉群万岭。
四方山脉五条龙，
东西南北都有名。
第一山名昆仑山，
第二太荒山老岭。
山岭直达东海处，
又取瀛洲、方壶、方丈、岱舆、员峤名。
更有一山叫蓬莱，
上有金阙金银台，
玉楼紫阁好仙景。
蓬莱虽好无人去，
就是神仙也不能。

周围弱水三千里，
丢片羽毛也下沉。
中有旸谷深万丈，
后有日月在此升。
玄黄说与众徒听：
不觉遨游昆仑行。
山中有城为九重，
九重城里有九井。
九重城里有城门，
神兽把守严又紧。
十二宫殿十二楼，
俱有瑶台与玉阙。
后为天地之都城，
纵使神仙也难进。

一、天地玄黄 I.Before Creation

In the mountain was a clear-spring cave,
with a pool of clear-spring water that was the origin of water.
As the ancestor of all famous mountains,
Mount Kunlun branched off to tens and thousands of smaller ones.
They extended in four directions and, with Kunlun, looked like five dragons,
and they were well-known in all four directions.
The first was Mount Kunlun,
and the second was the old Taihuang Mountain range.
The mountains reached all the way to the East Sea,
where they had the name of Yingzhou, Fanghu, Fangzhang, Daiyu, and Yuanqiao.
Of course there was Mount Penglai,
on top of which were the gold watchtower and the abode of the fairies.
It was a good fairyland with the jade building and purple pavilions,
but no one ever went there,
not even the immortals.

It was surrounded by three thousand *li* of weak water,
so weak that a feather was too heavy for it and would sink.
In the middle was Yanggu that was boundless *zhang* deep,
and from behind Yanggu the sun and moon rose.
As Xuanhuang explained all this to his followers,
they did not realize they were already in Mount Kunlun.
There were nine cities in the mountain,
and nine wells in them.
All cities had the city gate,
guarded tightly by mythical creatures.
There were also twelve palaces and twelve towers,
with Yao Tai and jade palaces.
They later became the capital cities of heaven and earth,
and even the immortals could not enter them.

众人游玩观山景，
忽然三阵狂风生。
刮得云雾腾空起，
霎时黑暗惨淡形。
顺手抓住风的尾，
知道其中有原因。
原是山中有一兽，
生得奇怪甚惊人。

诗曰：头黑项绿毛色青，
六足白色红眼睛。
长尾好似黄金色，
二角五尺头上生。
其兽高有四尺五寸零，
长有九尺三寸身。
獠牙四颗如钢剑，
此兽名字叫混沌。
头如碾盘样，口张簸箕形。
角长有五尺，高有四丈五。

长有百丈零，獠牙三尺剑，
目中放光明，鼻孔似水桶，
行走云雾伴，一动狂风生。
异香三阵过，出气山川震，
六足云雾起，顷刻万里程。
满身鳞甲九九数，
能吐火光照虚空。

一、天地玄黄 I.Before Creation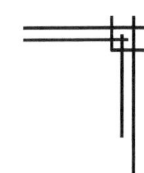

As the group went on sightseeing,
three strong gales of wind struck suddenly.
They blew up the clouds,
and instantly the daytime turned dusky and the clouds menacing.
Seizing the tail of the wind,
they found out what was happening.
It was a monster in the mountain,
a strange and frightening beast.

The Poem says: It had a black head, a green neck and blue hair,
with six white feet and red eyes.
Its long tail seemed to be golden in color,
and its two horns on the head were each five *chi* long.
The beast was four *chi* and five *cun* tall,
and nine *chi* and three *cun* long.
Its four fangs were like steel swords,
and its name was Chaos.
Its head was like a grinding stone, and its mouth opening like a dustpan.
Its horns were five *chi* long, and it was four and a half *zhang* tall.

It was more than a hundred *zhang* long and its fangs were like three-*chi*-long swords.
Its eyes shined with lights, and its nostrils were as big as the water buckets.
Its walks were accompanied by the clouds, and its every move stirred up the wind.
Its odd smell was strong, and it shook the mountains when it breathed.
Its six feet stirred up clouds, and it traveled tens of thousands of *li* instantly.
Its body was protected by an armor with eighty-one scales,
And it could spit fire to light up the sky.

背上又生双翅翼,
翅膀一展狂风生。
要与玄黄来争斗,
昆仑山中定输赢。
此兽张口朝天吼,
一股黑气往上升,
黑气之中有鸟叫,
好似乌鸦一大群。
玄黄一一认分明,
一只名叫鳼鴙①鸟,
嘴壳红色黑的身,
二只名叫毕方名,
身子墨黑头色青,
第三名叫鴂鵂②鸟,
三个头来六只眼,
伸出六翼和六足,
抓住玄黄顶门头。
第三鸺鹠③有九头,
口一张来火光起,
要烧玄黄众徒身。
第四名叫玡鷦④鸟,
六目四翅赛大鹰。
第五名叫人面鸟,
口吹黑气毒雾生。
玄黄取出小葫芦,
倒出大水火灭净,
四只恶鸟无踪影。

---

① 鳼鴙（音"介雌"）
② 鴂鵂（音"决付"）
③ 鸺鹠（音"休留"）
④ 玡鷦（音"玉焦"）

一、天地玄黄 I.Before Creation

On its back were two wings,
the spreading of which caused fierce wind.
Chaos was to fight with Xuanhuang,
to decide the winner in Mount Kunlun.
The beast roared towards the sky,
sending a whiff of black fume rushing upward.
In the midst of the black fume the sound of some birds was heard,
like a big crowd of crows.
Xuanhuang distinguished every kind of the birds clearly.
One had the name of Jieci,
with a red beak and a black body.
A second had the name of Bifang,
with a black body and a blue head.
A third had the name of Juefu,
with three heads and six eyes,
its six wings and six feet stretched out,
to grab the head of Xuanhuang.
One of them, Xiuliu, had nine heads,
spitting fire every time it opened its mouth,
and trying to enflame Xuanhuang and his followers.
A fourth kind had the name of Yujiao,
with six eyes and four wings, as large as those of an eagle.
The fifth had the name of Human-Faced Bird,
that blew black fume with poisonous mist.
Xuanhuang took out the little gourd,
the water pouring out and putting out the fire,
and four evil birds vanished immediately.

混沌一兽慌张了，
变一白蝶飞不赢。
一飞飞到葫芦口，
一股狂风顿时生。
不是朔风和罡风，
不是东西南北风，
不是杨柳松竹风，
此风名叫"无形风"。

诗曰：无形风来不见风，
无影无形又无踪。
又名耳风真厉害，
神仙逢此必遭凶。
吹入六腑丹田内，
穿透九窍骨空中。
骨肉俱酥身自化，
化为青烟影无踪。

玄黄打开葫芦口，
把风收在葫芦内。
混沌一见忙跪下，
要叫玄黄饶性命。
这时猛兽摇身变，
变一陒①狸要吃人。
玄黄祭起开天剑，
一条电光杀混沌。

---

① 陒（音"虎"）

一、天地玄黄 I. Before Creation

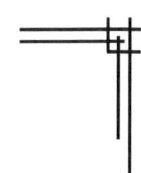

The bestial Chaos panicked,
trying to escape by changing into a white butterfly.
But he flew right to the mouth of the gourd,
and instantly a gale of wind started blowing.
The wind was not cold nor strong,
not east, west, south or north,
not aspen-, willow-, pine-, nor bamboo-wind,
but known as the "invisible wind".

The Poem says: The invisible wind came, but one could not see it,
for it had no shadow, no form and no trace.
It was also known as the truly powerful ear wind,
a sure sign of disaster for the immortals when they ran into it.
It entered the internal organs and the pubic region,
penetrating the nine orifices and the bone marrow.
It caused the bones and flesh to be brittle and the body melted
into the blue smoke vanishing without a trace.

Xuanhuang opened the gourd,
to recall the wind to return inside it.
On seeing this, Chaos knelt down immediately,
to beg Xuanhuang to spare his life.
But suddenly, the fierce beast transformed itself,
into a tiger-raccoon to eat up the group.
Xuanhuang turned to the sky-opening sword,
to kill Chaos with a lightning bolt.

这时混沌来跪下，
俯首帖耳泪淋淋。
玄黄收它为坐骑，
又取名字叫开明。
玄黄骑了混沌兽，
师徒又在山中行。
只见山中一仙女，
美貌端正裸体身。
名叫朦朧女妸仙①。
她是一个产育神。
见了玄黄忙下拜，
叫声玄黄救性命，
手按肚腹口呻吟，
一连生下两个蛋，
活蹦乱跳地上滚。
玄黄劈开蛋来看，
蹦出小孩一大群。
十个男孩十二女，
个个机灵甚喜人。
天干地支出了世，
玄黄一一取了名。
一群小孩见风长，
霎时个个长成人。
玄黄一一做婚配，
从此才有天干地支名。

---

① 朧（音"当"）妸（音"可"）

一、天地玄黄 I.Before Creation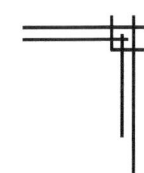

Finally, Chaos knelt again,
completely surrendering itself in tears.
Xuanhuang then accepted him as his personal riding beast,
naming him Kaiming.
Xuanhuang now riding the Chaos the beast,
the master and apprentices resumed their excursion in the mountain.
Presently they met a female fairy,
who was beautiful and naked.
Her name was Fairy Meng Dang Nv Ke,
a fertility immortal.
On seeing Xuanhuang, she bowed,
and asked him to save her life.
With her hands pressing on her stomach, groaning,
she gave birth to two eggs,
which rolled and jumped all over on the ground.
Xuanhuang split them in half to look inside,
and out jumped a big crowd of children.
There were ten boys and twelve girls,
everyone being smart and lovely.
This was the beginning of the Heavenly Stems and Earthly Branches①,
and Xuanhuang gave each of them a name.
All the children grew on being exposed to the wind,
so they grew into adults in no time.
Xuanhuang arranged the marriages among them,
and the names of the Heavenly Stems and Earthly Branches came into being.

---

① A Chinese system that calculates the movements of the astronomical bodies such as the sun, the moon, and the stars in order to determine, for example, the four seasons.

诗曰：在天为星在地为神，
在人心肝脾肺肾。
名属金木水火土，
又配宫商角徵羽五音，
青黄赤白黑五色。
东西南北中五方名，
各归其位尽其责，
五方五地守护神。

鸿濛洞中奇妙子，
玄黄出游心纳闷。
忽然心中灵机动，
挖来黄泥做泥人。
眼睛所见心里想，
各类形象要做成。
做一男来做一女，
眉清目秀好端正。
又让他们成婚配，
世世代代有子孙。

一、天地玄黄 I.Before Creation

The Poem says: What are stars in heaven are immortals on the earth,
and are the heart, liver, spleen, lung and kidney in humans.
They correspond to Metal, Wood, Water, Fire and Earth, respectively,
accompanied by Do, Re, Mi, Sol, La, the five notes,
and blue, yellow, red, white and black, the five colors.
The names of the five directions are east, west, south, north and center,
so all have their places and responsibilities,
all five directions and places are guarded by the immortals.

Qimiao was at Cave Hongmeng by himself,
while Xuanhuang went out to think about things.
Suddenly Qimiao got an idea,
to dig the yellow mud to make clay figures.
According to what he saw and what he thought,
he was making all sorts of figures.
He made a man and a woman,
each with fine features.
He wanted them to marry,
so that they could have offspring generation after generation.

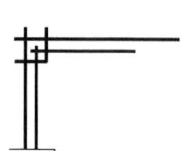

奇妙正把泥人塑,
口吐涎水捏泥人。
抬头一看吃一惊,
玄黄骑兽转回程。
随后众徒无其数,
奇妙慌忙前去迎。
玄黄一见泥人笑,
此是前缘与后因。

对着泥人吹仙气,
要使泥人还原形。
化成一个土珠子,
滚来滚去成一人。
取名就叫泥隐子,
日后人世有泥神。

昆仑山上碧水池,
碧水池中生红莲。
红莲九朵生红烟,
红烟里边九火蛇。
火蛇口中吐火焰,
玄黄抛出一根绳,
捆住九蛇在山巅。
九蛇口中含火珠,
照得山上放光明。

一、天地玄黄 I.Before Creation

Moulding the clay figurine,
he spit saliva to construct them.
When he raised his head, he was surprised,
to see that Xuanhuang was already returning on his beast-ride.
Following Xuanhuang were countless followers,
and Qimiao hurried forward to meet with them,
Xuanhuang smiled on seeing clay figurines,
because there was a reason for everything.

The magic breaths were blown at a clay figurine,
to change it to its original form.
It changed into a clay bead,
which rolled around and around and then became a person.
He was named Niyinzi,
who was the clay immortal for the human race.

On Mount Kunlun was a clear-water pool,
in which grew the red lotus.
There were nine of them, and they produced red smoke,
and in the red smoke were nine fiery snakes.
The fiery snakes were spitting fire,
so Xuanhuang used a rope,
and tied the nine snakes to the top of the mountain.
The nine snakes now held the fiery beads in their mouths,
illuminating the mountain top.

太荒山上一桃树,
树高万丈无比粗。
同时开花又结果,
青桃未黄早桃熟。
七个仙桃真可爱,
七桃裂口现七核。
七彩紫气不见了,
跳出七个小娇娇。
一见玄黄微微笑,
玄黄老祖问根苗。

七童当时来答道:
我来本是仙桃精,
灭天之时劫逃过,
孕化万物传人苗。
七童手指仙桃云,
此物不是非凡品,
混沌黑暗起的根。
说罢七童不见形,
玄黄老祖心纳闷。
回到洞中观分明,
石台上面飘香气,
台上现出七果仁。
玄黄拿起观仔细,
桃仁忽然来跳起,
顿时落地生了根。

一、天地玄黄 I.Before Creation

On Mount Taihuang was a peach tree,
which was tens and thousands *zhang* tall and incomparably thick.
It blossomed and bore fruits at the same time,
so some peaches were still green when early fruits were already ripe.
Seven of the miracle peaches were particularly lovely,
with seven seeds showed through the cracked peaches.
When the seven shades of purple disappeared,
seven little children jumped out.
They smiled the moment they saw Xuanhuang,
and the ancestor asked them about their origin.

The seven children replied:
We are the peach spirits,
who escaped the last heavenly disaster,
and now help the reproduction of myriads of things and humans.
They continued, pointing to the magic peach cloud:
this is not some ordinary cloud,
because it caused the rise of Chaos and the darkness.
When the seven children finished talking, they disappeared,
leaving Xuanhuang quite baffled.
Returning to the cave to figure it all out,
he sensed the fragrance wafting from the stone table,
where there were seven peach pits.
When Xuanhuang picked them up to examine them,
the seeds suddenly jumped up,
and then fell to the ground, taking root at once.

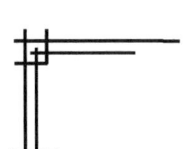

长出七根仙桃苗，
七色鲜花朵朵开，
朵朵鲜花如伞盖。
玄黄弟子吃桃子，
桃核丢在山里头，
不知桃核有物体，
许多神灵日后出。

昆仑山上一棵槐，
青枝绿叶甚可爱。
层层树叶如天盖，
密密树根通天脉。
槐树之中怀老母，
老母又把子孙怀。
百鸟百雀树上落，
五音五色分五彩。
有的鸟儿来献果，
有的鸟儿报信来。

一日玄黄昆仑行，
见一景致好惊人，
一棵古树高万丈，
树上百鸟叫连声。
有的好像乌鸦叫，
有的好比凤凰鸣。

一、天地玄黄 I.Before Creation

There grew seven peach seedlings,

with fresh flowers of seven colors blooming,

all in the shape of an umbrella.

The disciples of Xuanhuang ate the peaches,

and threw away the peach pits in the mountain,

not knowing that the pits contained matter,

which later produced many spirits.

On Mount Kunlun was a locust tree,

a truly lovely tree with its dark branches and green leaves.

Each layer of its leaves was like the cover of the sky,

and the thickness of its roots connected it to the pulse of heaven.

The locust tree nurtured an old mother,

who in turn brought up her children and grandchildren.

Hundreds of birds came to alight on the tree,

the birds that were of five notes, five colors and five kinds.

Some birds came to offer fruits,

while others came to send messages.

One day Xuanhuang was on a walk in Mount Kunlun,

he was stunned by the view,

of a tree tens and thousands *zhang* tall,

with hundreds of birds on it singing.

Some sounded like crows,

others, like the Phoenix.

树下有个碧玉洞，
住了一群老妖精。
大怪张口无比大，
四颗獠牙往外伸。
二怪头上一只角，
四只眼睛如铜铃。
三怪两头生四角，
分开两半合一身。
四怪人头鸟雀样，
张开翅膀飞黑云。
五怪狮头人身样，
大吼一声如雷震。
六怪独角四只手，
膀子三丈有余零。
七怪人身老虎头，
竖起尾巴九丈零，
围住玄黄不放行。
大怪张开血盆口，
伸出獠牙要吃人。
二怪一角撞将来，
力大无穷本事能。
三怪现出四只手，
要捉玄黄众徒生。
四怪飞在半天里，
要抓玄黄一个人。
六怪昂头来得快，
咆哮一声如雷鸣。

一、天地玄黄 I. Before Creation

Under the tree was a jade cave,
where lived a crowd of old monsters.
The first monster had a huge mouth,
with four fangs protruding outside of its mouth.
The second monster had a horn on its head,
with four eyes like copper bells.
The third monster had two heads and four horns,
one body that was two conjoint.
The fourth monster had a human's head and a bird's shape,
the opening of its wings bringing black clouds.
The fifth monster had a lion's head and a human's body,
its roaring like the shattering thunder.
The sixth monster had a single horn but four hands,
with its shoulders more than three *zhang* broad.
The seventh had a human' body and a tiger's head,
with its tail standing nine *zhang* long.
They surrounded Xuanhuang and would not let them through.
The first monster open its bloody mouth,
stretching its fangs and ready to kill.
The second monster charged with its one horn,
showing off its immense power and ability.
The third monster reached out its four hands,
attempting to catch Xuanhuang and his followers.
The fourth monster flew up into the sky,
trying to capture Xuanhuang himself.
With the head up, the sixth monster ran up quickly,
letting out a roar that was like a thunder rumbling.

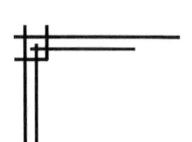

玄黄见了吃一惊,
原是山中怪物精。
连忙祭起开天剑,
一道闪电起红云。
六怪一见忙跪下,
口称玄黄饶性命:
"我们都是太荒生,
有的是金石来成形,
有的树木来长成,
有的山精并水怪,
有的爬虫与飞兽。"
说罢一一现原形,
五颜六色放光彩。
玄黄一见心中喜,
众怪以后有用处,
收为弟子一路行。

玄黄回到洞府门,
收的弟子一大群。
排在两边讲道法,
宇宙洪荒讲原因。
先天后天讲一遍,
阴阳变化万物生。
玄黄坐在灵台上,
画天画地画风云,
口吐祥云透九霄,
指头上面绕彩云。

一、天地玄黄 I.Before Creation

Xuanhuang was taken aback,
Ah, these are the spirits of the mountain monsters!
He turned to the sky-opening sword,
and a lightning struck with red clouds.
The six monsters hurriedly knelt down,
begging Xuanhuang to spare their lives:
"We were all born to Tai Huang.
We came from gold and stones,
trees,
mountain spirits and water monsters,
or the crawling worms and flying birds."
On finishing these words, they transformed into their original forms,
all shining with rich colors.
Xuanhuang was glad to see this,
for they could come in handy in the future,
and so he accepted them as his disciples.

By the time Xuanhuang returned to the cave,
he had gathered a big crowd of disciples.
They lined up on both sides of him,
as Xuanhuang explained cosmic floods and famines.
He detailed how before and after heaven was formed,
Yin and Yang interacted so that myriads of things came into existence.
When Xuanhuang was sitting on the magic platform,
he drew heaven, earth, wind and clouds,
spoke words that floated like auspicious clouds penetrating the sky,
with his fingers circled colorful clouds.

玄黄老祖洞中坐,
手执金鞭化条河。
一条黄龙水上行,
一只天龟来相迎。
黄龙盘在金龟背,
龟负黄龙重万钧。

天河有块五行石,
天龟含在口中吞,
每回吞吐三千次,
天龟借它养性命。
天龟不慎把石吐,
"咕咚"一声落凡尘。
落在黑水潭中心,
黑水一时鼓大泡,
现出一个大山林,
此山名叫五行山。
五行山,五条岭,
五岭像是五龙形,
一条黄龙中间卧,
口含一珠放光明。
照亮七十二昆仑,
后出多少稀奇文。

一、天地玄黄 I.Before Creation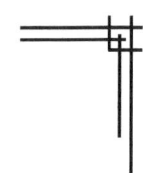

Sitting in the cave,
Xuanhuang, with a gold whip in hand, conjured up a river.
On the river a yellow dragon was walking,
and a heavenly tortoise came to greet it.
When the yellow dragon coiled up on the back of the gold tortoise,
the two together weighed tens and thousands of *jun*①.

In the Milky Way, there was a Five-Element stone,
which was kept in the mouth of the heavenly tortoise.
The tortoise swallowed and spit the stone three thousand times each time,
to sustain its own life.
It once dropped the stone by accident,
so with a thud, the stone dropped to the earth.
It fell to the center of a Black Water Pond,
where instantly a big bubble rose from the black water,
and a big mountain forest appeared,
whose name was the Five-Element Mountain.
The Five-Element mountain had five ridges,
like five dragons,
with a yellow one couching in the middle,
who held a shining pearl in its mouth.
The pearl shined upon all corners of Mount Kunlun,
and produced many a story.

---

① A *jun* is about 75,000 kilograms.

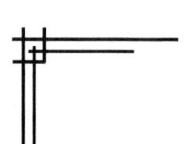

玄黄叫声泥隐子,
葫芦一个传与你,
后收洪水葫芦存。
天干地支入葫芦,
交与泥隐一神人,
藏在昆仑石洞内,
要躲洪水一难星。
洪水一万八千载,
葫芦存在昆仑顶。
等到盘古开天地,
天干地支得重生。
玄黄留下诗一首,
说泥隐子你且听:
先天一世要灭尽,
后天盘古才出生。
盘古举起开天斧,
一斧劈开太阳洞,
天上才有太阳神。
二斧劈开太阴府,
天上才有太阴星。
三斧劈开葫芦壳,
天干地支满天星。
玄黄老祖元气化,
混沌初开第一神。

一、天地玄黄 I. Before Creation

Then Xuanhuang called for Niyinzi:

I pass on to you this gourd to keep,

for the floods that will happen later.

The secret of the Heavenly Stems and Earthly Branches,

which was stored inside,

was also entrusted to Immortal Niyin,

for him to hide in the cave of Mount Kunlun,

for the escape of the catastrophic flood.

The flood lasted for eighteen thousand years,

while the gourd was kept intact on the top of Mount Kunlun.

It was waiting for Pengu to re-separate heaven and earth,

and for the Heavenly Stems and Earthly Branches to be reborn.

Xuanhuang was going to leave behind a poem,

and asked Niyinzi to listen carefully:

An entire generation must perish,

before Pangu is born.

Pangu will raise the creation axe,

and split open Cave Tai Yang with one strike,

so that there will be Immortal Tai Yang in heaven.

With a second strike, he will split open the Yin Palace,

so that there will be the Yin Star in heaven.

At a third strike, he will split open the gourd,

spreading the Heavenly Stems and Earthly Branches stars all over the sky.

The ancestor Xuanhuang was the Primordial Qi,

and the first immortal before Chaos.

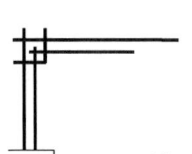

诗曰：未开天地玄黄尊，
他是开辟第一神。
地气化身收众徒，
天地一体万物生。
天下名山初具形，
九大名山好风景。
收伏红魔转化神，
诸多物体初长成，
可怜洪水泡天地，
所创世界一扫平。
一看黑水三巨浪，
大浪淘去多少神，
多少神仙成泥沙，
一波未平一波生，
九九劫难又逢春。

一、天地玄黄　I.Before Creation

The Poem says: Before the separation of heaven and earth was Xuanhuang,
the first ever immortal.
In an earthly form he accepted many disciples,
and heaven and earth became ones body to give rise to myriads of things.
All the famous mountains under heaven started to take shape,
especially the nine most famous ones with beautiful sceneries.
Xuanhuang subdued the red monster and turned it into an immortal,
and many things began to form.
It is a pity that the flood inundated heaven and earth,
leveling the world that had been created.
The black water surged over and over,
sweeping away countless immortals,
grinding countless fairies into silt,
one cycle after another,
but time and again life follows calamities.

二、黑暗混沌①

玄黄过后出混沌，
依然黑暗少光明，

---

① "黑暗混沌"标题为整理者所加。资料来源：一是1983年编辑《神农架民间歌谣集》时，发现松柏镇敬老院院长张忠臣有《黑暗传》抄本。张忠臣抄本为李鹤亭抄录于1964年，李鹤亭系有名的火居道士和私塾先生，因张忠臣的底本残缺不全，李鹤亭在抄写时加进武当祖师的内容。李鹤亭有《黑暗传》全传，"文革"时交出被烧毁。类似张忠臣抄本在林区发现10余种，最早是阳日镇钱家湾村贾邦修的清代抄本，此书分为两大部分：《黑暗大盘头》和《黑暗纲鉴》，为神农架一带最为流行的抄本。二是1993年在林区宋洛乡梨子坪村村民陈相玉处，他口述浪荡子吃荷叶一段。陈相玉系篾工，不识字，陈相玉于1954年在房县西蒿坪八寨给一老火居道士做篾工时听他唱的。采录时已记不全了。时年陈相玉60余岁。三是1984年在新华乡黄成彦处得到的"玄黄""昊天"两个清代抄本，收入《神农架〈黑暗传〉资料汇编》。1995年委托唐运青在兴山县平水乡石鹅岭收集到祝天照清代抄本（残缺）、甘溪坪村姜德龙钢笔转抄本。昊天杀五黑龙的抄本书名为《混元传》有为"记"。唐运青，40余岁，林区宋洛乡莲花村人，高小文化，其父唐文灿，有《黑暗传》失于"文革"中，其子唐运红、唐运青、唐运华均为著名歌手。唐运青于1985年移居兴山县平水乡石鹅岭村，他还提供了不少资料。作为口头记录，只采用部分资料。

二、黑暗混沌 II.Darkness and Chaos

II. Darkness and Chaos[1]

After Xuanhuang, Chaos came,

and it was darkness with little light,

---

[1] The title "Darkness and Chaos" was added by people who sorted it out. This material originated: one was from Zhang Zhongchen's manuscript of *The Legend of Darkness*. Zhang Zhongchen was the dean of a nursing home in Songbo Town. When people editing *Ballad Folk Song Book in Shengnongjia* in 1983, they found his manuscript, which was copied by Li Heting in 1964, who was a famous Huoju Taoist and private tutor, adding Wudang founder since Zhang Zhongchen's manuscript was not complete. And Li Heting had the full story of *The Legend of Darkness*, but was burned during the "Cultural Revolution". There were more than ten kinds of transcripts similar to Zhang Zhongchen's, among which Jia Bangxiu's in Qianjiawan Village, Yangri Town in Qing Dynasty was the earliest and the most popular in Shennongjia region. It was divided into two parts: *Darkness Inquiry* and *Darkness Principles Guide*. The second was from Chen Xiangyu, a villager in Liziping, Songluo Town of the forest region in 1993. Chen Xiangyu, an illiterate craftsman by making articles from bamboo strips, gave an oral account about Loafer eating lotus leaves at the age of over 60 in 1954, which he learned from an elderly Huoju Taoist in the Eighth Stockaded Village, Xihao Village, Fang County in 1954, so it was not complete. The third was from the two manuscripts of "Xuanhuang" and "Haotian" in Qing Dynasty from Huang Chenyan in Xinhua Village in 1984, which were collected in *The Document Assembly of Legend of Darkness in Shennongjia*. Tang Yunqing was commissioned to collect Zhu Tianzhao's Qing-Dynasty manuscript (incomplete) in Shi'e Mountain Range, Pingshui Village, Xingshan County in 1995 and Jiang Delong's manuscript with pen in Ganxiping Village. In the manuscript of *Legend of Hunyuan*, there was the story about how Haotian killed the five black dragons. Tang Yunqing, over 40, a villager in Lianhua Village, Songluo Town, was educated six years in elementary school. His father was Tang Wencan, had *Legend of Darkness*, but lost in the "Cultural Revolution". His children—Tang Yunhong, Tang Yunqing and Tang Yunhua all became famous singers. When Tang Yunqing moved to Shi'e Mountain Range Village, Pingshui Town, Xing Shan County in 1985, he provided many materials, but only part of them was adopted because it was all oral records.

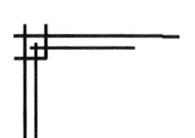

天地相连无人分。
混沌九九八十一劫难,
混沌之后盘古生。

混沌本来一头颅,
无鼻无腔甚是神。
多少玄妙里头存?
歌师记得清不清?
恭请歌师讲分明。

诗曰: 混沌无有天和地,
古祖灵山出世起,
寒阳洞里参禅机。
乾坤混沌几万秋,
度下开天辟地斧。
昆仑山上讲根由,
乾坤黑暗黑无边,
传下徒弟混沌仙。
混沌未分有一山,
天心地胆在中间。
盘古老祖他在先,
活了一万八千年,
那时洪水才泡天。

二、黑暗混沌 II.Darkness and Chaos

and no one could separate because heaven and earth were fused as one.
Chaos went through many hardships,
and after Chaos came Pangu.

Chaos used to be a skull,
without nose nor any aperture, a truly supernatural being.
How many mysteries were there about it?
Does the master singer remember them?
Please clarify it for us.

The Poem says: Under Chaos there was no heaven or earth,
with only the ancient miraculous mountain emerging,
the most profound Chan mystery formed in Cave Hanyang.
Heaven and earth were in Chaos for tens and thousands of years,
a time during which the axe that separated heaven and earth came into being.
It started at Mount Kunlun,
when heaven and earth were in complete darkness,
where the immortals and disciples came into being.
During Chaos there was a mountain,
where stored the cores of heaven and earth.
The ancestor Pangu lived first,
who lived for eighteen thousand years,
after the flood had just destroyed everything.

讲起混沌有根基，
我有一句来问你：
洪水泡天有根源，
叫声歌师听我谈，
洪水泡天有几番？
自从洪水泡天地，
混沌黑暗谁在先？
清水泡天有几番？
从头至尾讲根源，
那时才算得你为先。

自从洪水泡了天，
玄黄老祖他在前。
洪水泡天有三番，
三五老祖他在先。
清水泡天出古祖，
才有古祖在灵山。
清水泡天有几番？
清浊相连无有天。
我把天地谈一谈，
乾坤暗暗如鸡蛋，
千层万层包得严，
谁人知得这根源？

二、黑暗混沌 II.Darkness and Chaos

Speaking about the origin of Chaos,
I have some questions:
the flood had a long story,
so please help me understand:
how many times did the flood happen?
After the floods,
who was first, Chaos or Darkness?
How many times did the clear water inundate heaven?
Only if you can tell us from the beginning to the end,
do you deserve the extolled title of a master.

Prior to the flood,
ancestor Xuanhuang was first.
The flood came three times,
and the San-Wu ancient ancestors were first.
During the clear-water flood the ancient ancestors appeared,
the reason for the magic mountain for the ancient ancestors.
How many clear-water floods were there, you ask?
The water, clear or not, was mixed, so it's hard to tell.
Let me tell you about heaven and earth back then.
They were shelled like an egg,
with layers upon layers of covering, wrapped up tightly.
Who can know their very beginning?

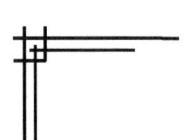

密密匝匝几千层，
三五相交看不清，
听我一一说混沌。
混沌山上十八祖，
青龙岭上昆仑山，
昆仑山上起青烟，
三千七百神仙洞，
八百洞中降真仙，
听我一一说根源。

玄黄死后留头颅，
天地灵气里头存，
预示天地未形成，
后来转变为混沌。
无鼻无眼心里明，
如似一个鸡蛋形。
划天老祖来彩画，
取出神笔画图形。
五气六气画眉毛，
八字蛾眉两边分。
七孔八窍安停当，
睁开双目看分明。
凿开混沌开七窍，
才有三光与三才。

二、黑暗混沌 II.Darkness and Chaos

Despite thousands of packed layers,
entangled obscurity,
let me tell you about Chaos in more detail.
In Mount Chaos there were eighteen ancient ancestors.
In the Qinglong Range was Mount Kunlun,
from which the light blue smoke arose.
Among the three thousand seven hundred fairy caves,
eight hundred of them saw true immortals.
Let me tell you about them one by one.

Xuanhuang died and left behind a skull,
within which stored his knowledge of heaven and earth,
foreseeing that heaven and earth would not take shape,
before it first turned into Chaos.
With no nose nor eyes but a clear mind,
Chaos had the shape of an egg.
Then came the ancestor to do color painting on it,
who pulled out the miraculous brush to paint with a design.
With five movements and six essentials the eyebrows appeared,
two of them like the character eight standing apart from each other.
Once the seven orifices and eight openings were arranged,
it opened its eyes and could now see clearly.
Only when Chaos was open up like this,
could there be the sun, the moon, the stars and heaven,
earth, humans.

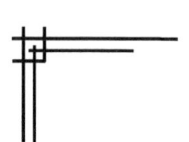

黑暗传　The Legend of Darkness

混沌头破似天开，
化一老祖有气概。
混沌老祖初出世，
无有天地五行势，
一气三化将人置。
站住仔细四下观，
举目抬头看一看，
四方都是黑暗暗，
清浊二气上下连，
无有人影在世间。

混沌一气降世起，
生在青梅山前地。
青梅山上把道传，
聚拢三百六十员，
寒阳洞里讲神仙。
都是天地变化成，
乾坤黑暗得自然。

混沌辞别洞府去，
太荒山前走一程，
只见乌云沉沉黑，
不知南北与西东。
混沌便把旗来绕，
现出太荒一座山。
转身住在太荒地，
不觉又是五百春。
只见太荒金石现，
石斧铁锤现原身，
赐与盘古把天分。

二、黑暗混沌　II.Darkness and Chaos

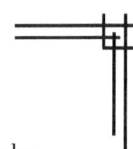

The opening of Chaos's head was like the opening of the sky,
turning itself into an ancestor with impressive appearance.
At ancestor Chaos' birth,
there was no heaven, earth and the Five Elements,
so he made humans with the vital energy.
Standing still, he looked around carefully,
and he raised his head to look up.
He saw darkness all around him.
Pure and unclean energy connected from top to bottom,
with no sight of human beings in the world.

Chaos' birth,
took place on the ground in front of Mount Qingmei.
He thus preached on that mountain,
gathering thirty six disciples,
talking about the immortals in Cave Hanyang.
Everything resulted from the changes of heaven and earth,
so darkness of heaven and earth was a natural course of event.

Then Chaos left the cave,
to visit Mount Taihuang,
but there he saw only the dark clouds overhead,
getting no sense of the four directions.
Therefore, Chaos waved the flag,
and then Mount Taihuang appeared.
He turned around and settled there,
and five hundred years passed without him realizing it.
This was the time when the gold stones appeared on Mount Taihuang,
the original stone axe and iron hammer appeared as well,
the axe and hammer were given to Pangu to separate heaven and earth.

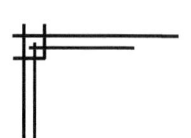

玄黄头颅化混沌，
混沌里面盘古生。
盘古生在头颅内，
头颅好似天地形。
盘古随着头颅长，
又有神祖画成形。
混沌转化成盘古，
实为三度转化身。

北方壬癸化水星，
东方甲乙化木星，
西方庚辛化金星，
南方丙丁化火星。
四方星辰来助阵，
要助盘古显威能，
北方水星化海池，
东方木星化斧柄，
西方金星化石斧，
南方火星霹雳震，
中央戊己是昆仑，
脚踏太荒一山林。
盘古来在山顶上，
一斧劈开混元石，
清气浮而九霄去，
重浊落在地下沉，
天高地厚才形成。
老祖老母神两个，
一个红精黑暗祖，

二、黑暗混沌 II.Darkness and Chaos

Xuanhuang's skull became Chaos,
and Chaos gave birth to Pangu.
Pangu was born inside of the skull,
which had the shape of heaven and earth.
Then Pangu grew with the skull,
with the pattern painted by the ancestor.
That's why the change of Chaos to Pangu,
actually entailed three transformations.

In the north, Ren Gui became Mercury.
In the east, Jia Yi became Jupiter.
In the west, Geng Xin became Venus.
In the south, Bing Ding became Mars.
The stars in all four directions came to help,
to bolster Pangu's morale and showcase his prowess.
In the north, Mercury turned into a pool of seawater.
In the east, Jupiter turned into the handle of an axe.
In the west, Venus turned into a stone axe,
In the south, Mars turned into the roaring of the thunderbolts.
In the middle, Wuji was Mount Kunlun,
which stood firmly on a forest in Mount Taihuang.
Pangu came to the top of the mountain,
with one strike, he chopped open the muddled original stone,
pure air sent floating high into the sky,
heavy debris sent sinking onto the ground,
the moment the high sky and thick earth were being formed.
There was two immortals, a forefather and a foremother,
one the red spirited forefather of darkness,

一个黑精红暗母。
洪水之时金石化，
黑水之时成神祖，
收下三百六十子，
都是先天化童顽。
老祖老母来讲道，
要将顽童都从善，
都成正果知天然。

洞房门前一石兽，
像虎像狮像狻猊。
非虎非狮不一般，
一对眼睛红光闪，
龇着獠牙吐舌端。
一日顽童来玩耍，
见了石兽眼流血，
越流越多甚惨然。

老祖一见事不好，
石兽流血为哪般？
老祖老母来观看，
原是洪水要泡天。
洪水要淹昆仑山，
吩咐子弟快躲避，
最后剩下三个半，
哪三个，哪半个？
要请歌师找答案。

二、黑暗混沌 II.Darkness and Chaos

the other the black spirited foremother of redness.
During the flood, the gold stone melted,
and during the black water the immortal ancestors came to be.
They adopted three hundred and sixty disciples,
all being naughty children by nature.
The forefather and foremother preached to them,
to guide them to pursue goodness,
and to be good and understand nature.

There was a stone animal in front of the cave,
that looked like a tiger, a lion, or a lion dragon.
Neither a tiger nor a lion, it was no ordinary being,
with a pair of eyes shining with the red light,
fangs showing, the tongue stretched out.
One day when the naughty children came to play,
they saw the stone animal's eyes bleeding,
blood running on and on, a very heartbreaking sight indeed.

The forefather saw this and became worried,
wondering, why does the stone animal bleed?
The forefather and foremother figured,
that the flood was coming.
Since Mount Kunlun was to be flooded,
they ordered the children to seek refuge,
except for three and a half of them.
Who were the three? Who was the half?
Master singer please find the answer.

老祖老母未淹死，
半个弟子是混元。
弟子慌忙去躲难，
有的藏在深洞内，
有的忙往石缝钻，
有的爬在高树上，
有的长翅飞上天。
有一个葫芦连藤长，
忽然喳开忙开口，
快到口里躲难星。
有的连忙往里钻，
化为鱼龙把水翻。

有一个弟子叫混元，
混元弟子不一般，
日后混元有造化。
清水之时有一缘，
连忙来把混元叫，
来到石兽腿中间，
石兽腿后有一孔，
此是昆仑一地眼。
你今躲在地眼内，
扯菀茅草来盖严。
还有弟子无处躲，
昆仑山中地方宽，
山中有山山上山，
无数洞府神祖占。
有一洞府甚奇异，
各样景致看不完。

二、黑暗混沌 II.Darkness and Chaos

The forefather and foremother did not drown,
and the half disciple was Hunyuan.
All the disciples rushed to escape:
some hid deep in the cave;
some got into the cracks of the stone;
some climbed high up to the trees;
and some grew wings and flew into the sky.
Presently, a gourd with long vines,
opened its mouth all of a sudden:
come into my mouth to escape the disaster!
Some rushed into it,
and changed into fish and dragon to stir up the water.

The disciple whose name was Hunyuan was no ordinary disciple,
and he had a great future.
During Clear Water, there was a time for Hunyuan,
so he was called quickly,
to come between the legs of the stone animal.
Behind the legs of the animal was a hole,
and it was an earth's eye in Mount Kunlun.
He hid in the earth's eye,
and covered it tightly with thatch.
Other disciples had nowhere to hide,
even though Mount Kunlun was big and wide,
with mountains within mountains,
countless caves of the ancestral immortals,
even a fantastic one,
with more various scenery than one could see.

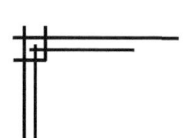

提起混元一老祖,
躲在地眼三千年。
这时他把头来探,
洪水未退泪几点。
望了四次仍未退,
四滴眼泪滴下边。
化成四个水爬虫,
万丈长来千丈宽,
又出浪子不一般。
四个浪子无比怪,
浮在水上像大船。
四个浪子四下分,
摇摇摆摆水上玩。

四个浪子四个怪,
又吞日月又吞天。
第四浪子他最好,
常常回来见混元。
混元问他哪里去?
浪子回答水上玩。

水上看见什么景?
一蓬荷叶大又圆,
一蓬荷叶有九匹。
一匹荷叶一重天,
荷叶上面有一景,
露水珠儿亮闪闪。
滚来滚去有灵性。
放出五色祥云团。

二、黑暗混沌 II. Darkness and Chaos

Ancestor Hunyuan,
hid in the earth's eye for three thousand years.
He then stuck his head out to look,
only to find the flood not subsiding, so he was in tears.
And he did this four times and, with the flood persisting,
four drops of tears fell.
The tears transformed into four water crawlers,
tens and thousands of *zhang* long and thousands of *zhang* wide,
and they changed themselves into unusual loafers.
The four loafers were unsurpassed in oddity,
floating on the water like large ships.
They divided the water into four areas,
amusing themselves swaying up and down.

The four loafers were four monsters,
they swallowed the sun, the moon and the sky.
The fourth loafer was the kindest,
returning often to visit with Hunyuan.
When Hunyuan asked him where he had been,
the loafer answered that he had fun on the water.

What did you see on the water?
I saw a lotus leaf huge and round,
as large as nine bolts of cloth.
The leaf was like the sky,
with the view,
of the shiny dewdrops glistening and glittering.
The drops rolled here and there with magic,
letting out auspicious cloud in five colors.

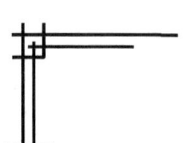

黑暗传　The Legend of Darkness

混元听了多有趣，
天地之根已出现。
荷叶在天分九重，
露珠像似雨露般。
荷花已谢莲籽落，
莲籽将来化神仙。
正是浪子口中渴，
七颗甘露一口吞。
喝了七颗甘露水，
一朵莲花还未谢。
一个莲蓬结籽生，
荷叶失了甘露水，
枯了荷叶和花心。

荷叶老祖一苦莲，
混元忙把浪子问：
见了荷叶你怎办？
浪子回答我吃了，
吃了荷叶往回转。
荷叶好吃水好喝，
撑得肚皮圆又圆。

混元一听心大怒，
来把浪子撕两段。
只分两段不打紧，
露出荷叶屎一团。
人间万物包在内，
一团混沌分清难。
屎团一堆见风长，
陡然长起山一座，
名字就叫青龙山，
后头慢慢说根源。

二、黑暗混沌 II. Darkness and Chaos

Hunyuan was very happy to hear all this,
because that meant that the beginning of heaven and earth
had already appeared.
The lotus leaf had the nine layers of high heaven,
and the dewdrops were like the raindrops.
When lotus flower withered, down fell the lotus seeds,
which were to change into immortals.
When the loafer was thirsty,
he swallowed the seven sweet dewdrops at one gulp.
He drank all the seven dewdrops,
but one lotus flower was still blooming.
Even though the lotus seedpod was bearing fruit,
the lotus leaf lost the sweet dewdrop,
and then both the leaf and the lotus dried up.

Poor lotus ancestor!
Hunyuan asked the loafer hurriedly:
what did you do to the lotus leaf?
The loafer said that he had eaten it:
after eating the lotus leaf,
the delicious leave, he drank the sweet dewdrops,
filling up the belly round and round.

On hearing it, Hunyuan was furious,
and tore the loafer in half.
From between the two halves,
came a ball of lotus droppings.
It contained everything in the world,
although it was difficult to tell one thing from another.
The pile of droppings grew with wind,
and suddenly became a mountain.
Its name was Mount Qinlong.
Later I will explain the origin by and by.

金鼓一停我接住,
提起昊天一段古,
歌师听我从头数。
无有乾坤无有天,
只有古祖他在先,
自从洪水泡了天,
渺渺茫茫无自然,
山中十万八千年,
才出昊天老神仙。
讲起古祖来出世,
提起昊天老祖母,
一无父来二无母,
你看怪古不怪古?

黑黑暗暗,混混沌沌,
渺渺冥冥,昊天此时生,
只有昊天圣母生得恶,
头上长出一对角,
打败黑龙平洪波。

洪水泡了天和地,
提起灵山虚妙洞,
昊天圣母一段情,
圣母原是金石长,
清水三番成人形。
石人得道称圣母,
名唤昊天是她身。
圣母坐在虚妙洞,
要到灵山走一程。

二、黑暗混沌 II. Darkness and Chaos

Gold drum stopped, so let me go on.
There was a long story about Haotian.
Master singer, listen to me to tell it from its beginning.
Before there was heaven and earth,
the ancient ancestor was born.
Since the great flood,
there was nothing but boundless water.
Only one hundred eighty thousand years later,
did the ancient immortal Haotian appear in the mountain.
Speaking of the birth of the ancestor,
the ancient grandmother Haotian,
you will find it odd,
because she had neither a father nor a mother.

It was dark, chaotic,
and indistinct, when Haotian was born.
Goddess Haotian was born ugly,
with a pair of horn on her head,
and she defeated the Black Dragon and quelled the melee.

While heaven and earth were flooded,
there was Cave Xumiao in Mount Ling,
where a story about Goddess Haotian happened.
The goddess was originally grown out of the gold stone,
adopting the human shape after living through the clear water flood three times.
Enlightened, this stone became a goddess,
and Haotian was her name.
The goddess, sitting in Cave Xumiao one day,
wanted to take a walk in Mount Ling.

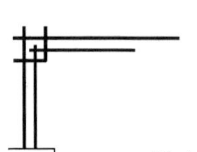

站在灵山四下望,
洪水滔滔怕煞人,
两条长龙在争斗,
二龙相斗气腾腾。
只见空中黑云现,
黄龙当时逞威武,
抓得黑龙血淋淋。
黑龙当时来聚会,
弟兄五个显威能,
黄龙一时败了阵,
直奔灵山洞府门。

圣母观了多一会,
定天珠在手中存,
抛在空中雷电闪,
黑龙一见忙败阵。
便把黑龙来打败,
七窍流血逃性命。

漫天黑云不见形,
往西边走不见了,
这时洪水稍平静。
黄龙落在灵山上,
感念圣母有恩人。
生下三个龙蛋子,
三个龙蛋放光明。

二、黑暗混沌 II.Darkness and Chaos

Standing on Mount Ling, she look down around her,
and saw frighteningly torrential floodwater everywhere.
Two big dragons were fighting,
both aggressive and belligerent.
Suddenly black clouds appeared in the sky,
and the Yellow Dragon, to show off its strength,
clawed Black Dragon bloody.
The Black Dragon gathered its brothers,
five of them all powerful and ready.
When the Yellow Dragon was defeated,
it ran straight to the cave in Mount Ling.

The goddess watched for a long time,
holding the lulling pearl in her hand.
She then threw the pearl into the sky causing thunder and lightning,
and the Black Dragons to retreat.
The Black Dragons were defeated,
fleeting for their lives and covered with blood.

The all encompassing black clouds disappeared,
to the west.
Then the flood calmed down a little.
The Yellow Dragon landed on Mount Ling,
grateful to the goddess, the savior of its life.
It gave birth to three dragon eggs,
three shiny eggs.

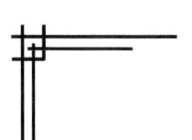

圣母一见心欢喜，
将蛋吞在腹中存。
吃了三个龙蛋子，
腹中有孕在其身。
怀孕不觉三十载，
正月初七降下身，
一胎生下人三个。
圣母一见甚欢心。

长子取名为定光，
次子后土是他身，
第三取名为婆娑，
虚妙洞中生长成，
三个儿子已长成，
不觉已过五百春。

圣母便把孩儿叫，
灵山景致多得很。
一座石岩高万丈，
朵朵梅花在中间。
三十六匹叶子长，
有座仙山生得妙，
更比群山高远了。
此山名字叫虚妙，
虚妙山上长仙草。
色分七彩好奇妙。
树高只有三尺三，
时时都把毫光现，
结颗宝珠似仙丹。

二、黑暗混沌 II.Darkness and Chaos

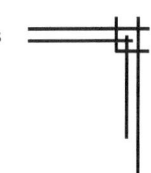

The goddess was glad at the sight of them,
and she swallowed them to store them in her belly.
Having swallowed the three dragon eggs,
she became pregnant.
Quickly thirty years had passed,
before she gave birth on the seventh day of the lunar January,
to triplets.
The sight of them delighted the goddess.

The eldest was named Dingguang;
the second, Tashen,
and the third, Posuo.
They grew up in Cave Xumiao,
and when they became grown-ups,
five hundred years had passed.

Then the goddess asked them to come with her,
to appreciate the diverse sceneries of Mount Ling.
A rocky cliff reached up tens and thousands of *zhang* high,
with many plum blossoms.
There were thirty six bolts of long leaves.
An exquisite fairy mountain,
stood higher and farther away than all other mountains.
Its name was Xumiao,
where there were prairies of magic grass,
with seven wonderful colors.
The trees were only three *chi* three *cun* tall,
but they gave out light constantly,
bearing a treasure pearl like an elixir of life.

李子开花白又鲜，
根深叶青自先天。
后世自有神仙出，
上古神来下古仙。
杏树开花碗口大，
杏子黄了四时鲜。
杏仁里面有一物，
洪水之后出世间。
桃树花儿红艳艳，
花开不谢三千年。
三千年后结桃子，
桃核里头藏众仙。
后来王母蟠桃会，
自有核仁落人间。

一蔸青草正扬花，
花开花落一瞬间。
此草名叫天仙草，
后叫稻米五谷先。
一万八千春过后，
传与农夫好种田。
此事虽是后来事，
说与孩儿记心间。

二、黑暗混沌 II. Darkness and Chaos

The plum tree blossomed white and fresh,
with deep roots and green leaves by nature.
Immortals came out of here later,
ancient immortals and then fairies.
Apricot flowers were as big as a bowl,
ripened apricots remaining fresh all year long.
And inside the apricot pit was an object,
which came out after the floods.
The peach flowers were brilliant red,
blooming for three thousand years without withering.
They bore fruits at the end of three thousand years,
and hiding inside the peach pits were all kinds of immortals.
Later on when the Heavenly Queen Mother hosted the Festival of Immortal Peaches,
no wonder almonds fell to the mortal world.

A handful of green grass was just flowering,
but blooming and then instantly fading.
Its name was Heavenly Immortal Grass,
which later was called rice and other grains.
They were handed down to farmers to grow,
eighteen thousand years later.
Though this was a later event,
I mention it for later generations to bear in mind.

母子来到丹桂树,
看见树下红光现。
圣母一见高声问:
你是什么妖魔怪?
烧死丹桂为哪般?
忽然两人来跪拜,
一男一女忙开言:
"一男一女人两个,
又叫与子贞天贤。
原在荷花池内住,
金水相生结仙缘。
只因三番洪水后,
俱在灵山躲难星。
桂花树下藏其身。"
圣母听了此言语,
笑在眉头喜在心,
"原是太阳与太阴,
后来日月就是你,
一阴一阳照乾坤"。

二人听罢忙点头,
辞别圣母不见形。
一男回到太阳洞,
一女又归太阴门。
都在咸池深海内,
并蒂莲花海上存。
有一根古在后头,
浪荡吃了遭难星。

二、黑暗混沌 II. Darkness and Chaos

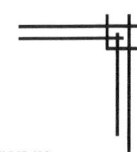

Presently the mother and her children came under an orange osmanthus tree,
which was seen glittering with red light.
The goddess demanded with a forceful voice:
What kind of monster are you?
Why did you burn the orange osmanthus tree?
Suddenly, two persons appeared kneeling in front of her,
a male and a female, and answered hurriedly:
"We two are a male and a female,
also called Yu Zi Zhen and Tianxian.
We used to live in the lotus pool,
born to the gold water to be an immortal couple.
Because of the three floods,
we are in Mount Ling to escape the catastrophic event.
We are hiding under the orange osmanthus tree as our shelter."
On hearing these words,
the goddess was pleased, smiling:
"I see. You are Tai Yang and Tai Yin.
You will later be the sun and the moon,
shining upon heaven and earth with Yin and Yang."

Listening, the two nodded promptly,
taking leaving of the goddess and vanishing instantly.
The male returned to Cave Tai Yang,
while the female, Gate Tai Yin.
Both dwelled deep in the Xian Pool at the sea,
as two sea lotus flowers connected at the roots.
There is another story later,
when a loafer suffered miserably after eating them.

母子游到菊花殿,
各种菊花开得鲜。
面对一个雪花洞,
雪花纷纷顿觉寒。
将来以花来分月,
一十二月结花缘。

梅树开花报春早,
桃李开花正春天。
稻花一开谷结穗,
菊花一开霜雪连。
此是灵山四季景,
传在后世在人间。
忽听树上嘤嘤叫,
原是黄鸟万万千。
黄鸟一叫报时辰,
黄鸟报时有根源。
黄鸟一叫天就明,
黄鸟二叫太阳升,
黄鸟三叫正午时,
黄鸟再叫天黄昏。

母子观罢灵山景,
要回天山洞府门,
定光看得正高兴,
要到灵山顶上行。

二、黑暗混沌 II.Darkness and Chaos

Now the mother and her children came to the chrysanthemum palace,
all kinds of chrysanthemums were in full bloom.
They were in front of a snow cave,
with the chilling snow falling down profusely.
The months would be divided by flowers later,
and the twelve months and various flowers were meant for each other.

Plum blossoms heralded early spring,
while peach blossoms heralded high spring.
The bloom of the rice flower promised the hanging ears of the millet,
and the bloom of chrysanthemums promised the falling of the frost and snow.
These were the four-season sceneries of Mount Ling,
that were handed down to the mortal world later.
Suddenly, there was chirping from the tree,
by tens and thousands of yellow birds.
Yellow birds' singing gave the correct time,
following a regular pattern:
the first chirp showing the daybreak,
the second chirp showing the sunrise,
the third chirp showing the noon,
the fourth chirp showing the dusk.

Mother and children were done sightseeing in Mount Ling,
getting ready to return to the gate of Cave Tianshan.
Dingguang was not yet ready to end the joyful outing,
so he climbed to the top of Mount Ling.

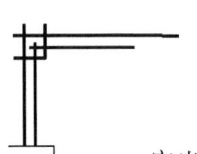

定光来到山顶上，
洪水滔滔怕煞人。
黑雾腾腾空中旋，
忽听空中喊一声。
叫声定光你且听，
太虚洞中多热闹，
请到太虚走一程。

定光跟着黄龙走，
太虚殿中看分明。
只见宫殿多齐备，
亭台楼阁色色新。
定光来到太虚殿，
紫云腾腾放光明。
黄龙跪下称老祖，
定光圣祖你且听，
可恨黑龙来作乱。
又翻洪水水连天，
他与吾龙来作对，
灵山顶上躲灾星。
太虚洞中九天外，
不遭洪水救众生，
敬请圣祖发号令。
五条黑龙多厉害，
兄弟五个本事能，
大哥手执开山斧，
二哥口内吐红云，
三弟能把山搬走，
四弟搅得海翻腾。
只有五弟手段狠，
天地日月一口吞。

二、黑暗混沌 II. Darkness and Chaos

While there at the top,
he saw the frightening torrential floodwater.
From the black fog circling in the sky,
a voice unexpectedly was calling at him.
Dingguang, listen to me.
Cave Taixu was bustling with fun,
so please take a trip there.

Thereupon, Dingguang followed the Yellow Dragon,
to have a look at Cave Taixu.
There, he saw a variety of palaces,
brand new pavilions and towers.
When Dingguang entered the Taixu Hall,
he saw purple clouds rising and brightening.
The Yellow Dragon suddenly knelt in front of him, saying:
Ancestor Dingguang, please listen to me,
about the vile Black Dragons who created a disturbance.
They stirred up the floodwater sky high,
just to make trouble for me,
so I am hiding on the top of Mount Lingshan to escape the disaster.
In Cave Taixu, out of the Ninth Heaven,
I am beyond flood's reach and can save lives.
Therefore, I beg Ancestor to give an order.
The five Black Dragons were fierce,
all of the five brothers having powerful skills:
the eldest brother can wield a mountain-chopping axe;
the second brother can spit red clouds from his mouth;
the third brother can move mountains;
the fourth brother can stir up the sea.
The fifth brother being the cruelest,
he can swallow heaven and earth, the sun and the moon at one gulp.

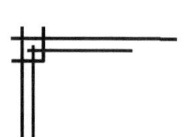

五条黑龙有来因,
它是上古洪荒生。
当日石龙一老母,
住在洞内闷沉沉。
下到昆仑来游玩,
洪水之中起黑云,
黑云遮住老母身,
老母当时肚子疼,
产下一个龙蛋子,
龙蛋炸开两边分。

蛋里跳出五黑龙,
五条黑龙吐黑水,
一股黑水淹昆仑。
如果收了黑龙精,
天下洪水得太平。
定光听得这言语,
怒目圆睁冒火星。
忙招鹰龙来领命,
来到昆仑高山顶。

二、黑暗混沌 II. Darkness and Chaos

The five Black Dragons have their own stories,
and they were born during the ancient chaotic times.
Once an old woman of the stone dragon,
was bored staying in her cave.
She went out to Kunlun to have some fun,
but the black clouds rose from the flood,
which covered the stone mother,
who instantly felt a stomachache
and then gave birth to a dragon egg,
which burst into two halves.

Out of the egg jumped five Black Dragons,
all of them spewing black water,
that drowned Mount Kunlun.
If the Black Dragon monsters are under control,
the flood will subside and peace be restored.
On hearing this,
Dingguang was so angry that his eyes were blazing with sparks.
Quickly, he ordered Eagle Dragon,
to run to the top of Mount Kunlun.

说起鹰龙大得很,
千片羽毛万丈长,
遮天盖地本事能。
原是天上大鹏鸟,
一声吼叫如雷鸣。
两道目光如闪电,
爪如铁钩万般能。
名叫鹰龙无敌手,
专为定光听号令。
当时鹰龙听吩咐,
黑龙抓到爪中心。
便把龙头来拿下,
拿到定光面前呈。
当时洪水来平定,
黑龙散去不见影。
黄龙当时把恩谢,
连忙献出宝和珍。
献上化云珠一颗,
化为九天一朵云,
落定尘埃天地清。
黄龙最后为天师,
掌管龙神它为尊。

昊天圣母知此事,
便叫次子幽冥听。
你把黑龙来收伏,
九泉地狱去安身。
叫他托起五方地,
地高水退得安宁。

二、黑暗混沌 II.Darkness and Chaos

About this Eagle Dragon, it was huge,
with thousands of feathers tens and thousands *zhang* long,
that could cover heaven and earth.
It used to be a roc in the sky,
its roar comparable to the thunderbolt.
Its eyes were like lightening,
and its claws were like powerful iron hooks.
Named Eagle Dragon, it was invincible,
and took orders only from Dingguang.
The Eagle Dragon was told,
to seize the Black Dragons by the claws,
remove their heads,
and present them to Dingguang.
As soon as the flood subsided,
the Black Dragons were gone.
The Yellow Dragon expressed his gratitude,
and immediately presented the treasure,
of a cloud-changing pearl,
which turned into a cloud in the Ninth Heaven,
settling the dust in heaven and earth alike.
Eventually, the Yellow Dragon became the honorable Celestial Master,
in charge of all dragon immortals.

When Goddess Haotian learned about all this,
she gave an order to the second son Youming.
Go bring the Black Dragons under control,
and send them to settle in the nine-spring underworld.
Tell them to hold up the earth in all five directions,
so that there will be peace on the high land and in the low waters.

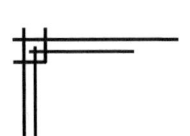

圣母又把幽冥叫，
你把幽都走一程。
赐你斩关剑一口，
分开五关到幽都。
幽冥来到幽都地，
此为地府十八层。

五条黑龙阴魂在，
见了幽冥怒气生。
今日要把仇来报，
为何斩我五性命？
说罢现出五龙爪，
要抓幽冥一仇人。
幽冥取出翻天印，
五龙吓得战兢兢。
幽冥一见传下令，
封为幽都守门人。
又赐夜明珠五颗，
照的幽都地狱城。

二、黑暗混沌 II.Darkness and Chaos

The goddess also ordered Youming,
to pay a visit to the nether world.
She bestowed upon him a special sword for the guards at the passes,
which there were five on the way to the nether world.
Youming came to the nether world,
where there were eighteen levels.

The ghosts of the five Black Dragons were haunting the place,
furious on seeing Youming.
We will avenge ourselves today,
for why did you kill us five?
Then they extended their five dragon talons,
to grab Youming, their enemies.
Instantly, Youming took out the heaven-turning seal,
which sent the five dragons trembling with fear.
When Youming saw this, he gave the order,
to offer them the post of gatekeepers of the nether world.
In addition, he awarded them with five luminous pearls,
to illuminate the nether world.

幽都城里冤魂多，
都因洪水丧性命。
上古神仙水中死，
许多龙蛇也丧生。
大大小小三千万，
聚在幽都等超生。
幽冥做了幽都主，
主管幽都一座城。
来把冤魂一一问，
打发阳世来托生。
掌管五关并六部，
又管阴阳二界门。
又赐夜明珠五颗，
照见幽都放光明。

昆仑山上鸿清洞，
鸿清洞中一段情。
白妃娘娘洞中坐，
她的出生怪得很。
远古太荒洪水起，
一番洪水那时生，
一块白石化人体，
白化老母出世根。
原在昆仑山上生，
一块白石大又圆，
黑暗之中放光明。

二、黑暗混沌 II.Darkness and Chaos

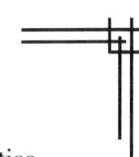

In the nether world were many souls that suffered injustice,
because they lost their lives to the flood.
Many ancient immortals died,
so did numerous dragons and snakes.
Big and small, there were altogether thirty millions of them,
awaiting reincarnation.
Now that Youming was the chief of the nether world,
he was in charge of the whole nether world.
He inquired into the cases of the wronged ghosts one by one,
to arrange their rebirth.
He was also in charge of five passes and six departments,
together with the two gates to the worlds of Yin and Yang.
Again, he was granted five luminous pearls,
illuminating the nether world bright.

In Mount Kunlun, there was Cave Hongqing,
the home of another legend.
In the cave sat an Empress Baifei,
whose birth was quite peculiar.
During the ancient floods and in Taihuang,
she was born,
as a white stone, which then changed into a human body,
which was the origin of the ancestress.
A native to Mount Kunlun,
the white stone was large and round,
giving out light in darkness.

久而久之石头炸,
一道红光如彩霞,
变出一个女娇娃,
后名白妃就是她。
长子名字叫洪儒,
次子取名是洪浩。
只有三子他最小,
取名就叫小洪钧。
谈起三子根基深,
元始上古宝石珍。
金水相生得精气,
三番洪水有了灵。

昆仑山中三口井,
原是地眼品字形。
一井黑水苦又腥,
一井红水如血汁,
一井清水如甘霖。
原是三番洪水留,
灵气聚到三口井。
白妃喝了三井水,
借得白妃腹长成。
九九三精附一体,
白妃娘娘来育生。

二、黑暗混沌 II. Darkness and Chaos

Eventually the stone exploded,

with a ray of red light like rosy clouds,

and a baby girl appeared.

She was the one who was later named Empress Baifei.

Her eldest son was named Hongru,

and second son, Honghao.

The third son was small in size,

so he was named little Hongjun.

This third son had deep roots,

in the ancient precious gem stones.

His spirit was molded by gold and water,

and his soul, tempered by the three floods.

In Mount Kunlun were three wells,

originally three of the earth's eyes in a triangle arrangement.

The water in the first well was black, bitter and smelly;

the water in the second well was red like the thick blood;

the water in the third well was clear and sweet.

They were left behind by the three floods,

with spirit-Qi collected in them.

After Empress Baifei drank from the wells,

her belly grew.

All three spirits stuck to one body,

and were borne by Empress Baifei.

不觉三子都长大，
各到各处显威灵。
一日洪钧把山上，
玉虚洞中走一程。
一见定光洞中坐，
见了洪钧来相迎。
两个在此来相会，
原是上古缘分定。

以后再把根古论，
多少根古讲不清。
玄黄老祖生青气，
浪荡出世吞了天。
黑龙黄龙两相战，
三番洪水天地淹。
昊天圣母战洪水，
洪钧称为第一仙。
金龟吐石生昆仑，
九天老祖降凡间，
洪末，末叶，与荷叶，
定光，玉虚，与幽冥。
神仙之中第一贤，
九斩昆仑三妖龙，
混沌出在洪荒间。
盘古出世分天地，
更比玄黄高得远。
有人知得这根源，
能在歌场称上仙。

二、黑暗混沌　II.Darkness and Chaos

Quickly all three sons had grown up,
going to different places to show their talents.
One day, when Hongjun went to the mountain,
he visited Cave Yuxu.
He saw Dingguang sitting in the cave,
and, on seeing Hongjun, coming up to greet him.
The two meeting here,
was meant to happen and determined in the ancient times.

I can tell stories about ancient times later,
so many of them that some are hard to sort out.
The ancestor Xuanhuang was the Qi,
while the Loafer was born to swallow heaven.
The Black Dragons fought with the Yellow Dragon,
and the three floods drowned heaven and earth.
The Goddess Haotian subdued the floods,
as Hongjun was honored as the first fairy.
The gold tortoise spit the stone that became Mount Kunlun,
and the ancestors of the Ninth Heaven descended to the earth:
Hongmo, Moye, and Heye,
Dingguang, Yuxu, and Youming.
The best of the immortals,
nine times slew the three dragon monsters in Kunlun,
while Chaos appeared in the ancient chaotic times.
Pangu was born to separate heaven and earth,
surpassing Xuanhuang.
The one who knows the reason of all this,
can be called the immortal in the Song House.

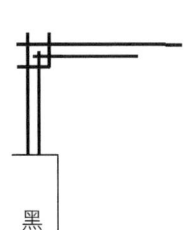

三、日月合明[①]

盘古初开几颗星？
几颗星斗放光明？
何星白日升上界？
何星夜中放光明？
何神出世日月升？
轻气上浮为何因？
浊者下沉为何名？
不知为何生无极？
为何又有太极生？

[①] "日月合明"标题为整理者所加。资料来源：一是《黑暗大盘头》《黑暗纲鉴》部分内容。特别是陈世奎口述记录，如盘古到咸池请日月升天重要唱段，并参阅了他的《日月合明经》《盘古真经》《女娲真经》《神农五谷经》《地母妙经》《太阳真经》等经书。陈世奎，松柏镇蔬菜村村民，民间火居道士，民间歌手，他在青年时期打薅草锣鼓时与人合唱过《黑暗传》。笔者1982—1995年多次采访过他，他提供了不少口头资料。1998年1月去世，享年94岁。据陈世奎的赡养人——孙婿施明贵讲，陈世奎确有一部《黑暗传》，秘不示人，去世时和《道教经》一起被盗。

三、日月合明 III. The Sun and the Moon Illuminating Together

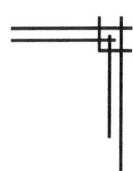

III. The Sun and the Moon Illuminating Together①

How many stars were there when Pangu first separated heaven and earth?

How many of them gave out light?

Which stars rose to heaven during the daytime?

What glittered at night?

Which immortal was born with the sun and moon rising up?

Why did the light air ascend?

Why did the heavy air sink?

Why was Wuji born?

Why was Taiji born as well?

---

① The title "The Sun and the Moon Illuminating Together" was added by people who sorted it out. The resources were: one from part of *Darkness Inquiry* and *Darkness Principles Guide*, especially from the record of Chen Shikui's oral account, such as the important song of Pangu's invitation of the sun and the moon to Heaven in Xian Chi. This also consulted his sacred books like *The Sun and Moon Illuminating Scriptures*, *Pangu Scriptures*, *Nvwa Scriptures*, *Shennong Patron of Agriculture*, *Mother Earth Scriptures*, and *The Sun Scriptures*, etc. Chen Shikui was a villager in Shucai Village, Songbo Town, a folk Huoju Taoist and a folk singer. When he was young, he sang *The Legend of Darkness* together with others while playing weeding drumming. The writer interviewed him many times from 1982-1995, and got a lot of material. He died at the age of 94, in January, 1998. According to Shi Minggui, a grandson-in-law of Chen Shikui, Chen Shikui did have a book of *The Legend of Darkness*, though being kept secret, stolen with *The Tao Teh King* when dying.

163

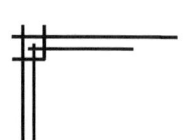

混沌初开分天地，
盘古出世此时起，
谁人知得这根底？
盘古出世神又神，
站在九霄云里层，
手拿一把开天斧，
斧头用来开天门。
又有一把开山斧，风火钻，
还有斩龙剑一根。
盘古开辟天地明。
两手举斧安日月，
开天辟地定乾坤。
盘古知道地理与天文，
开天开地定乾坤。

阴阳二气搅一团，
二气不分成混沌。
二气来分开，才成天地形，
气之轻清往上升，
气之重浊往下沉，
方才成了天地样，
才算开天第一人。

三、日月合明 III. The Sun and the Moon Illuminating Together

Heaven and earth in Chaos was to be separated,

the time Pangu was born.

Who knows about this story?

Pangu was born, amazingly,

standing in the clouds of the Ninth Heaven,

holding a creation axe,

the axe for opening the heavenly gate.

He also had a mountain-chopping axe, a wind-fire drill,

also a dragon-slaying sword.

Pangu cleft apart heaven and earth, brightening both.

With both of his hands holding the axe, Pangu set the sun and the moon,

heaven and earth.

Pangu, understanding geography and astronomy,

separated heaven and earth.

With Yin and Yang mixed up,

indistinguishable was Chaos.

Only when the two were separated, heaven and earth took shape.

Light air rising,

and heavy air sinking,

heaven and earth being formed.

He was therefore the first person on earth and under heaven.

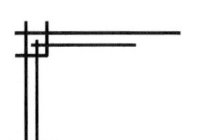

歌师你请慢消停，
我把歌师称一声，
盘古怎么来出身？
提起盘古问分明，
盘古怎么来出世？
怎么来把天地分？
盘古应天而出世，
生于太荒有谁知？
混沌世界怎开辟？

说盘古，讲盘古，
多亏混沌一老祖。
九十一气费尽心，
五行方位安其身，
浑身上下元气足，
盘古他在哪里走，哪里行？
怎么得的开天斧？
那斧是宝还是精？
或是木头来砍就？
还是钢铁来打成？
你把根源说我听，
才算歌场第一人。

三、日月合明 III. The Sun and the Moon Illuminating Together

Master singer, please slow down,

and I am sorry to interrupt you, master singer.

How was Pangu born?

I would like to know the following:

how was Pangu born?

How did he separate heaven and earth?

Pangu was born according to heaven's will,

but does anyone know where in Mount Taihuang he was born?

How was Chaos separated into heaven and earth?

Pangu,

owed it to Ancestor Chaos.

He strained himself to the limit,

settled with the Five Elements and in five directions,

and was full of the primordial Qi.

Where did Pangu go or on what did he walk?

How did he get the creation axe?

Was that axe a treasure or a demon?

Was it made of wood?

Or was it made of iron and steel?

If you can tell me that story,

you will be number one in the Song House.

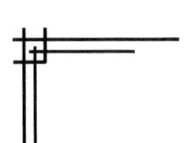

黑暗传　The Legend of Darkness

歌师听我说分明，
我把根由说你听，
今日鼓上遇知音。
混沌之时出盘古，
洪荒之中出了世，
说起盘古有根痕。
当时乾坤未成形，
青赤二气不分明，
一片黑暗与混沌，
金木水火土，五行未成形。
乾坤暗暗如鸡蛋，
密密匝匝几千层，
不知过了多少年，
二气相交产万灵。

盘古怀在混沌内，
此是天地产育精。
混沌里面是包罗，
包罗吐青气，昆仑才形成，
天心地胆在中心，
出生盘古一个人。
不知过了几万春，
盘古长大成人形。
盘古昏昏如梦醒，
伸腿伸腰出地心。
睁开眼睛抬头看，
四面黑暗闷沉沉，
站起身来把腰伸，
撑破黑暗与混沌。
天宽地阔无比伦。

三、日月合明 III. The Sun and the Moon Illuminating Together

Listen to me carefully, the master singer,
to tell you the origin,
since, in singing together, we have met today as bosom friends.
Pangu was born to Chaos,
in the ancient chaotic times,
so Pangu had his own story.
At that time heaven and earth were not yet formed,
blue and red energies being indistinct.
All were full of darkness and chaos,
and the Five Elements (Metal, Wood, Water, Fire and Earth) were not yet formed.
The mass of heaven and earth was as dark as the inside of an egg,
packed with thousands of layers.
No one knows how many years had passed before,
the two kinds of energy intersected and produced tens and thousands of spirits.

Chaos was pregnant with Pangu,
who was nurtured by the essence of heaven and earth.
Inside Chaos was Baoluo,
When Baoluo spit blue air, Kunlun began to form.
With the cores of heaven and earth in his center,
Pangu was born a person.
No one knows how many years had passed,
before Pangu grew into a human being.
He felt groggy like just waking up from a deep sleep,
stretching his legs and waist beyond his place.
Opening his eyes and raising his head,
he saw only darkness all around him.
He stood up to straighten up his back,
poking through Darkness and Chaos.
The sky was matchlessly wide and the earth incomparably broad.

一朵赤气往下落,
长出昆仑山一座。
自从昆仑它长成,
不知过了多少春。
昆仑山上绕黑龙,
把山绕了三转有余零。
盘古来把黑龙斩,元气化为精,
昆仑增高三千丈,长成五龙形。
昆仑生出五条岭,
生出一个五龙形,
曲曲弯弯多古怪,
五龙口中流红水,
聚在海洋内面存。
就在此处结仙胎,
多少古怪长出来。

盘古出世雷声响,
一股灵气透天光,
冲开黑暗云和雾,
冲破头颅一混沌。
定要把混沌来劈分。
这时盘古四下里寻,
上为盖来下为盆,
严丝合缝扣得紧,
混沌如同头颅形,
左寻右摸看不真,

三、日月合明　III. The Sun and the Moon Illuminating Together

One red cloud descended,
and turned into Mount Kunlun.
Since the formation of Kunlun,
no one knows how many years had passed again.
Then came the Black Dragons winding themselves on Kunlun,
circling it more than three times.
Pangu came and slew the Black Dragons, and the primordial Qi became spirit.
Kunlun grew another three thousand *zhang*, shaped like five dragons.
Kunlun had five ridges,
taking the shape of the five dragons,
twisting and turning, looking odd.
Red water ran from the mouths of the five dragons,
into the sea and stayed there.
This was where celestial beings were conceived,
producing many bizarre beings.

Pangu's birth was accompanied by a loud thunderclap,
and some miraculous brightness penetrating the sky,
through the black clouds and fog,
cracking open the skull of Chaos.
Pangu was determined to split Chaos.
He searched high and low.
But the top was like a cover and the bottom a basin,
the two clamping tightly without any seam.
Chaos was like a skull,
obscure inside,

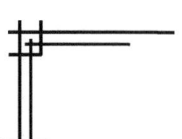

上无缝来下无门，
看来天地不好分。
盘古原名曰金坤，
身高万丈无比伦。
混沌里面生长成，
渐渐长大难容身。
金木水火土五行，
天河落的宝和珍。
落在地上万万年，
土之保养成五星。
水星化成大海池，
木星化成高山林。
金星化一把开天斧，
漂在海上不下沉。

盘古见了忙捞起，
一把石斧不差分。
盘古奔波一路行，
往东方，东不明，
往北方，看不清，
往南方，雾沉沉，
往西方，有颗星。
盘古摘来星星看，
西方金星来变化，
变一石斧面前存，
盘古一见喜十分，
不是金来不像银，
也不像铁匠来打成，
原是西方庚辛金，
金精一点化斧形。

三、日月合明 III. The Sun and the Moon Illuminating Together

with not a crack on top nor a door below.
It looked like it would be hard to separate heaven and earth.
The original name of Pangu was Jinkun,
and he was tens and thousands of *zhang* tall.
Growing inside Chaos,
Pangu gradually felt it hard to stay there.
The Five Elements—Metal, Wood, Water, Fire and Earth—
were treasures falling from the Milky Way.
Tens and thousands of years after they fell,
nurtured by the dirt, they became five stars.
Mercury turned into an ocean of seas.
Jupiter turned into the forests in the high mountains.
Venus turned into the creation axe,
floating on the sea without sinking.

When Pangu saw the axe, he fetched it out of the water right away,
which seemed exactly like a stone axe.
Pangu was on his way.
he looked at the east, it was dark;
he looked at the north, it was obscure;
he looked at the south, it was foggy;
he looked at the west, there was a star.
When Pangu picked the star to examine it,
this Venus of the west started to change,
and turned into a stone axe.
Pangu was excited to see it,
which was neither gold nor like silver,
not like something forged by a blacksmith.
It was Gen Xin Venus of the west,
who transformed the Venus spirits into an axe.

盘古连忙把斧拎,
拿在手中万斤重,
喜在眉头笑在心,
拎起斧子上昆仑。
一座高山来阻路,
盘古开言把话论。
此山像把斧子形,
拿起不重也不轻,
盘古得了宝和珍。
一把斧子拿在手,
盘古来到东山上,
黑黑暗暗四下连。
不觉来到高山岭,
雾气腾腾怕煞人,
不知天地怎么分?
手执开天斧一把,
劈开天地上下分,
高山挡路一扫平。
盘古来到昆仑山,
抬头睁目四下观,
四下茫茫尽黑暗,
看是哪里连着天。

东边砍,西边砍,
南边砍,北边砍,
声如炸雷冒火星,
劈山填海开地平。
盘古他把天地分,
此处还有好诗文。

三、日月合明 III. The Sun and the Moon Illuminating Together

Pangu hurriedly picked it up,
which weighed, in his hand, tens and thousands of *jin*①.
With excitement on his face and in his heart,
he went up Mount Kunlun carrying the axe.
On his way, he was blocked by a high mountain.
Pangu reasoned to himself, saying,
this mountain looks like an axe.
When I hold it in my hand, it is neither too heavy nor too light.
He decided to keep the treasure.
With the axe in hand,
Pangu came to the top of the east mountain,
where it was pitch-dark on all four sides.
Before he knew it, he came to the Gaoshan Ridge,
where it was thick with fog and frightening.
How to separate heaven and earth?
Wielding the creation axe,
he divided heaven on top and earth at the bottom,
leveling the high mountains that was in his way.
When he arrived at Mount Kunlun,
he raised his head and strained his eyes to look around,
only to find the vast darkness,
which was one with heaven.

He chopped to his east, hewed to his west,
struck to his south, hacked to his north,
with thunderous noises and sparkly stars,
splitting mountains and leveling the sea.
Pangu seperated heaven and earth,
brought forth many a fine song.

---

① *A jin* is half of a kilogram.

诗曰：举斧开天真奇异，
善能安排天和地。
两指一伸开天剪，
剪开云雾往前行。

四句诗儿不打紧，
多少歌师不知情。
歌师听我说分明，
我把根由说你听，
今日鼓上遇知音。
混沌之中出盘古，
鸿蒙之中出了世，
盘古石斧化雷电，
千秋万代镇天庭。

盘古根古说你听，
不知知情不知情？
歌师唱得可是真？
我今还要问几声，
不知仁兄听不听？
盘古既把天地分，
还是天黑地不清，
还要什么照乾坤。
太阳太阴怎么行？
天有日月来相照，
怎么又有满天星？
怎么又有风云会？
怎么又有雨淋淋？
你把根由说我听，
才算歌中一能人。

三、日月合明 III. The Sun and the Moon Illuminating Together

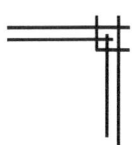

The Poem says: The separation of heaven with an axe was truly amazing,
heaven and earth well arranged.
It was like two fingers that opened up like a pair of creation scissors,
cutting open the clouds and fog for the path ahead.

These four lines are quite general,
because master singers know very little.
Master singers, listen to me to explain clearly,
from the beginning of the story,
since I met my bosom friends in singing today.
Chaos gave birth to Pangu,
in other words, Pangu was born to Hongmeng, the primordial world.
Pangu's axe turned into thunders and lightenings,
controlling heavenly court from generation to generation.

We will listen to you tell the story of Pangu,
hoping you indeed know it.
master singer, is what you know indeed true?
Let me ask a few questions.
Would you allow me to do so?
If Pangu had already separated heaven and earth,
why is the world still dark without distinction,
and what is the use to illuminate heaven and earth?
How about Tai Yang and Tai Ying?
And with the shining sun and moon in the sky,
why are there stars all over it?
why is there the meeting of wind and cloud?
Why is there rain?
Only if you can tell me all the answers to these questions,
can you be the best among the singers.

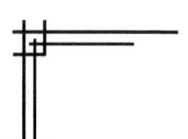

歌师你且慢消停,
我把根由说你听,
看我说得真不真?
盘古分了天和地,
天地依然是混沌,
还是天黑地不明。
盘古想得心纳闷,
要找日月与星辰,
来到东方看分明,
有座高山毫光现,
壅塞阻拦不通行。

提起日月上天庭,
此中奥妙无穷尽。
日月又是什么来长成?
谁人得知日月升?
歌鼓场中拜上尊。

说起当年天河岸,
石龙吃沙炼宝珍。
一口喷出天地生,
石龙卷在地中心。
石龙头上一双眼,
乃是宝中之宝珍。
洪水泡天随波滚,
冲洗磨炼亮晶晶。
一日长起两座山,
东昆仑来西昆仑。
一座日山一月岭,
两山相对万里远,
像对眼泡目未睁。

三、日月合明 III. The Sun and the Moon Illuminating Together

Master singer, be patient,
wait for me to tell you the origins,
and then judge whether my story is true.
Indeed, after Pangu separated heaven and earth,
it was still chaotic,
and full of pitch-darkness.
Pangu was perplexed,
so searching for the sun, the moon, and the stars,
he went to the east to look for them,
and found a high mountain giving off light,
that blocked his way.

About the sun, the moon, and the heavenly court,
they were unfathomable mysteries.
What were the sun and the moon made of?
Who know how they came to be?
Those who do will be the most respectable in the Song House.

About the bank of the Milky Way at that time,
it was where the stone dragon swallowed the sandstone to produce treasures.
It spat out heaven and earth,
wrapping itself up in the center.
On his head were a pair of eyes,
which were the treasure of all treasures.
When the waves rolled during the flood,
they polished those eyes shiny and bright.
One day, two mountains arose,
east Kunlun and west Kunlun.
They were the Sun Mountain and the Moon Ridge,
facing each other while tens and thousands of *li* apart,
like a pair of upper eyelids unopened.

盘古开砍众山岭,
谁敢阻挡一扫平。
左劈右砍汗淋淋,
一滴汗水一朵云。
见到左右山一对,
原是日山月山两山岭。
一斧劈开太阳洞,
一颗珍宝耀眼明。
一斧劈开太阴府,
一团清光亮莹莹。
盘古一见用手捡,
霎时二珠腾空起,
向东飞去如流星。

盘古开步去追赶,
一步跨有百里程。
二珠越飞越是快,
盘古后边追得紧。
越过高山和水洼,
追过一程又一程。
只见二珠落东海,
地眼咸池万里深。
咸池顿时波涛起,
祥云朵朵水色清。
水上金莲开万朵,
每朵花中有图形。
原来是二珠阴阳太极象,
原来是二气生化来成形,
原来是二珠尚得长修炼,
原来是日月升天有时辰。

三、日月合明　III. The Sun and the Moon Illuminating Together

When Pangu chopped away mountains and ridges,
he leveled anyone who dared to block his way.
Hewing left and right, he was dripping with sweat,
each drop of sweat forming a cloud.
When he saw the pair of mountains flanking on his sides,
he knew they were the Sun Mountain and the Moon Ridge.
He then split open Cave Tai Yang with one chop,
and saw a pearl dazzling bright.
He next split open Cave Taiyin at one chop,
and saw a swirl of clear light glistening bright.
The moment Pangu tried to pick up the two pearls,
they rose up to the sky,
and flew east like two meteors.

Pangu started to run after them,
every step one hundred *li* long.
The pearls flew faster and faster,
while Pangu chased closer and closer.
He passed high mountains and low marshes,
persisting one *li* after another.
Then he saw the pearls falling into the east sea,
the earth's eye, the deep Xian Pool, measuring tens and thousands of *zhang* deep.
At once waves in the Xian Pool surged high up,
clear water that formed pieces of auspicious clouds.
Tens and thousands of gold lotus flowers blooming,
each flower contained with it some pattern and design.
It turned out to be the image of the Yin Yang Taiji of the two pearls.
It turned out to be the pattern formed by the two energies.
It turned out the two pearls were to be further cultivated.
It turned out the sun and the moon had their set time to rise up.

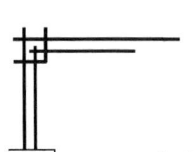

盘古这时睁慧眼，
慧眼长在额中心，
一看知得未来世，
功果未满转回程。

盘古回到太荒林，
眼观四方黑沉沉。
只有东方有光色，
定是咸池二珠明。
盘古又往西方寻，
西方天地连得紧。
大步流星往前走，
前边有一万丈坑。

万丈坑里有一物，
好似怪物大得很，
口吐黑雾毒气生，
一对眼睛绿莹莹。
见得盘古张大口，
一口要把盘古吞。
盘古举起开天斧，
对着怪物下无情。
怪物名曰混沌兽，
吞天吞地本事能。
先天黑暗玄黄收，
后天黑暗又逢盘古神。

三、日月合明 III. The Sun and the Moon Illuminating Together

Now Pangu opened his discerning eye,
which was in the middle of his forehead.
With his foresight he saw,
he hadn't achieved all, so he returned to finish his work.

Pangu returned to the Tai Huang Forest,
where all he saw was duskiness.
Only in the east was shining some light,
which must come from the two pearls in the Xian Pool.
He searched to the west,
where heaven and earth were fused tight.
He walked ahead with vigorous strides,
and found a chasm ten thousand *zhang* deep.

In the chasm of ten thousand *zhang* was an object,
which was huge like a monster,
spitting black smoke that poisoned the air.
It had green and glossy eyes.
When he saw Pangu, he opened his huge mouth,
wanting to swallow Pangu once and for all.
Pangu raised the creation axe,
facing the monster with absolute resolve.
The monster was Chaos' pet,
who was capable of swallowing heaven and earth.
In the first period of darkness, it was adopted by Xuanhuang,
and in the later period of darkness now, it encountered Pangu.

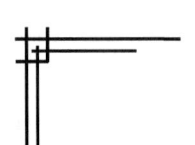

玄黄之后一万八千岁，
又出盘古收混沌。
一个浪荡吞天珠，
一个浪荡吞地灵。
这个怪物吞万物，
就连盘古也敢吞。
盘古举斧将它砍，
一股黑水又翻滚。

此时黑水又泡天。
怪物逃生不见形。
此兽不除有后患，
后来又把日月吞。
盘古劈山来填水，
止住黑水四下分。
蓄住黑水归海池，
万里为圆千丈深。
盘古又到北方行，
北方泉山连天凌，
砍开冰山沉大海，
此是北溟无比冷。
砍开冰凌现一物，
一条鱼龙像山岭，
长有千里生银甲，
双目红光晃晃明。

三、日月合明 III. The Sun and the Moon Illuminating Together

Eighteen thousand years after Xuanhuang,
Pangu came to change Chaos.
A loafer could swallow the heavenly pearl,
and another could swallow the earthly spirits,
but this monster could swallow everything,
even if it was Pangu.
Pangu raised the axe and killed it,
a stream of black water flowing out.

The black water flooded heaven again,
and the monster escaped without a trace.
Alive, it remained potential trouble for the future,
because it would swallow the sun and the moon again.
Pangu split the mountains to block the floodwater,
stopping the black water from spreading in four directions,
The black water was stored in the pond of the sea,
which extended ten thousand *li* across and thousands *zhang* deep.
Pangu then went to the north,
where Mount Quan was touching the icicles from the sky.
Pangu smashed the ice-mountain, which sank into the sea.
It was the northern dark ocean, the coldest place.
When the icy columns were crashed, something appeared,
a fish dragon like a hill.
It was thousands of *li* long and had a silvery shell,
with two eyes shining with red light.

张开大口狂风起,
盘古也难稳住身。
鱼龙来与盘古斗,
要与盘古比输赢。
盘古举斧高劈下,
砍得鱼龙逃性命。
盘古后边忙追赶,
鱼龙跃起变化身。

化成一只大苍鹰,
抓住盘古往上拎。
盘古把爪来捉住,
又啄盘古双眼睛。
盘古松手护双眼,
苍鹰挣脱逃性命。
展翅高飞追不上,
此为鹰龙出世根。

盘古又往南方行,
南方一片红火云。
一座高山冒焰火,
下有火海难拢身。
千只火鸟齐扑来,
要烧盘古一个神,
他是金刚不坏体,
不怕火来不怕冷。

三、日月合明 III. The Sun and the Moon Illuminating Together

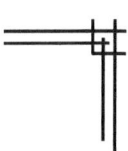

It opened its huge mouth, and the ferocious wind was blowing,
even Pangu found it hard to stand still.
The fish dragon came to fight with Pangu,
until a winner was declared.
Raising his axe high, Pangu then struck so hard,
that the fish dragon fled for its life.
Pangu chased after it,
and the fish dragon leaped up to transform itself.

It turned into a huge goshawk,
seizing Pangun and lifting him up.
Pangu grabbed its claws.
Then it tried to peck Pangu's eyes.
Pangu let go his grip to protect his eyes,
so the goshawk struggled away and freed itself.
It spread its wings and soared so high that it was hard to catch.
This was the origin of the Eagle Dragon.

Next, Pangu walked to the south,
where there was a piece of flaming cloud.
It was fire coming down from a high mountain,
creating a fiery sea that was impossible to get close to.
Thousands of fire birds attacked him all at once,
to burn Immortal Pangu,
but his body was diamond-built,
impervious to fire and coldness.

盘古扑鸟鸟飞散,
引水灭火热气蒸。
从此南方有大海,
才有南海对北溟。
盘古四方开三方,
只剩东方等时辰。
一日等得时辰到,
要请日月上天庭。
盘古开辟费辛勤,
不觉又是八千春。
日月二星已修成,
十磨九难才成形。
盘古来到东方地,
来到咸池把神请。
咸池大海九万里,
波又平来水又清。

日月二珠成人形,
修起日宫和月殿。
宫中无数宝和珍,
聚结天精和地灵。

三、日月合明 III. The Sun and the Moon Illuminating Together

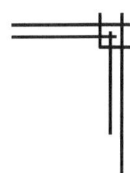

Pangu shooed the birds away,
and put out the fire by inducing water, which turned into a steam.
From then on there was the sea in the south,
the South Sea pairing with the North Dark Ocean.
By now Pangu had opened up three directions,
leaving only the east awaiting Pangu.
Once the time was favorable,
Pangu asked the sun and the moon to enter heaven.
Pangu worked so hard to create the world,
that another eight thousand years passed without him realizing much of it.
The two stars of the sun and the moon were ready,
after many a mishap and setback.
Now Pangu came to the east,
to invite the immortals in the Xian Pool.
The sea, where the Xian Pool was, extended ninety thousand *li*,
with calm ripples and clear water.

The two pearls of the Sun and the Moon took on the human shape,
to build their Solar Palace and Lunar Palace,
The palaces had collections of countless treasures,
assembling all heavenly spirits and earthly essences.

日神为阳月为阴,
化为俊男美女身。
男掌日珠女月宝,
金龙看护保安宁。
不知盘古来相请,
但愿永久不离分。
盘古来到咸池地,
站在一山观风景。

此山半圆为不周,
山清水秀飘祥云。
水深万里能见底,
日宫月殿放光明。
山上一棵大古树,
树上果实重千斤。
此树高有万丈余。
树枝如盖分九层。

盘古这时忙打望,
每片树叶现图纹,
上有天文并地理,
点化盘古分五形。
这时树上有鸟叫,
声音洪亮甚惊人,
盘古见鸟生得美,
金色羽毛红冠顶。

三、日月合明 III. The Sun and the Moon Illuminating Together

Immortal Sun was Yang and Immortal Moon was Yin,
in the figures of a handsome male and a beautiful female.
The male held the Sun Pearl while the female held the Moon Gem,
while the gold dragon kept both safe and peaceful.
They didn't know Pangu was coming,
but wanted to stay together without separation.
When Pangu first arrived at the Xian Pool,
he stood on a mountain, enjoying the scenery.

The mountain was half of a circle,
with bright mountains, clear waters and auspicious floating clouds.
The water was ten thousand *li* deep but the bottom could be seen,
while the Solar Palace and Lunar Palace were shining brightly.
On the mountain was a large ancient tree,
on which the fruits weighed a thousand *jin*.
The tree was more than tens and thousands of *zhang* tall,
branches like a cover with nine layers.

Pangu looked at the tree carefully,
finding patterns on each leave,
patterns of astronomy and geography,
which inspired Pangu to form five forms.
Presently, a bird on the tree began to sing,
with a startling and sonorous voice.
Pangu saw the beautiful bird,
with golden feathers and a red crest.

这时金鸟叫一声，
对着盘古点头鸣。
此鸟不像是恶鸟，
定是祥鸟报好音。
三声鸟啼落了音，
传入日月宫殿门。
连忙出了咸池水，
见是盘古老神尊。

日月双双来下拜，
二人到此喜相迎。
开天辟地多辛苦，
吾等至此保安宁。
迎得盘古进日殿，
殿里景色难说尽。
千里宽来万里阔，
上有青天日珠明。

殿旁无数七宝树，
玉枝宝花色色新。
月宫更是现奇景，
玉石栏杆镶宝珍。
盘古说声来相请，
来请二神上天庭。
二神说声不答应，
不愿上天遭难星。

三、日月合明 III. The Sun and the Moon Illuminating Together

Then the gold bird chirped again,
and it also nodded at Pangu.
It didn't look like an evil bird,
so it must be an auspicious one, announcer of good news.
When its third chirp just came to a pause,
that entered the gates of the Solar Palace and Lunar Palace.
They hurriedly went out of the Xian Pool,
and found out it was Ancestor Pangu.

Both the Sun and the Moon knelt,
to greet Pangu joyously.
You worked so hard to create the world,
so that we can have peace and safety here.
They welcomed Pangu to the Solar Palace,
whose scenery was hard to describe in words.
It was extremely extensive and spacious,
under the shining Solar Pearl in the sky.

By the palace were innumerable seven-treasure trees,
with new jade branches and fresh treasured flowers.
The scenery in the Lunar Palace was even more stunning,
the jade handrails were inlaid with treasured jewels.
Pangu explained his reason for coming,
to invite both of them to the heavenly court.
The two immortals refused,
unwilling to suffer separation there.

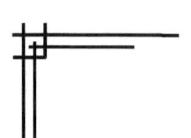

盘古再次说声请,
要请二位照乾坤。
四方天地已开辟,
如今洪水已波平。
天地黑暗无光明,
缺少日月和星辰。
只有你等当此任,
这是天意不容情。

见得盘古此言语,
面带怒容显威灵。
日月二神点头应,
盘古开言带笑云:
你们升天安排定,
我来保护无难星。
一月夫妻会一面,
月爱阳来日爱阴。

山上那棵扶桑树,
当作天梯往上登。
树上金鸡报时辰,
普天之下有黎明。
叫来金龙来护送,
架起云车十二乘。
手执化云珠一颗,
脚踏风火二车轮。

三、日月合明 III. The Sun and the Moon Illuminating Together

Pangu invited them again,
inviting the two to illuminate heaven and earth.
Now the four directions have all been created,
and the floods subdued.
Yet heaven and earth are still dark without light,
in need of the Sun, the Moon and the Stars.
Only you two are competent for this task,
the will of heaven which allows no excuse.

Hearing Pangu utter such words,
seeing the anger on his face that showed his authority,
the two immortals agreed with a nod.
Pangu responded with a smile, saying:
That's settled, and you both will ascend to heaven,
and I will protect you from any disaster.
Once a month you couple will meet,
the Moon-loving Yang and Sun-loving Yin.

A large mulberry tree on the top of the mountain,
was used as the high ladder for them to go up.
The gold rooster on the tree could give the correct time,
so that all under heaven could have dawn.
Gold dragon was ordered to escort them,
with twelve cloud vehicles.
They held a cloud-changing pearl in hand.
and stood on two hot wheels.

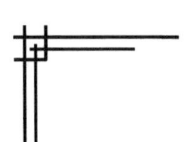

日穿宝衣火焰甲,
万道金光万化身。
月披水晶衫一领,
夜洒甘露济众生。
日神月神来领命,
披挂齐备要起程。
一声响亮天地开,
九重天堂顿时明。

日月初升不安宁,
西方怪物毒气喷,
霎时黑云满天庭,
乘机要把日月吞。
日神抛出化云珠,
霎时黑云往下沉。
月神洒下甘露水,
消了毒气和妖氛。

这时鹰龙来飞起,
遮住日月难照明,
盘古挥起斩龙剑,
一声雷电丧性命。
日月升上九霄云,
照亮青天一日轮。
这时才有昼和夜,

三、日月合明 III. The Sun and the Moon Illuminating Together

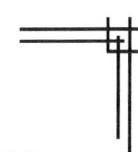

The Sun was wearing the treasured clothes with fiery armors,
ten thousands of the golden rays becoming its body.
The Moon was wrapped in a crystal cape,
spraying sweet dew at night to relieve the suffering of all living creatures.
The Sun and the Moon had accepted the order,
and they were ready to set out.
With a loud sound, heaven and earth were open,
and the nine levels of heaven were instantly lit up.

At the beginning after the sun and the moon had just ascended it was not peaceful,
because monsters in the west blew the poisonous smoke,
to fill the whole heaven with black cloud,
attempting to swallow the Sun and the Moon.
The Sun threw out the cloud-changing pearl,
which in a wink sank the black cloud.
The Moon sprayed the sweet dew,
cleansing the poisonous gas and evil spirit.

After that, the Eagle Dragon flew up,
keeping the Sun and Moon from shining upon the earth.
Pangu wielded his dragon-slaying sword,
killing him with the sound of a thunderbolt.
The Sun and the Moon now rose up to the ninth cloud,
with the sun shining during the day.
This is when the day and night came into being,

才有四季有阴晴。
周天三百六十零五度,
极地一百八十二度零。
天有六天青黄赤红黑,
上下六合二仪成。

诗曰：天地合德,日月合明,
盘古开混沌,苦难救众生。
日月升天有岁序,天地万物从此生,
夜有雨露昼有晴,千秋万代转金轮。
盘古老祖来分水,
手拿一个葫芦瓶。
分开葫芦瓢两把,
连忙舀水忙不停。
一瓢水叫天上水,
化作天河雨淋淋。
二瓢水作江河水,
向东流去永不停。
三瓢化为湖中水,
湖水不干水族生。
四瓢水作大海水,
大海鱼龙好藏身。
五瓢水作无根水,
在山为雾在天云,
万物有它养性命。

三、日月合明 III. The Sun and the Moon Illuminating Together

the four seasons and the elements.
Each day, the sun moved three hundred and sixty five degrees,
reaching the north pole at one hundred eighty two degrees.
There were six days sapphire, indigo, yellow, crimson, red and black,
and the two poles and six directions came into being.

The Poem says: heaven and earth combined make virtue;
the sun and the moon combined make light.
Pangu broke up Chaos to save all living creatures.
There was a time when the sun and the moon ascended to heaven,
the time when all living creatures came into being.
There was the rain at night and the sun during the daytime,
the golden wheel that turns generation after generation.
Then Ancestor Pangu came to assign waters,
with a gourd vase in his hand.
He first split the gourd into two ladles,
and right away he started ladling out water ceaselessly.
The first ladle of water was called heaven's water,
turning into the Milky Way to form raindrops.
The second ladle of water was called the river water,
flowing eastwards without stopping.
The third ladle of water was called the lake water,
not drying up so that the aquatic animals could thrive.
The fourth ladle of water was called the ocean water,
where fish and dragons could hide themselves in it.
The fifth ladle of water was called the rootless water,
turning into the fog in the mountains and clouds in the sky,
nourishing all things.

盘古老祖取黑水,
黑水装进葫芦瓶,
葫芦瓶儿长三寸,
以后发芽再生根。
此时江沽已为鲲鹏,
口吐泥丸把水平,
九颗泥丸化九州,
九州九处出神灵。

歌师唱歌莫消停,
再把盘古问一声,
方才算你有学问。
盘古分开天和地,
又有何人来出生?
盘古还是归天界?
还是人间了终身?

盘古过世一首诗,
七言四句正相应。
你把诗句说我听,
我今拜你为师尊。
歌师听我说分明,
我把根由说你听。
不知说得真不真?

三、日月合明 III. The Sun and the Moon Illuminating Together

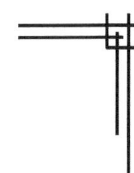

Ancestor Pangu then fetched the black water,
and put it into a gourd,
which was three *cun* long,
and would sprout and take roots later on.
Right then, Jianggu had grew into a roc,
spiting mud balls to calm down the water.
Nine mud balls turned into nine continents,
and immortals came into being from these nine continents.

Master singer, don't stop, please,
I still have questions about Pangu,
even though what you have said does show your knowledge.
After Pangu separated heaven and earth,
who else were born?
Did Pangu return to heaven when he died,
or did he stay on earth?

The elegy on the death of Pangu,
put aptly with four sentences each of seven words.
If you can recite it to me,
I will salute you as my honorable teacher.
Master singer, please listen to me,
and allow me to tell you the whole story.
You can then decide if it is true.

盘古分了天和地，
又有天皇出世根。
盘古得知天皇出，
有了天皇治乾坤。
盘古隐匿而不见，
浑身配与天地形。
头配五岳巍巍相，
目配日月晃晃明，
毫毛配着草木枝枝秀，
又按日月照天地。
天皇出世分昼夜，
又分天干与地支。
上定天盘星有序，
下受乾坤有地理。
地皇接住管九州，
才有人烟子孙兴。
人皇出世人分群，
才分礼仪与人伦。

三、日月合明　III. The Sun and the Moon Illuminating Together

After Pangu separated heaven and earth,
the Heavenly Emperor was born.
When Pangu learned about his birth,
he knew that heaven and earth were now in good hands.
He therefore went into hiding,
his whole body adopting the shape of heaven and earth.
His head resembled the Five Mountains, dignified.
His eyes were like the Sun and the Moon, illuminating.
His body hair took after the blades of grass, gentle,
and he shined upon heaven and earth as did the Sun and the Moon.
Emperor Heaven, since birth, separated day and night,
and set up the Heavenly Stems and Earthly Branches.
In heaven above, the stars were arranged in order,
while on earth below, geographical details were planned.
Emperor Earth was charged with running the nine continents,
the reason humans came into existence and prospered.
Since the birth of Emperor Human, people were grouped,
and etiquette and relations were elucidated.

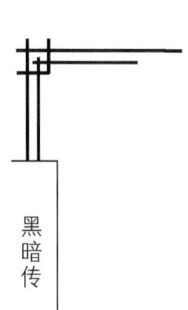

四、人祖创世①

盘古分了天和地,
又请日月上天庭,
又收黑水平天下,
重创世界万物生。
这时天地啥模样?

---

① "人祖创世"标题为整理者所加。资料来源一是书名为《黑暗传》的秭归县新滩镇抄本。1984年委托熊鹰桥收集,熊鹰桥为林区医药公司退休职工,秭归新潭人。1988年去世,时年60余岁。该抄本系清末抄本,其中有立引子(泥隐子)作泥人一节。二是2001年8月16日在阳日镇龙溪村村民杨有才和史光裕处口述记录,并有录像资料。杨有才,73岁,读过私塾,笔者于1984—1986年两次采访过他,他口述过《黑暗传》唱段。史光裕,中学文化程度,火居道士,青年时期在龙溪中武当山、保康县望佛山等庙观从师学过道经。五年前他曾从新华乡亲戚家借来《黑暗传》木刻本一书。三年前他双目失明,才把书还去,下落不明。整理时采用了杨有才、史光裕部分口述唱段。三是采用委托唐运青收集的祝天照、姜德龙抄本和唐运青采录的部分资料。四是采用贾邦修、张忠诚《黑暗大盘头》《黑暗纲鉴》资料,以及1999年3月在林区下谷土家族民族乡石磨村戊子垭刘茂森处摘录转抄本片段资料。

四、人祖创世 IV.Human Ancestors' Inventions

IV. Human Ancestors' Inventions[①]

After Pangu separated heaven and earth,
he invited the Sun and the Moon into the heavenly court,
subdued the black water to bring peace to earth,
and recreated the world with all living creatures.
What did heaven and earth look like then?

---

① The title "Human Ancestors' Inventions" was added by people who collected. The first resource was the manuscript of *The Legend of Darkness* in Xintan Town, Zigui County. Xiong Yingqiao was commissioned to collect in 1984, who was a retiree from medical corporation in forest region, a local in Xintan, Zigui County. He died at the age of over 60 in 1988. The manuscript was copied at the end of Qing Dynasty including the chapter of Ni Yinzi making clay figurine. The second was the oral records from Yang Youcai and Shi Guangyu in Longxi Village, Yangri Town on August 16th, 2001 with video records. Yang Youcai, 73, accepted old-style private school education and made oral records of *The Legend of Darkness* in the two periods of my interview from 1984-1986. Shi Guangyu, a Huoju Taoist, had secondary education level, and learned Taoist scriptures when he was young from Wudang Mountain and Wangfo Mountain. Five years ago, he had borrowed wood-carving *The Legend of Darkness* from his relatives in Xinhua Town. Three years ago, he was blind in both eyes, and returned the book, but the whereabouts was uncertain. Therefore, the part of oral records form Yang Youcai and Shi Guangyu was used when sorting out the material. The third was what Tang Yunqing collected from Zhu Tianzhao and Jiang Delong and part of what he interviewed. The fourth were the materials from *Darkness Inquiry* and *Darkness Principles Guide* by Jia Bangxiu and Zhang Zhongcheng and part of the excerpt copy from Liu Maosen in Shimo Village, Tujia nationality town of the forest region in March, 1999.

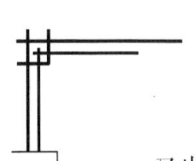

又出哪些众仙神？
歌师如果讲得真，
《红黑传》上走一程。

东海仙山有红池，
有一鳌鱼池中生。
吸取天地之灵气，
修成滇氾一仙神。
统管水族三千万，
三番红水①漫乾坤。

鳌鱼蛟龙来争斗，
都想称霸不安宁。
滇氾一见怒生嗔，
平叛水妖红水平。
滇氾挥起分水旗，
鳌鱼蛟龙水底沉。
抽出山水剑一把，
水妖水怪逃性命。

---

① 本书中红水与黑水、清水均系创世时期中的洪水神话，此处因情节发展，洪水又分为红、黑、清三种形态。

四、人祖创世 IV.Human Ancestors' Inventions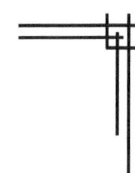

What immortals lived at the time?
If the master singer could tell us what really happened,
please take us on the journey of *The Legend of Red and Black*.

In the celestial mountain in the east sea was a Red Pool,
in which a tortoise-fish was born.
After absorbing the anima of heaven and earth,
it cultivated itself into Immortal Diansi.
It was in charge of about thirty million aquatic animals,
and later red-water① flooded heaven and earth three times.

Tortoise-fish and flood dragons fought with each other,
both of whom wanted to assume hegemony.
On seeing this, Diansi was furious,
determined to suppress water monsters and restore peace to the red water.
Diansi waved the water-dividing flag,
and the tortoise-fish and flood dragons sank to the bottom of the water.
Diansi then drew out the mountain-water sword,
and the water monsters fled for their lives.

---

① The red-water, black-water and clear-water in this book all come from the flood mythology in the creation period, but here for the development of the plot, the flood is divided into three forms: red, black and clear.

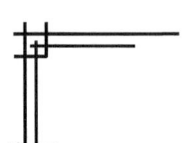

红水波平浪静后，
滇汜忽然变了形，
变成红花如仙神。
一日游玩花山上，
满山百花好风景。
花丛坐着石龙母，
滇汜连忙拜师尊。

石龙老母花丛坐，
神通广大无比能。
她知天地有进程，
红水三番要消退，
清水三番波涛平。

石龙忙把红花问，
你是哪的女仙神？
红花仙神忙答应，
红水之中来修成。
平息红水成女神，
特拜老母为师尊。
石龙说道随我去，
怕的性命难保身。

四、人祖创世 IV. Human Ancestors' Inventions

After the red water regained its calm,
Diansi suddenly transformed,
into a red flower like a fairy god.
Taking a walk on the flowery mountain one day,
Diansi enjoyed the beautiful scenery with flowers all over the mountain.
At the sight of ancestress stone dragon sitting among the flowers,
Diansi hurriedly made a courtesy bow.

The ancestress stone dragon, sitting among the flowers,
had far-reaching supernatural power.
She knew that heaven and earth had its own course,
the three red-water floods would recede,
and the three clear-water waves would calm down.

The stone dragon asked Diansi, the red flower:
Where did you come from, fairy goddess?
The red flower fairy replied:
I was cultivated in the red water,
and became a fairy goddess after subduing the red water,
so I came only to bow to you as my ancestress.
The stone dragon asked the goddess to come along,
for fear that she could not keep herself alive.

提起红花女仙神，
她是滇汜转度人。
老母给她取下名，
铁角老母是名号，
引你去见名台真，
又拜台真师父称。
台真一见心欢喜，
开言便把弟子称。
我今与你取下号，
又叫玄天你的名。
赐你几颗灵丹子，
天河砂子来形成。
你把灵丹来埋下，
一股紫烟如祥云。
紫烟袅袅化一人，
见了玄天忙下拜，
连忙又把师父尊。
玄天一见心欢喜，
我今与你取个名。
取名滇元赐丹灵。
埋下又出开天神。
滇元用丹化人才，
后出多少开辟人。

四、人祖创世 IV. Human Ancestors' Inventions

About Goddess Red Flower,
she was transformed from Diansi.
The ancestress gave her a name,
Goddess Tiejiao,
and then led her to see Taizhen,
so that Goddess Tiejiao could acknowledge him as her tutor.
Taizhen was so delighted at the sight of Tiejiao,
that he called her his disciple immediately:
Today I give you an assumed name,
which is Xuantian.
I also grant you a few pellets of panacea,
that were originally the sand in the Milky Way.
She buried the panacea,
presently a column of purple smoke of auspicious clouds rose up.
The curling purple smoke changed into a person,
who knelt down to Xuantian at the sight of her,
and greeted the Master at once.
Xuantian was delighted to see this:
Today I give you a name,
Dianyuan, and grant you some panacea.
Once buried, the panacea again sprouted creation immortals.
Dianyuan produced many talents by using the panacea,
many pioneering talents in the later ages.

先天唱起泥隐子，
后天唱起末叶神。
海蛟他把天来灭，
洪水泡天无有人。
只有先天泥隐子，
他是先天创世人。
知道天地已该灭，
蓬莱山上坐其身。
天地俱无少世界，
四座名山雾沉沉。
昆仑蓬莱山二座，
太荒山对泰山林。
四大名山无人住，
只有泥隐子一神。
紧打鼓，慢逍遥，
黑暗根源从头道：
昆仑山有万丈高，
二山相对真个好，
两水相连响潮潮。
泥隐子观看荷叶发，
二水冲成一河泡。
化成人形三尺八，
荷叶上面起根苗。

四、人祖创世 IV. Human Ancestors' Inventions

We sing about Niyinzi of the former times,
and we sing about Immortal Moye of the latter times.
When the flood dragon drowned heaven,
no one was left but the floodwater.
Only Niyinzi of the former times,
was the creator of that time.
He knew that heaven and earth would be destroyed,
so he sat himself on Mount Penglai.
There was neither heaven, earth, nor the world,
only four famous mountains, full of dense fog.
Kunlun and Penglai were two of them,
Mount Taihuang and Mount Tai the other two.
The four famous mountains would have been completely empty,
if not for Immortal Niyinzi.
Hit the drum now as we continue to saunter throughout time,
from the beginning of the darkness.
Mount Kunlun was tens and thousands *zhang* high,
facing Penglai and making a nice pair with it,
flanked on each side by water with bubbling sound.
When Niyinzi watched lotus sprouting,
he saw the water from the two sides forming a river bubble.
The bubble took on the shape of a human, three *chi* and eight *cun* tall,
taking roots on the surface of the lotus.

泥隐子,抬头看,
忽见水泡成人形。
水泡成人真古怪,
随时与他取了名,
取名"末叶"二字文,
又称无极是他身。

末叶得了姓和名,
就问泥隐名和姓。
泥隐子来回言道:
"我今一一说你听:
吾是先天泥隐子,
故此给你取姓名。"
正在说时抬头看,
阴山流水响沉沉。
一具浮尸水上漂,
生下孩儿人三个,
天翻地覆聚会中。

四、人祖创世 IV.Human Ancestors' Inventions

Niyinzi, raising his head,
saw the bubble changing into a human.
Amazed by the strange happening,
he named it immediately,
with a two-character "Moye",
which was also known as Wuji.

After Moye was named,
he asked about Niyinzi's name.
Hence Niyinzi replied,
"Let me tell you in detail:
I am Niyinzi from the former times,
so I gave you your name."
While talking, he raised his head,
and saw Mount Yin's water running with a heavy sound.
A floating corpse on the water,
gave birth to three children,
who gathered within themselves the vicissitudes of heaven and earth.

洪儒他在西昆仑,
放下葫芦收红水,
红水消退现山岭。
子会一万八千春,
红水泡天无世界,
后来天地有红尘。
二弟洪浩来出世,
放下葫芦把水平,
葫芦里头装黑水,
黑水淹地无有人,
黑天黑地黑混沌。

第三洪钧来出世,
洪钧出世现人形。
她为人形是女身。

泥隐子,把媒做,
配合夫妻两个人。
二人低头来下拜,
谢了泥隐子做媒人。
泥隐子,开言道,
口称末叶你是听,
今来无天又无地,
先天世界传你身,
你传后天世上人。
说话将身只一变,
隐入青山不见形。

四、人祖创世 IV. Human Ancestors' Inventions

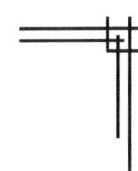

One was Hongru of the western Kunlun Mountain,
who would put down the gourd to collect the red water,
so that water would recede and the mountains ridges appear.
For a period of eighteen thousand years,
there was nothing but the red water, not a world,
which only came later.
The second brother Honghao then came into being,
who would put down the gourd and calm the water,
with the black water collected in the gourd.
While the black water flooding everything there was no human,
but black heaven, black earth and black chaos.

Next the third, Hongjun, was born,
in the human form,
a female human form.

Niyinzi, acting as a matchmaker,
Married Hongbao and Hongjun as husband and wife.
The two knelt and bowed,
to Niyinzi thanking him for being their matchmaker.
Niyinzi then said:
Moye, listen to me please.
There is neighter heaven nor earth today,
but I impart to you the former world,
so that you can hand it down to the world later.
With these words Niyinzi disappeared,
hidden in the green mountains without a trace.

末叶出世教人伦，
不觉数代有余零。
顶上还挂一葫芦，
葫芦放出是绿水，
绿水青山到如今。
三人出世会人寅，
天翻地覆未生成，
犹如鸡蛋一个形，
昏昏暗暗不得明。
末叶口称泥隐子，
我今不拜你为尊。
泥隐子听了心中怒，
口骂忘恩负义人。
"你是西北一块土，
是我塑你一人形。"
"这些胡言我不听，
你今若有真手段，
再塑一个才算能。"
泥隐子当时塑一人，
摇摇摆摆甚斯文。
一口仙气吹将去，
土人睁眼笑盈盈。
身长三丈零一尺，
横眉竖眼獠牙生，
土人一见心欢喜，
拜他二人为世尊。

四、人祖创世 IV. Human Ancestors' Inventions

After his birth, Moye taught human relations,
for many generations, time that went by him quickly.
He had always had a gourd, hanging from his head,
which could pour out green water,
which is the reason for the green mountains till today.
The three of them were born to their time to produce people,
when heaven and earth had yet to experience drastic changes.
It is similar to the inside of something like an egg,
full of shadow and darkness without light.
Moye said: Niyinzi,
I won't honor you as my master today.
Hearing this, Niyinzi was livid,
abusing Moye as ungrateful.
"You used to be a piece of clay in the northwest,
and it was I who moulded you into a human."
"I will not listen to such nonsense!
Only if you can mould another human today,
are you indeed the true talent."
Niyinzi made another right away,
who moved with a sway of refinement.
When Niyinzi blew a magic breath at it,
the clay person immediately opened his eyes, beaming with delight.
He was three *zhang* and one *chi* tall,
with leveled eyebrows, titled eyes and fangs protruding.
This clay man was filled with joy,
honoring the two as his masters.

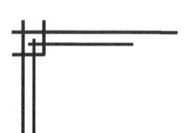

泥隐子一见心欢喜,
师徒三人上山林。
真空之中无一物,
无物之中有物生。
空者一概无所立,
图名皎洁一轮回。
"我今无影本无形,
无父无母本来人。"
捏不成形眼不开,
看来看去难成胎。
有人道我先天地,
沙泥沙石脱仙胎。
渺渺茫茫道为主,
身居雷霆坐灵台。
冷眼无边看世界,
黑暗憔悴怎得开?

西天老母随后跟,
一十八人说不尽。
三父八母谁人晓?
几人知得这根苗?
三灾八难来讲起,
大海九连窝一座。
一个老母窝中生,
原是海鸟蛋一个。
蛋破产出一个人,
树根穿身灾难尽,

四、人祖创世 IV. Human Ancestors' Inventions

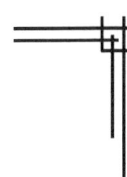

Niyinzi was glad on seeing this,
and then the master and two disciples went to mountain.
There was not an object in the empty space,
but from the void an object was born.
Born of emptiness, it relied on nothing,
and was to live out its own time as pure as the moonlight.
"I have no shadow, because I have no shape,
no father or mother, but an originator."
Impossible to be moulded into any shape, its eyes would not open,
hard for a foetus to be conceived.
It was said that I was born before heaven and earth,
as a magic foetus formed from sand and stones.
Distant and indistinct, the way of nature dominated,
while I sat on the Ling Platform amidst the thunderbolts.
Looking at the world with a calm eye,
I wonder how to break the darkness?

The heavenly ancestress in the west followed next,
but even eighteen people would find it hard to explain clearly.
Who knew about the three fathers and eight mothers?
How many people knew about the beginning of this object?
Let me start with the three sufferings and eight hardships,
with the nest of the nine seas.
An old ancestress was born in the nest,
an egg of a seabird originally.
When the egg cracked open a person appeared,
who suffering the tree roots threading through his body,

头顶鹰鸟不动身,
随来土长是真人。
无天无地无乾坤,
又无日月两边分,
他母怀他十六岁,
四月初八午时生。

一眼观定乾坤界,
身坐西方半边天。
十八神仙旁边站,
众多老母站台前,
左边站定四十八老母,
右边站立四十八祖先。

秦氏老母站右边,
又向元古来表明,
元古坐在灵山岭,
天愁地惨实难忍,
万里乾坤不自然。
收下弟子把道传,
差了洪钧去开山,
洪水滚滚满山川,
洪钧昆仑自修炼,
三花仙斧劈开山。

四、人祖创世 IV. Human Ancestors' Inventions

and motionless with an eagle above his head,
was a true person growing with the earth.
With neither heaven nor earth,
neither the sun nor the moon on either side,
his mother carried him for sixteen years,
and gave him birth at noon, the eighth of April according to
the lunar calendar.

Surveying heaven and earth at one glance,
he sat on half of the western sky.
Around him stood eighteen immortals,
and in front the platform stood many ancestors,
forty-eight ancestresses on the left,
forty-eight ancestors on the right.

Ancestress Qin on the right,
said to Yuangu,
who was sitting on the ridge of Mount Ling,
looking at the unbearable sight,
of heaven and earth not being themselves:
Accept disciples to pass on the way of nature,
and send Hongjun to cut open the mountains,
and to let the floodwater flow;
Hongjun, having prepared himself in Mount Kunlun,
can cut open the mountains with the magic three-flower axe.

洪钧老祖降世起,
出洞不见天和地,
乾坤暗暗混二气。
老祖抬头把眼睁,
清浊二气不分明,
转身回到古洞门,
忙差徒弟下山林,
蓬莱山上开天门。
洪钧、洪浩二老祖,
出洞不见天地势,
惨惨乾坤将何治?
二仙上山同游玩,
遇着亚琐古祖仙,
来到蓬莱山上看。
蓬莱原是一条船,
原是上古沉香木,
盘古老祖把树砍,
为救神仙造大船。
洪水滔天船被翻,
淹死神仙无计算。
此船沉在洪水底,
洪水浸泡几千年。
大船化为沉香木,
后来长成蓬莱山。

四、人祖创世 IV. Human Ancestors' Inventions

When Ancestor Hongjun was born,
there were no heaven and earth outside of the cave,
but a dark world shrouded in the two kinds of energy.
He raised his head, opened his eyes,
and saw the two kinds of energy obscure and indistinct,
so he turned around, went to the mouth of the cave,
and sent his disciple to go down the hills,
and open the heavenly gate of Mount Penglai.
When the two ancestors Hongjun and Honghao,
came out of the cave, they saw neither heaven nor earth.
They wondered how to create the world out of such a sad state of affairs.
One day when the two immortals went on a walk in the mountains,
they met Ancestress Yasuo,
who came to visit Mount Penglai.
Penglai was at first a boat,
made of ancient eaglewood,
which was cut by ancestor Pangu,
for building the big boat to rescue the immortals.
But it capsized in the torrents of the surging floodwater,
drowning countless immortals.
The boat sank to the bottom of floodwater,
and immersed in it for several thousand years.
It later turned into eaglewood,
from which grew Mount Penglai.

一丛树木朝天长,
青枝绿叶花朵鲜。
花谢又结长生果,
长生果儿如珠圆。
树长百鸟来啼叫,
树中又生众神仙。
树中又有大洞门,
洞里又住二神仙。
名叫洪钧和洪浩,
又是亚琐一老母,
观看洪水几时退,
又有谁个出世间?

三番洪水渐渐平,
自生一根天地藤,
天地相连一脉承。
中间结个大葫芦,
五龙捧着为何因?

洪水之时生洪儒,
洪儒传洪梅,洪梅传洪浩,
洪浩传洪末,洪末传洪钧。
洪末住在石洞内,
洪水未消闭沉沉。
昏睡之中做一梦,
梦见两个女佳人。
此梦做得真蹊跷,
蹊跷梦中有原因。

四、人祖创世 IV. Human Ancestors' Inventions

A clump of trees grew toward the sky,
with fresh branches, green leaves and bright flowers.
When the flowers withered, it bore the longevity fruit,
which was round like the bead.
As the trees grew, hundreds of the chirping birds came,
and numerous immortals were born to the trees.
Among the trees was a big gate to a cave,
where lived two immortals.
These were Hongjun and Honghao,
who, with Ancestress Yasuo,
were watching to see when the flood would recede,
and wondering who would come into being next?

With the three floods slowly subsiding,
there grew naturally a vine,
which connected heaven and earth.
A big gourd grew in the middle,
but why were there five dragons holding it in their hands?

There was a Hongru who was born to the floods.
Hongru was followed by Hongmei, who was followed by Honghao,
who was followed by Hongmo, who was followed by Hongjun.
Hongmo, living in the stone cave,
was besieged by the floodwater that hadn't receded.
Slumbering, he once had a dream,
dreamed of two beautiful ladies.
It was really a curious dream,
but there was reason for it.

原来是东边有个张氏女,
西边住李氏女佳人。
忽然梦中怀了孕,
先生男儿后女婴。
一男一女甚聪明,
一日玩耍到昆仑。
只见洪水扑山顶,
吓得连忙逃性命。
只见葫芦口张开,
接住童男童女身。
二童进了葫芦内,
葫芦合得紧沉沉。
咔嚓一声断了蒂,
好比断了脐带根。
葫芦漂在洪水上,
里有五龙来护身。
洪钧老祖在蓬莱,
只见一物起祥云。
他把葫芦捞上岸,
五龙逃去不见形。

四、人祖创世 IV. Human Ancestors' Inventions

They turned to be Lady Zhang of the east,
and Lady Li of the west.
They suddenly became pregnant one day while they were asleep,
and then they gave birth to a boy first and then a girl.
The boy and the girl were very smart,
and went to Kunlun one day on an excursion.
This was when they saw the floodwater surging to cover the top of the mountain,
and frightened, they ran hastily for they lives.
At this time a gourd was seen opening its mouth,
and caught the boy and the girl.
The moment they went into the gourd,
it closed tightly.
With a click, the stem broke,
like the umbilical cord was cut off.
The gourd floated with the floodwater,
escorted by five dragons.
When Ancestor Hongjun came to Penglai,
he saw an object accompanied by an auspicious cloud.
When he fetched the gourd out of the water,
the five dragons disappeared.

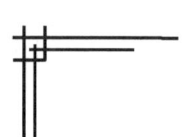

混沌之时还未分,
有一金龟出了生。
金龟本是天龟化,
有意点化传后人。
洪水三番起波涛,
遇着洪钧把水平。
来到蓬莱洪庆洞,
洪庆洞中称洪钧。
洪钧收它为弟子,
当着坐骑水上行。

金龟说与洪钧听:
"洪水之后想安顿,
九大名山都复现,
九大部州荒无人。
洪水过后神仙少,
许多神仙化沙尘。
有的神仙变禽兽,
有的神仙要成人。"

洪钧答曰说得是,
要找男女配婚姻。
要找阴阳来相合,
要找有血有肉人。
眼前人类还未出,
不知要到何处寻?

四、人祖创世 IV. Human Ancestors' Inventions

During the chaotic period,
a gold tortoise was born.
It was originally a heavenly one,
but was meant for humans later.
The flood surged three times,
and was subdued by Hongjun.
The tortoise came to Cave Hongqing on Mount Penglai,
where it came to see Hongjun.
Hongjun accepted it as a disciple,
and rode on it to get around on the water.

The gold tortoise spoke to Hongjun:
"After the flood, settlement would be a priority,
since the nine famous mountains will have reappeared,
but they will be desolated and uninhabited.
And there will be much fewer immortals,
since many turned into sand and dust.
While some will become birds and beasts,
others will be humans."

Hongjun expressed his agreement:
we need to find, match, and marry men and women.
To integrate Yin and Yang,
we need to find humans with flesh and blood.
So far they haven't appeared,
so where can I find them?

金龟答曰有啊有,
五龙捧着葫芦行,
飘飘荡荡八千载,
内装一对男女身。
来到东海蓬莱下,
打捞起来问原因。
洪钧问道怎知情?
何以见得男女身?
金龟答曰我所见,
老祖听我说原因。

昆仑山上黑暗母,
她与老祖结成婚,
生下一对双胎子,
一男一女甚聪明。
方才长到八岁整,
整日玩耍在山林。
看见山中一根藤,
结一葫芦重千斤。

葫芦见了童男女,
张口说话叫连声,
快叫两人躲进去,
洪水泡天天地倾,
两人一听慌忙进。
葫芦闭口紧又紧。
一声霹雳来打下,
葫芦离了天地藤。

四、人祖创世 IV. Human Ancestors' Inventions

The gold tortoise answered: Oh yes!
There are five dragons who have held a gourd,
which has been floating for eight thousand years.
Inside the gourd are a boy and a girl.
Therefore, we can go to the east sea at the foot of Penglai,
to fetch the gourd from the water and to find out more about it.
Hongjun asked: how do you know this,
and how do you know they are a boy and a girl?
The gold tortoise answered: I saw it,
and let me explain.

Mother Darkness on Mount Kunlun,
was married to an ancestor,
and they gave birth to twins,
a boy and a girl, very smart.
When they were eight years old,
they spent all day playing in the mountain forests.
One day they saw a vine in the mountain,
which bore a gourd that weighed a thousand *jin*.

When the gourd saw the boy and the girl,
it opened its mouth and called out to them,
to let them hide inside quickly,
because the flood would cause heaven and earth to collapse.
On hearing this, the two hurried in,
and the gourd closed tightly at once.
With a loud thunderbolt,
the gourd broke off of the vine.

兄妹两个昏沉沉，
随着洪波乱翻滚。
唱起葫芦根基深，
葫芦生长在昆仑。
洪水淹了昆仑山，
葫芦里面救残生。
蓬莱山上出洪钧，
洪庆洞中观风景，
千里波涛怕煞人，
水翻黑泡为何因？
来到蓬莱山脚下，
眼看汪洋大海清，
只见海中红水现，
五龙抱着葫芦行。
捞起葫芦千斤重，
劈开葫芦两半分，
两股雾气化祥云。
洪钧老祖忙相问，
来把根古说我听。
当日海中有五龙，
青黄赤白蓝五色形，
捧一葫芦水上行，
葫芦藏着两兄妹，
以后兄妹成了婚。
五龙听得老祖叫，
弃了葫芦不见形。
洪钧当时来收住，
带回洞中看分明，
忙将葫芦来打破，
现出两个小孩童。
一男一女人两个，
兄妹二人八岁春。

四、人祖创世 IV. Human Ancestors' Inventions

The brother and the sister were in a daze,
rolling around with the surging waves.
About the gourd, it was deeply rooted in Kunlun,
native to it.
When the flood inundated Mount Kunlun,
the gourd saved what was left of the living creature.
When Hongjun appeared on Mount Penglai,
and enjoyed the scenery in Cave Hongqing,
frightening waves of a thousand *li* long were billowing,
and he wondered, why are there black bubbles on the overturned water?
He went down to the foot of Mount Penglai.
Looking at the clear water in the boundless sea,
he saw in the sea the red water surging,
with five dragons holding a gourd swimming.
He fetched up the gourd that weighed a thousand *jin*,
and as he divided it into two parts,
two whiffs of vapor rose and then changed into an auspicious cloud.
Ancestor Hongjun then asked,
for more details.
But the five dragons in the sea—
who were in green, yellow, red, white and blue,
who swam on the water carrying the gourd,
wherein the brother and sister were,
who later married each other,
on hearing the ancestor calling out to them—
gave up the gourd and vanished without a trace.
Hongjun took the gourd,
back to the cave to examine it.
When he broke the gourd,
out came two little children.
A male and a female,
the brother and the sisiter were eight years old.

如何生在葫芦内？
二人如何海中行？
老祖就把二人问，
叫他二人说原因。
二人上前讲根由，
昆仑山中岩石缝，
忽生一根葫芦藤，
藤子牵有万丈余，
无有叶子只有藤，
结了一个大葫芦，
见了我俩把话明，
叫我钻进它肚内，
里面天宽地又平，
马上洪水要泡天，
藏在里头躲难星。

俩人钻进葫芦内，
不知过了几年春。
当时天昏地也暗，
洪水滔滔如雷鸣。
漂漂荡荡不计年，
随着波涛到处行。
亏得老祖来搭救，
两个孩童忙谢恩。
老祖便把男童叫：
"我今与你取了名，
取名就叫五龙氏。
如今世上无男女，
怎传后代众黎民？
我今与你把媒做，
配合二人传后人。"
童女这时把话应：
"哥哥与我同娘养，
哪有兄妹结成婚？"

四、人祖创世 IV. Human Ancestors' Inventions

Why did you live inside the gourd?
How come you traveled in the sea?
The ancestor asked at once,
and told them to explain clearly.
They walked up to him and explained:
From a rock crack on Mount Kunlun,
a gourd vine one day came up all of a sudden.
The vine was tens and thousands of *zhang* long,
but it had no leaves but only the vine,
It bore a huge gourd,
which, on seeing us, spoke to us,
and asked us to enter its belly.
Inside the gourd the sky was wide and the ground was flat.
Since the flood was to destroy everything,
we hid there to seek refuge from the disaster.

The two children entered the gourd,
unaware how many years had passed,
During those years, the sky was dim and the earth was dark,
and the flood surged high, sounding like thunderbolts.
Floating around and unable to count the years,
they went wherever the waves took them.
They were so fortunate that the ancestor came to their rescue,
so they expressed their gratitude at once.
Then the ancestor told the boy:
"Today, I will give you a name.
Your name is Five Dragon.
The world today has neither a man nor a woman.
How can there be offspring?
Let me be the matchmaker,
marring you two so that you have posterity."
At this time the girl refused:
"My brother and I have the same mother.
How can we get married?"

老祖这时来劝说:
"只因洪水泡天后,
世上哪有女子身?
世上虽有人无数,
却非父母赋人形。
也有金石为身体,
也有树木成人形,
也有水虫成人像,
也有鸟兽成人形。
只有你们人两个,
一男一女正结姻。
你们都有肉身体,
有血有肉是真人。
劝你们二人成婚配,
生男育女传后人。"

童女一听忙言语,
"请听我来说原因:
若要兄妹成婚配,
要你的金龟把话应。"
"叫声童女你是听,
混沌初开有男子,
世上哪有女子身?
一来不绝洪水后,
二来不绝世上人。"
童女一听怒生嗔,
石头拿在手中心,
将石就把金龟打,
裂成八块命归阴。

四、人祖创世 IV. Human Ancestors' Inventions

The ancestor explained:
"Since the catastrophic flood,
where is a female person in the world?
Though there seem to be countless humans,
they were not born of a father and a mother.
Some have the gold stone bodies,
while others are human-shaped trees,
human-imaged water bugs,
human-looking birds and beasts.
Only the two of you are,
a man and a woman who can marry.
Both of you have the fleshy body,
and only those with blood and flesh are truly human.
I urge you to get married,
to give birth to sons and daughters so as to have descendants."

On hearing this, the girl said promptly:
"Allow me to explain:
to marry us brother and sister,
you need to have your gold tortoise answer to me."
"Little girl, please listen to me.
Chaos has just been split so there were only men;
where are women in the world?
There need to be humans after the flood,
and offspring in the future."
The girl was angered by these words,
so with the stone in her hand,
she hit the gold tortoise hard,
cracking it into eight pieces, dead.

童男来把金龟合,
八块合拢用尿淋,
金龟顿时又活了,
开口又把话来明:
"叫声童女你且听,
生也劝你成婚配,
死也劝你为婚姻。"
童女这时心思量,
难得逃躲这婚姻。
二童无奈才答应,
又怕反悔事不成。

洪钧来把二人引,
人皇正想置人伦,
此是人苗来出世,
才有世上众百姓。
二人见了人皇面,
人皇一见喜十分。
来叫二人成婚配,
以后产下后代根。

一日二人闷沉沉,
要到山上散精神。
夫妇二人观山景,
此名华胥山之名。
华胥山中有一洞,
太昊圣母在洞门。

四、人祖创世 IV. Human Ancestors' Inventions

The boy then pieced the gold tortoise whole again,
by holding the eight pieces together and then peeing on them.
Instantly, the gold tortoise revived,
opened its mouth and said:
"Listen to me, little girl.
Living, I will advise you to get married.
Dying, I will still advise you to get married."
At this time the girl thought to herself,
that she could hardly escape this marriage.
Out of no choice, the two agreed,
afraid also of regretting the consequences if they didn't marry.

Hongjun then introduced them to Emperor Human,
who was just considering proper human relations.
Now that the human seedlings had been born,
it is possible to have people in the world.
They met with the Emperor Human,
who was delighted to see them.
He married the two of them,
who later give birth to all the generations of humans.

One day, they were in low spirits,
so they want to go up the mountain to relieve their boredom.
They enjoyed sightseeing on the mountain,
which was named Huaxu.
On Huaxu was a cave,
wherein lived Ancestress Taihao.

见得一男一女多美貌,
笑在眉头喜在心。
连忙召来一仙神,
山上引路留脚印。
脚印一尺有二寸,
夫妇二人跟着行。
不知不觉到山顶,
见一虹霓五色新。
打一冷噤动春心,
不知不觉怀了孕。
生下双胎男与女,
取下伏羲女娲名。

长大兄妹成婚配,
又有五龙来托生。
女娲出世一美女,
身高一丈有余零。
出世学会观天象,
又察地理手段能。
为何天塌与地陷?
为何洪水三番成?
为何诸神来相争?
为何禽兽斗输赢?
只因出世心不善,
霸占名山把利争。
有的贪吃欲不尽,
有的作恶丧性命。
三番洪水分善恶,
恶的死灭善者存。
也是天意来注定,
天地重开置人伦。

四、人祖创世　IV. Human Ancestors' Inventions

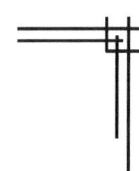

Seeing the beautiful girl and handsome boy,
the ancestress was visibly pleased,
and summoned an immortal,
to lead them by footprints.
Each stride was one *chi* and two *cun* long,
and the couple followed the footprints closely.
Quickly they arrived at the hilltop,
where they saw a rainbow with five colors.
Suddenly the girl felt a chill and the desire to make love,
and without realizing it she was pregnant.
She gave birth to twins, a boy and a girl,
and she named them Fuxi and Nvwa.

The twins grew up and married each other,
and they gave birth to five sons to continue the human race.
Nvwa was born beautiful,
more than a *zhang* in height.
She was learned about astronomy
as well as geography.
Why did the heaven fall and the earth sink?
Why was there the flood for three times?
Why do all immortals fight each other?
Why do birds and beasts compete to win?
The reason is the evil heart,
the greed for fame and personal interest.
Some were gluttonous with endless desire,
and some lost their lives by doing evil.
Good and evil appeared after the three floods,
with the evil to die and the good to remain.
It was also the will of heaven,
so as to restart heaven and earth and to set the proper human relations.

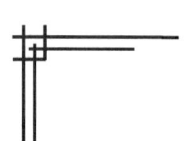

九山九海无人住,
需要传衍子孙孙。
自传子孙也有限,
需要千千万万人。
需要人来创世界,
自思索来自纳闷。
思量如何把人造,
起个念头心中喜,
不如挖泥做泥人。
洪水之后淤泥多,
就着沙滩做泥人。
比着自己一般样,
泥人泥手泥眼睛,
有牙齿,有嘴唇,
有腿有脚无灵性,
不走不动不开眼,
做去做来做不成。

这时来了泥沽神,
泥沽传授做泥人。
说起泥沽有根本,
生于上古洪荒时,
长在洪荒养其身。
原为水中一条虫,
千年修炼成了精。
一个女貌鳞甲身,
荷叶老祖一门人。
荷叶为家水上荡,
漂流四海过光阴。

四、人祖创世 IV. Human Ancestors' Inventions

No one was living in the nine mountains and nine seas,
though there needed to be generation after generation of humans.
There was a limit to the pace of human self-reproduction,
but there needed to be tens and thousands of people soon.
To create world, Nvwa,
must think hard and come up with some answers.
Pondering on the ways to make people,
she hit upon the delightful idea,
of digging the mud and making clay figurines.
There was much sludge after the floods,
so she made figurines on the beach.
According to her own image,
she moulded the clay person with clay hands and eyes,
with teeth and lips,
legs and feet but without the soul.
With the figurine not being able to walk or open the eyes,
she failed at last.

At this time came Immortal Nigu,
who taught her how to mould persons.
About this Nigu,
she was born to the former chaotic deluge,
brought up during that period.
She used to be a worm in the water,
and perfected herself into a spirit after a thousand years of cultivation.
With a female appearance and with scales and a shell,
she was the disciple of Ancestor Lotus,
living in lotus leaves, drifting on water,
and spending her time wandering among the four seas.

一日老祖来吩咐，
看守荷叶保安宁，
此是天根并地苗，
通天达地元气生。
泥沽当时领了命，
急急忙忙下昆仑。
泥沽坐在荷叶上，
逍遥自在快乐神。
随着波涛千层波，
困了睡在荷叶心。
忽然一阵黑风起，
吓得泥沽战兢兢。
泥沽这时好伤心，
不觉两眼泪淋淋。
泪水滴在荷叶上，
化为甘露亮晶晶。
等待风平与浪静，
一股清香扑鼻根。

只见一朵荷花开，
霎时花谢结莲蓬。
莲蓬结了七颗籽，
顺手摘来口里吞，
陡然精神长十分。
蹦蹦跳跳上昆仑，
来见荷叶老祖等。
禀知老祖说原因，
老祖一听笑盈盈，
吃了莲子长精神，
得了灵气有福分。

四、人祖创世　IV. Human Ancestors' Inventions

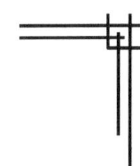

One day, Ancestor Lotus assigned her,
to take care of lotus leaves and keep peace,
because they were heavenly roots and earthly seedlings,
connecting heaven and earth and sources of the primordial energy.
Accepting the assignment,
Nigu went downhill in a great haste.
Sitting on the lotus leaf,
Nigu felt like a leisurely and carefree goddess.
As she floated with the waves of the rolling sea,
she fell asleep in the middle of the lotus-leaf.
Suddenly, a blast of black wind,
frightened Nigu.
Trembling, she became so upset,
that tears were streaming down her face.
The moment tears dropped on the lotus leaves,
they turned into sparkling sweet dew.
When the wind calmed down and the waves subsided,
wafts of delicate fragrance assailed the nostrils.

Behold, a lotus flower blossomed,
but instantly it withered and bore a seedpod,
with seven lotus seeds.
Nigu picked the seeds, ate them,
and immediately felt greatly energized.
Running by leaps and bounds, she went up Mount Kunlun,
to see Ancestor Lotus who was expecting her.
When she explained what had happened,
Ancestor Lotus smiled:
Your spirit is enhanced after eating the lotus seeds,
and this means you are destined to receive the spirit.

今日有话说你听，
也是造化缘分定。
当日有个浪荡子，
也是混元眼泪成。
那时荷叶才出世，
一棵荷叶才长成，
水中一枝并蒂莲，
藕根扎下万丈深。
吸收灵气于一身，
后变荷叶老祖身，
藏于藕内过光阴。
一时洪水滔天起，
随着波涛如浮萍。
后在水里扎下根，
一日漂到大海内，
正好风平与浪静。
吸取天精与地灵，
内有七孔通泉壤，
上有妙笔知天文，
此是天地一灵根。
才生几颗露水珠，
结聚天精与地灵。
浪荡把叶来吃净，
喝了露珠水不存。

四、人祖创世　IV. Human Ancestors' Inventions

The fact I can speak to you today,

is also predetermined by my deeds in my previous lives.

There used to be a Loafer,

born also from Hunyuan's tears.

At the time, the lotus leaf was just born,

and as it grew up,

it became a lotus stem in the water,

with a lotus root that reached tens and thousands of *zhang* deep.

After absorbing the spirits,

it turned into Ancestor Lotus,

hiding in the lotus root to pass his time.

When the floodwater surged up to the sky,

he floated with the huge waves like a duckweed.

Afterwards, it took roots in the water,

and one day floated into the ocean,

when it happened to be calm and smooth.

He inhaled the heavenly spirits and essences,

and its seven holes inside reached to springs and soil.

Being learned and knowing astronomy,

he therefore became a magic root of heaven and earth,

producing a few potent dewdrops,

with the spirit of heaven and earth.

Some Loafer came along and ate up the leaves,

with no drop of dew left.

浪荡吃了长精神，
贪吃贪喝把天吞，
想吃日月变天狗，
要与盘古斗输赢。
盘古举起开天斧，
杀了浪荡血水淋。

如今吃了莲蓬子，
神通广大本事能。
你今离我到一处，
自开洞府在门庭。
到了时候自有用，
多做善事少逞能。
再说女娲做泥人，
用心用意做不成。
来了泥沽一神女，
女娲一见称师尊。
女娲作为人始祖，
要随泥沽下山林，
要找黄土作泥人。
话说泥沽手段能，
五方五地来找寻。

青黄赤白黑五土，
金银钢铁锡之精，
此土也是非凡土，
洪水之后泥沙沉。
泥土原是神仙骨，
波涛之中化泥尘。

四、人祖创世 IV. Human Ancestors' Inventions

After the Loafer ate the dewdrops and felt stronger,
it became greedy and wanted to swallow up heaven,
the sun, the moon and to turn into a heavenly dog,
rivaling Pangu for being the best.
Raising the creation axe,
Pangu left Loafer dead in his blood.

Now that you have eaten the lotus seeds,
you have gained the far-reaching magic power.
I send you away to another place,
to open your own cave and to have your own court.
In time, your skill will find its use,
but be sure to do good and not to show off.
Let me return now back to Nvwa,
who worked hard but failed to make the clay figurines.
When Goddess Nigu appeared,
Nvwa immediately addressed her as the master.
As the Human Ancestress,
Nvwa wanted to accompany Nigu to go down the forest hill,
to search for loess to mould clay figurines.
Since Nigu was gifted in various ways,
she went to search in five directions and five regions.

The loess, varying in green, yellow, red, white and black colors,
was the essence of gold, silver, steel, iron and tin.
It was not some ordinary soil,
but the sandy sediment of the floods.
It was originally the bones of the immortals,
turning into the muddy dust after the surging waves.

泥沽采土走忙忙,
采到泥土上昆仑。
架起烈火烧丹鼎,
黄泥为丹炉中烧,
七天七夜才烧成。
七颗泥丹来炼就,
色分七彩放光明。
小小泥丹神力大,
一颗能化一山岭,
放在海里水淤平。

诗曰: 九烧九转天地精,
先天一点化泥尘。
无极太极浮尘聚,
轻者上浮为云雾,
浊者下凝泥土尘。

真精化气气化神,
精气化神入丹鼎。
具一气胎丹之始,
肇万殊生化之根,
九华玉液丹九转,
七宝黄丹七返生。
把丹抛在九霄云,
一时落地不见形,
化为黄泥到如今。
结丹化土养生灵,
才有黄土养黎民。

四、人祖创世 IV. Human Ancestors' Inventions

Nigu worked hard to collect the loess,
and then took it up Mount Kunlun.
In an alchemy furnace with raging fire,
the loess was tempered in the elixir furnace.
It was done in seven days and seven nights,
and seven mud pellets were produced,
with seven colors, giving off light.
Small as they were, the mud pellets had great magic power.
Each could turn into a mountain,
and level the sea when being put in it.

The Poem says: Tempered and turned nine times, the spirits shook heaven and earth,
and each dust came from the former chaotic period.
Wuji and Taiji assembled from the floating mud dust,
with the lighter dust flying up and changing into clouds and fogs,
and the heavier dust sinking down and changing into mud and sand.

True essence turned into spirits and spirits, into immortals,
by entering into the elixir furnace.
The conception of the pellets began with one spirit,
originating from the root that transformed from ten thousand special lives.
With splendid colors or as liquefied jade the pellets changed nine times,
and became seven yellow life-giving treasures.
Being thrown into the highest heaven,
they fell down without a trace,
and became today's loess,
to nourish living creatures,
so that there is loess that keeps people alive.

女娲取了黄泥土,
要接黄土做泥人。
做泥人来要血水,
没有血水无灵根。
女娲造人费辛勤,
内脏七窍都成形,
教他们说话知人性。
眼看都要成活人。
此时洪水又泛滥,
淹天淹地又淹人,
要将泥人淹干净。
这时女娲慌了神,
急忙登上太荒山,
太荒山上有树林。
盘古开辟过了后,
斧头还原为金星。
斧把插在太荒顶,
化为沉香树一棵。

女娲砍树来做船,
要做木船救泥人,
只因树大砍不倒,
砍下树枝有几根。
粗枝拿来做船底,
细枝拿来做船舷。
先装神,后装仙,
然后又装泥巴人。
装禽兽,装物品,
一个巨浪打翻船,
许多物品水中沉。

四、人祖创世 IV.Human Ancestors' Inventions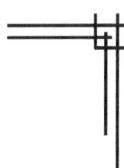

Nvwa got some loess,
to mould mud figurines with it.
To do so, she needed blood,
without which, there would not be soul.
Nvwa took on great pains,
to form the entrails and seven apertures.
She also taught them to speak and to adopt human nature,
and all of them were almost to become real humans,
when the flood came again,
threatening to submerg heaven, earth, and everything with them,
including the figurines.
Anxious,
Nvwa hurriedly went up Mount Taihuang,
where she found a forest.
Previously and after Pangu separated heaven and earth,
his axe reverted back to be the Venus,
infixed on the top of Mount Taihuang,
as an agallochum tree.

Nvwa wanted to cut down the tree,
to make a boat to rescue the figurines.
But the tree was too big to cut down,
and only a few branches were chopped off.
She used the thick branches to make the bottom of the boat,
and twigs for sides of it.
She put in the immortals first, then the fairies,
and then the clay figurines.
She also tried to save the birds, the beasts and the goods,
but a huge wave capsized the boat,
with many goods sunk into the water.

有的为水族,有的化飞禽。
女娲重新来造人。
谁个知得这个根?
歌场之中是能人。

红水之后是清水,
清水三番出人伦。
三皇出世定江山,
三番九次五帝生,
才有九州锦乾坤。

女娲要用自己血,
一点一滴做成人,
有血有肉有灵性。
比自己,画人形,
泥沽赐她笔一根。
此笔也是炉中炼,
炼出阴阳五形金,
一支神笔才炼成,
递与女娲画人形。

先画眉毛并七孔,
五脏六腑画完成。
画上三百六十人骨节,
又画血脉身上存。

四、人祖创世 IV. Human Ancestors' Inventions

Some became aquatic animals, while others became birds.
Nvwa had to restart the moulding.
Does anyone know what happened next?
He who knows will be the more knowledgeable.

After the red water was the clear water,
and after the third clear water were born the proper human relations.
The Three Emperors were born to stabilized rivers and mountains,
and Five Sovereigns were born over and over.
Only after these did the nine regions with heaven and earth take shape.

Nvwa used her own blood,
to mould clay figurines into humans,
with blood, flesh and the soul.
She drew the human shape according her own figure,
with a painting brush given to her by Nigu.
This brush was also refined in the the elixir furnace,
so it was of the Yin-Yang and five metals,
a truly magic brush,
with which Nvwa painted humans.

She first painted the eyebrows and the seven apertures,
and then finished painting the internal organs of the body.
She then pained three hundred and sixty bones,
and the blood vessels inside the body.

然后又把三清化，
金木水火土画人形。
五脏六腑画得清。
九十画得四肢出，
十一十二画眼睛，
二十六七从头画，
三十二三又提起，
汗毛十万八千根。
三十八九四十二，
顶头额角都画尽，
十指肝肺手连心。

五十一气停神笔，
犹如天上定盘星。
六十二三又提笔，
湖海江河又费心，
七十二气从头画，
五湖四海才安顿。
七十四气用笔点，
五谷禾苗尽生根。
左生毫毛二十九，
合共三十单六根。
两目犹如太阳像，
头顶四万头发青。
转身又画九十气，
八十一气画完成。
看我讲得真不真？

四、人祖创世 IV. Human Ancestors' Inventions

Then she painted the Triple Purity,
with the Five Elements for the human shape.
The internal organs of the body were painted clearly.
At the ninth and tenth breaths, she painted the four limbs,
and with the following two breaths, she painted eyes.
Then at the twenty-sixth and twenty-seventh breaths, she drew the head.
She kept on painting at thirty-second and thirty-third breath,
painting one hundred and eighty thousand body hairs.
Between the thirty-eighth to forty-second breaths,
she finished drawing the scalp and the forehead,
ten fingers, liver and lung all connecting to the heart.

At the fifty-first breath, she took a pause,
like the setting star in the sky.
She resumed at the sixty-second and sixty-third breaths,
to paint lakes and rivers.
At the seventy-second breath,
she finished painting the five lakes and the four seas.
At the seventy-fourth breath, she added the final touch,
and five grains all took root.
To the left were twenty-nine soft hair,
and there were thirty-six in all.
The two eyes were like two suns,
and on the head, the forty thousand hairs were black.
Turning around she took at the ninetieth breath,
but she finished painting with the eighty-first breath.
Don't you think what I told is true?

歌师傅，老先生，
果然书文记得清。
还有几句问一声，
说起三皇到尧舜，
共有八十女皇君，
哪一氏，生禽兽？
哪一氏，修平水旱道路行？
旱地有车水有舟，
人才能远行。
哪一氏，出凤凰，
几只凤凰一路行？
哪一氏，人多人吃兽？
哪一氏，兽多兽吃人？
哪一氏，架雀巢，蔽雨淋？
哪一氏，百姓专打鸟兽吞？
哪一氏，钻木火生，
生冷燥湿得烤蒸？

哪一氏，造字文，
万物各色都有名？
哪一氏，听鸟声，
作乐歌，神听和平人气和？

四、人祖创世 IV.Human Ancestors' Inventions

Master singer, senior teacher,
you really remembered it all clearly.
May I still ask that,
since from the Three Emperors to Yao and Shun,
there were eighty empresses,
who gave births to birds and beasts?
Who built the roads and waterways?
It was because the vehicles for the roads and boats for the waterways,
that people could travel afar.
During which time did the phoenixes come into being,
several of them traveling together?
During which time were there so many people that they ate the beasts?
During which time were there so many beasts that they at people?
During which time Sparrow Nests were built as shelters from the rain?
During which time did people catch only the birds for food?
Who made the fire by drilling the wood,
thus the raw, the cold and the damp could be toasted and steamed?

Who created characters,
and named all things?
Who, by listening to birds chirping,
made music to bring peace to the gods and make humans amiable?

哪一氏，造出五弦琴，
阴阳调和天下平？
哪一氏，用葫芦来造笙，
开化愚昧人聪明？
八十余氏问不尽，
略叫歌师答几声。

洪水泡天怎么起，怎么平？
谁又传下后代根？
歌师问得有学问，
讲起三皇到尧舜，
八十余氏果是真。
讲古还要讲根痕，
前后才能说得清。

五龙氏，生禽兽，
豺狼虎豹遍地行。
钜灵氏，开险处，
修平水旱道路平，
造车船，才远行。
皇覃氏，出凤凰，
六只凤凰一同行，
后分六处传子孙。
有巢氏，人多人吃兽，
兽多兽吃人，
架雀巢，蔽雨晴，
百姓专打鸟兽吞。

四、人祖创世 IV.Human Ancestors' Inventions

Who made the banjo,
whose sound harmonizing Yin and Yang and bring peace to the world?
Who made the Sheng instrument with the gourd,
with which people became enlightened and intelligent?
There are countless questions about the eighty empresses,
so I hope the master singer could address some of these.

Why did the flood start and how was it subdued?
Who gave birth to the offspring?
The master singer asked good questions.
From the three Emperors to Yao and Shun,
there were indeed eighty empresses.
To speak about the ancients,
we must inquire into their origin to speak clearly.

The five Dragon Queens gave birth to all birds and beasts,
and wolves, tigers and leopards roamed everywhere.
The god of rivers Juling braved dangerous places,
repairing the waterways and roads,
so that vehicles and boats could travel afar.
From Tribe Huangtan came phoenixes,
six of them going out together,
who were later separated into six places with their offspring.
During the period of Youchao, people ate the beasts when outnumbered the beast,
but, when outnumbered by the beasts, they were eaten by the beasts.
Building the Sparrow Nests to escape from the elements,
people hunted and lived on birds and beasts.

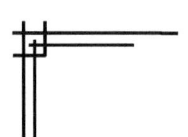

燧人氏，钻木来取火，
烧烤食物得烹饪。
史皇氏，有仓颉，
看鸟兽，观脚印，
观天象，察人形，
造下文字记事物，
万物各自都取名。
祝融氏，听鸟音，
作乐歌，神听和平人气和，
能引天神和地灵。
女娲氏，她用葫芦造成笙，
开教化，育子孙，
百姓听了开智化愚都聪明。
伏羲氏，山中听风声，
风吹木叶美声音，
就削树木来制琴，
面圆底平天地形，
五条琴弦相五行，
长有七尺三寸零，
上可通天达地神，
又修人身调气平。

四、人祖创世 IV. Human Ancestors' Inventions

Ancestor Suiren made fire by drilling wood,
so that roasting and barbecuing people started eating cooked food.
Sage Shihuang, named Cangjie,
watching birds, observing footprints,
tracing heavenly bodies and studying humans,
invented characters to keep records,
and named each and every objects.
The god of stoves and fire Zhurong, listening to birds singing,
made music and songs to bring peace to the gods and make humans amiable,
and to attract heavenly immortals and earthly spirits.
It was Nvwa who made the Sheng instrument with the gourd,
to educate and bring up the offspring,
so that common people were no longer ignorant but cultivated and intelligent.
Fuxi listened to the sound of the wind in the mountains,
and finding the wind rustling the leaves pleasant to hear,
he peeled the trees to make banjos,
which, like heaven and earth, had an arched surface and flat bottom.
The five strings corresponded to the Five Elements,
and it was seven *chi* and three *cun* long.
Its sound extended as far as heaven and earth,
and could improve people's health and cultivate their minds.

你问我，说你听，
不知说得真不真？
削桐木，来造琴，
作乐歌，传后人。
撞着共工掌乾坤，
女娲娘娘驾祥云，
杀了共工洪水平，
女娲娘娘她为神。

又把歌师问一声，
说起共工一段文，
共工怎么乱乾坤？
他与何人来交战？
不知谁输谁是赢？
何人输了气不过，
一头撞的什么山？
当时倒了什么柱？
何人一见怒生嗔？
何人又把天来补？
天补满天诛谁人？
何人一见气不过？
涌起洪水乱乾坤？

四、人祖创世 IV. Human Ancestors' Inventions

I have answered what you asked.
Do you think what I said is true?
Chipping the wood from the tung trees, Fuxi made the banjo,
composed music and songs to pass on to the offspring.
Facing off Gonggong, the god of flood, who dominated heaven and earth,
Nvwa, mounting the auspicious cloud,
killed Gonggong and subdued the floods,
this is the reason she is worshiped as a goddess.

I have other questions,
about Gonggong whom you mentioned.
How did he raise havoc in heaven and earth?
Whom did he fight?
Who won and who was defeated?
Who was too proud to admit defeat,
and rammed into a mountain and which mountain was it?
What kind of column collapsed?
Who was furious when seeing this?
Who then mended heaven?
Who was punished after heaven was mended?
Who was enraged on seeing this, enough
to send the flood to harass heaven and earth?

共工本是一帝君，
作恶无道失民心，
祝融一家怒生嗔，
领兵与他来相争。
提起祝融一段文，
他是天上火德星，
治理洪水有功勋。

当时有臣名共工，
共工出世手段能。
太荒山中一洞府，
五形精气孕化成，
能逃劫难洪水后，
三番洪水长成人。
养一鳌龙为坐骑，
洪水滔滔任游行。

祝融吹气如火焚，
要把鳌龙来烧死，
鳌龙一见心害怕，
化道彩虹逃性命，
鳌龙口中吐黑水，
要把灵山淹干净。

四、人祖创世　IV. Human Ancestors' Inventions

Gonggong used to be an emperor,
who did evil deeds and lost popular support.
Zhurong and the family were furious at this,
and led troops to fight him for justice.
As for Zhurong, there was a legend.
He was the Mars in heaven,
performing great feats by bringing flood under control.

At that time, Gonggong was an official,
who was born with great talent.
In a cave in Mount Taihuang,
he was conceived by the spirits of five shapes.
He escaped the calamitous flood,
and grew up to be an adult during the three floods.
He kept a tortoise-dragon as his ride,
traveling around in roaring flood at will.

Zhurong could breathe like blowing the burning fire,
so he wanted to burn the tortoise-dragon to death.
The tortoise-dragon was so frightened that,
it turned into a rainbow, fleeing.
It spat black water,
threatening to drown the whole Ling Mountain.

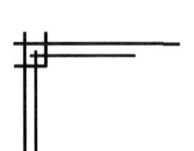

一见鳌龙发大水,
众神齐战鳌龙精,
不斩鳌龙气不平。
哪知鳌龙有道行,
众神与它战不赢,
共工撞倒不周山,
倒了擎天柱一根,
正是北边天塌下,
涌起洪水泡天庭。
女娲一见怒生嗔,
祭起斩龙剑一把,
一剑斩了鳌龙精。

说起女娲哪一个,
她是伏羲妹妹身,
洪水泡天结成婚。
当时她把天补满,
又斩共工这恶臣。
共工一见气不过,
涌起洪水乱乾坤。
共工遭斩百姓喜,
就尊女娲为上君。

四、人祖创世 IV. Human Ancestors' Inventions

Seeing the impending flood caused by the tortoise-dragon,
the immortals joined the fight,
to kill the tortoise-dragon and let justice prevail.
Who knew that the tortoise-dragon was acting according to the *dao*,
and the immortals couldn't defeat it.
Then Gonggong knocked down Mount Buzhou,
breaking a heaven-holding column,
causing heaven in the north to collapse,
and surging water flooding the heavenly court.
At the sight of this, Nvwa was filled with anger,
and wielding a dragon-slaying sword,
she killed the tortoise-dragon at once.

About this Nvwa,
she was the sister of Fuxi,
and the two married during the flood.
She mended heaven,
and executed the evil official Gonggong,
whose resentment,
caused him to send the flood to harass heaven and earth.
Common people were so delighted about Gonggong's death,
that they addressed Nvwa as Her Highness.

共工撞倒不周山,
上方倒了擎天柱,
下方裂了地与井,
洪水泛滥又混沌。
好个女娲有手段,
忙炼彩石去补天,
女娲学会炼彩石,
要炼彩石补天庭。
炼得彩石把天补,
女娲神力无比伦。
一把彩石手中拿,
口水喷在彩石上,
一把一把补天漏,
又吹冷气冰固凝,
又撒泥灰在大地,
聚灰止水洪水平。

地势得牢固,黄土固其身。
斩断鳌龙四只腿,
支起四柱立四极,
不周山缺了北边倾,
又把东北来支撑。
女娲吹冷气,天上雪纷纷,
北方天寒到如今。

四、人祖创世　IV. Human Ancestors' Inventions

Gonggong crashed into Mount Buzhou,
causing the collapse of the heaven-holding column in heaven,
the cracking of the ground and wells on earth,
and the flood and chaos everywhere.
But he met his match in Nvwa,
who quickly extracted colorful rocks to mend heaven.
After she learned how to extract the rocks,
she went to repair the heavenly court.
She used the rocks to mend heaven,
with her unparalleled magic power.
Holding the colorful stones in one hand,
sprinkling saliva on them,
she mended heaven little by little.
Afterwards, she blew cold breaths to solidify the patches.
She then spread the plaster on the ground,
and the dried plaster stopped the flood and brought peace.

Now the ground was firm, and the tortoise-dragon's body was fastened by loess.
Its four legs were cut off,
to be four columns that sustain the four poles.
Mount Buzhou was tilted to the north,
so she propped up the northeast.
Nvwa then blew some cold air, and snow started swirling down at once,
and it is still frozen in the north today.

当日又出浪荡子，
口咬北方一块天。
盘古追杀浪荡子，
一直追下昆仑山。
山下有个地眼洞，
浪荡子钻在洞里边。
盘古封了地眼洞，
变一天狗又翻天。
当日浪荡变天狗，
一只神狗上了天。
神狗它嫌月光明，
行走现形不方便。
它把日月吞半边，
女娲来把日月救，
月亮有缺才有圆。

歌师唱歌有学问，
有些事儿未说清。
女娲来把彩石炼，
什么石头分五彩？
彩石又在哪里寻？
炼石用的什么火？
取火又是哪个人？
为何取火烧自身？
歌师如果答得真，
才是歌场老先生。

四、人祖创世 IV. Human Ancestors' Inventions

One day a Loafer turned up,
and bit off a piece of heaven in the north.
Pangu chased the Loafer,
all the way down Mount Kunlun.
There was an earth-eye hole at the foot of the mountain,
so the Loafer wormed his way into it.
Pangu sealed off the hole,
and the Loafer turned into a heavenly dog and kept making trouble.
On the day he transformed into the dog,
a magic dog rose up to heaven.
It disliked the bright moonlight,
which revealed his true figure and made it hard to hide,
so he swallowed half of the moon.
Nvwa came to the rescue,
this is the reason the moon wanes first and then waxes.

Master singer, you are very learned,
but some things are still to be clarified.
Nvwa extracted colorful rocks,
but what kind of rocks had five colors?
Where did she find the colorful stones?
What kind of fire did she use for extracting the rocks?
Who went to fetch the fire?
Why did he fetch the fire and then burned himself?
If the master singer can provide true answers,
you will be a venerable master of the Song House.

歌师问起这段文,
说讲起来根古深。
女娲彩石如珍宝,
天河沙石来化成。
本来就是天上物,
洪水之时埋沙尘。
女娲采石不周山,
此山又名滑塘坑。
滑塘坑里多宝石,
坑中水深不可测,
又叫咸池旸谷名,
日月二神从此升。

咸池之中多珍宝,
女娲取石在此寻。
多亏女娲能变化,
上天入地般般能。
时变凤鸟上九天,
时变龙蛇入水深。

女娲采石多忙碌,
拣来彩石把天补,
补天补地补乾坤。
洪水之后无火种,
彩石怎么炼得成?

四、人祖创世 IV. Human Ancestors' Inventions

The text the master singer is asking about,
shows a long story.
The colorful stones Nvwa extracted were like gems,
formed by sand and stones in the Milky Way.
They belonged to heaven anyway,
buried in the sand during the floods.
Nvwa looked for rocks in Mount Zhou,
which was also named the Huatang Pit.
The pit was full of treasure,
but it is bottomless with its unpredictable water.
It was also named Xian Chi Yang Gu,
from which the Sun and the Moon rose up.

Xian Chi contained so many treasures,
so Nvwa went there to extract the rocks.
Owing to her transforming ability,
she could reach heaven above and earth below.
Now she turned into a phoenix flying into the ninth heaven,
and now she turned into a dragon swimming in the deep water.

Nvwa was busy,
extracting the colorful rocks,
to mend heaven and earth.
With no fire after the floods,
how would the colorful rocks be made?

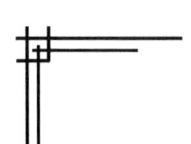

这时前边来一女,
见了女娲称师尊:
"吾是雷泽来长成,
先天金石来化身,
先天雷公化鸟形。
口吐一股霹雳火,
一怒放出巨雷声,
要与吾身成婚配,
不愿与他结婚姻。

女娲师尊搭救我,
我愿为你寻火根。
炼石需要三种火,
太阳,太阴和霹雳,
三昧真火炼宝珍。
吾愿取来三昧火,
炼得彩石补天庭。"

女娲一听喜十分,
不知如何取火根?
答曰上天取得太阳火,
又取月亮水晶阴中火,
又取雷公霹雳火,
愿为师母献其身。

四、人祖创世 IV.Human Ancestors' Inventions

Just at this time came a girl,
who respectfully addressed Nvwa as her master:
"I grew up in Leize,
and I was transformed from the gold stones.
The Thunder God turned into a bird,
spiting thunderbolt fire,
with a huge sound of thunder when he is in a rage.
He is forcing me to marry him,
but I am running away from him because I don't want to marry him.

Master Nvwa, you saved me,
so I would like to find the fire starter for you.
To make the rocks, you need three kinds of fire,
Taiyang, Taiyin and the thunderbolt.
Only by these three kinds of true fire can you make the treasure stones.
I would like to find these three kinds of fire for you,
to make the colorful rocks for mending the heavenly court."

On hearing this, Nvwa was joyful.
She asked: "how will you fetch the fire starter?"
The girl replied: "I am going to heaven to fetch the Taiyang fire from the sun,
the Taiyin fire from the crystal palace in the moon,
and the thunderbolt fire from the Thunder God.
I'd be happy to give myself to you."

女娲点头笑盈盈,
感念弟子一片心。
此女化为一朵云,
飘上重霄万里程。
这时雷公一声怒,
追赶那女九霄云,
一串炸雷震上下,
一道闪电化火根。
点燃彩石炼炉火。
彩石熔化升祥云。

女娲连忙把天补,
补天不是容易成,
哪里天穿哪里补,
哪里缺了哪修整。
彩石片片随心意,
北边天地才补成。

彩石补天止天漏,
止住天河往下淋,
天柱折了来接住,
昆仑山高做磉墩。
多亏女娲易变化,
一双巧手补天庭。
时化大鹏飞上下,
时化巨龙绕昆仑。

四、人祖创世 IV. Human Ancestors' Inventions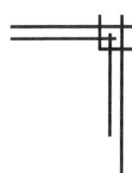

Nvwa nodded with a beaming face,
and thanked her for her devotion.
The girl then turned into a cloud,
floating far away.
It was heard then the Thunder God's angry roar,
as he chased after the girl in the clouds.
With an exploding clap of the thunder,
a flash of lighting turned into the fire starter.
The fire was started, and the rocks were burning,
the melted colorful rocks rose as the auspicious cloud.

Nvwa quickly began to mend heaven.
It was not an easy job,
for she must mend wherever there were holes,
and fill in what was missing.
Each colorful rock followed Nvwa's will,
and then the northern heaven was mended at last.

The colorful rocks were to stop the leaks in heaven,
preventing the heavenly river from showering down.
The broken heavenly columns were repaired,
with the high Kunlun Mountain being a pier base.
Thankfully, again, Nvwa was apt to transform,
she succeeded in mending heaven with her deft hands.
Sometimes she had to turn into a roc flying up and down,
while other times she had to turn into a huge dragon circling
Mount Kunlun.

诗曰：红水之时是红暗，
红水之后洪水清，
女娲补天止洪水，
闪电娘娘盗火根。
雷公电母成一体，
风婆雨师紧后跟。

女娲逝后化地母，
后土载物养黎民。
土生万物也生人，
不忘地母养育恩。

诗曰：盘古之后她为尊，
兄妹二人配成婚。
统天统地统三光，
包天包地包乾坤。
乾坤艮巽是为天，
坎离震兑为四柱。
女娲之后为地母，
厚德载物赖后土。
阴阳会合真造化，
造化天地产贤能。
虽然不言又不语，
俯察万物有神灵。
结胎原是卦爻定，
胎漏产出众黎民。

四、人祖创世 IV. Human Ancestors' Inventions

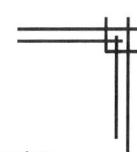

The Poem says: During the red water period, the floodwater was dark-red in color,
After the red water, the floodwater was clear.
It was Nvwa who mended heaven and stopped the flood,
and it was Goddess Lighting who fetched the fire starter.
God Thunder and Goddess Lightning joined into one,
followed by Goddess Wind and God Rain.

Nvwa died and turned into the Mother of Land,
nourishing the earth, carrying objects and benefiting people.
The land gives birth to everything and also us humans,
so we should always be thankful to the Mother of Land.

The Poem says: She was respected as the most honrable after Pangu,
the two, brother and sister, married to each other.
Managing heaven, earth and the Three Lights,
she cared for both heaven and earth.
In the Eight Diagrams, heaven included Qian, Kun, Gen and Xun,
and the Four Columns included Kan, Li, Zhen and Dui.
Nvwa then turned into the Mother of Land,
her great virtues carrying all things and nourishing the earth.
Yin and Yang united to bring good fortune,
the good fortune of bringing about heaven, earth and worthy talents.
Though quiet,
she had the miraculous power of observation.
Her original conception was determined by divination,
but she ended up benefiting the common people.

天皇地皇人皇氏,
燧人有巢与公孙。
东南西北两部州,
春夏秋冬四季分。
江河湖泊在她怀,
身负江河和山林。

天下五岳是仙境,
山林树木花草生。
黎民百姓靠耕种,
五谷六米才长成。
金银财宝是她生,
蔬菜药茶雨露生。
及时洒下甘霖水,
地上禾苗五谷生。

地母昼夜不合眼,
合眼生灵有灾星。
如果地母打个盹,
鳖鱼翻身一扫平。

要知地母名和姓,
鸿蒙未到老混沌。
造土造人多辛勤,
劳累而死为地平。

四、人祖创世 IV.Human Ancestors' Inventions

She reigned heaven, earth and humans,
leaving behind tribes like Sui Ren, You Chao and Gong Sun.
Because of her, there were four directions: east, west, south, north,
and four seasons: spring, summer, autumn and winter.
She embraces all rivers and lakes,
and carries all mountains and forests.

The Five Mountains are fairylands under heaven,
growing trees, grasses and flowers.
The multitudes lived by farming,
and so there are the five grains.
She is the one who made gold, sliver and precious things possible,
and who made the rain and dewdrops, vegetables, medicine and teas possible.
She is the one who sprinkled the timely sweet dewdrops,
to water seedlings of crops on the ground.

Mother of Land stays awake day and night,
to guard against any disaster.
If she takes a nap,
the beasts in the sea will make a comeback and destroy everything.

As for the name of Mother of Land,
she was born during Chaos before Hongmeng the primordial world.
She worked so hard to make earth and humans,
that she died of exhaustion while preparing the earth.

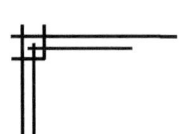

地母归土乃有灵,
养护万代之子孙。
水有源来木有根,
世代不忘地母恩。

再把天皇为师尊,
不知记得清不清?
天皇过后几多岁?
弟兄共有几多春?
又有何人来出世?
何人出世治乾坤?
你把根由说我听,
才算歌场高明人。

金鼓一住暂消停,
我把歌师尊一声,
慢慢听我讲根痕。
你问天皇来世出,
弟兄共有十三人。
天皇出世人民少,
淡淡泊泊过光阴。
又无岁数和年岁,
又无春夏与秋冬。
天皇那时来商议,
商议弟兄十三人,
创立天干定年岁,
又立地支十二名,
那时方才定年岁,
暑往春来一年春。

四、人祖创世　IV. Human Ancestors' Inventions

She returned to dust but her soul,
keeps nourishing her offspring from generation to generation.
Every river has its source, and every tree, its roots,
so her kindness should never be forgotten.

May I ask about Emperor Heaven:
do you remember his stories clearly?
How old was he when passed away?
How many brothers did he have?
Who was born after him?
Who was born to reign heaven and earth?
If you tell me those stories,
you will be the wise master in the Song House.

Stop the drum and take a break,
to let me address the master singer,
and talk about the origin by and by.
You asked about the birth of Emperor Heaven.
He had thirteen brothers.
When he was born, there were few others aroud,
so he lived a simple life with few desires,
without age and years,
without spring, summer and autumn, winter.
It was only after Emperor Heaven had discussed,
with his thirteen brothers,
and established the ten Heavenly Stems to fix the age,
and the twelve Earthly Branches,
were the years set up,
with four seasons within each year.

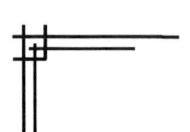

神笔三杆相传授,
听我从头说分明:
一支名叫画天笔,
画出日月与星辰;
二支名叫画地笔,
画出江河与山林。
天皇名字叫天灵,
出世就把干支配,
十二地支造分明。
一年又治十二月,
一生操了许多心,
管了一万八千春,
又该地皇来出生,
隐入青山不见形。

天皇隐匿不见形,
我把天皇说你听,
你说地皇行不行?
地皇出于什么地?
一姓共有几多人?
地皇怎么治天下,
什么方法定乾坤?
地皇过后几多岁?
又有何人来出生?
你把根由说我听,
歌场才算你为能。

四、人祖创世 IV. Human Ancestors' Inventions

The brothers had three magic paintbrushes,
and let me explain them to you from the beginning.
One was named Heaven-Painting Brush,
and it painted the sun, the moon and the stars.
One was named Earth-Painting Brush,
and it painted rivers, lakes, mountains and forests.
The name of Emperor Heaven was Tianling,
who, at birth, started to establish the Heavenly Stems and Earthly Branches,
arranging twelve distinct Earthly Branches.
He then set twelve months in each year,
working tirelessly,
for eighteen thousand years.
Then when Emperor Earth was born,
Emperor Heaven retired into the green mountains without a trace.

I have told you about Emperor Heaven,
who ended with making himself invisible.
Could you tell me about Emperor Earth?
Where was he born?
How many were there in his family?
How did he run the world?
What method did he use?
How long did he live?
Who was born after him?
If you could tell me about all this,
then you will be the most skilled in the Song House.

地辟于丑地皇君，
地皇一姓十一人。
弟兄十一管乾坤，
生于陕西叫龙门。
他的名字叫岳铿，
出世才把山川定。
他今才把昼夜分，
七十二候才来临，
二十四气是他分。
他以太阳把日定，
又以太阴把夜分。
三十日为一月，
十二月为一春，
那时才有年和月，
昼夜才能得分明。
地皇过了一万八千岁，
隐入青山不见形，
又有人皇来出生。

歌师傅，老先生，
又把人皇问一声：
仁兄是否记得清？
人皇出生什么地？
一姓共有几多人？
几人几处治天下？
他在何处教黎民？
人皇怎么现天象？

四、人祖创世 IV. Human Ancestors' Inventions

Emperor Earth was born second,
and he had eleven in his family.
Together these eleven brothers, born in today's Longmen, Shan'xi Province,
ran heaven and earth.
Emperor Earth, named Yuekeng,
settled mountains and rivers after his birth.
He then divided day and night,
and that was the beginning of the seventy two climates,
and we also owe the twenty-four Solar Terms to him.
He set the day according to the sun,
and the night according to the moon.
Since then there have been thirty days in a month,
twelve months in a year,
differentiating month and year,
dividing day and night.
Emperor Earth lived for eighteen thousand years,
and he then hid himself in the green mountains out of sight.
Emperor Human was born.

Master singer, senior master,
Could I ask about Emperor Human:
do you still remember his stories clearly?
Where was he born?
How many were there in his family?
How many people and regions did he rule?
Where did he teach the common people?
How did he observe the heavenly bodies?

黎民光景如何样？
几处太平不太平？
人皇共有几多春？
你把根源说我听，
才算歌场人上人。

人生于寅人皇主，
人皇兄弟九个人。
生于形马山中地，
弟兄九人分区明。
各管一州镇乾坤，
制纲常，立人伦，
才有三党共六亲。
天皇地皇人皇君，
共管四万五千八百春。

人皇弟兄为龙海，
又该五龙来出生，
一黄伯，二黄仲，
三黄叔，四黄季，
五黄五龙出世分，
金木水火土中存。
才有宫商角徵羽，
才把五音来分清，
五龙四帝五处分。

四、人祖创世 IV. Human Ancestors' Inventions

How were the common people's lives under him?
Where was peace and where unrest?
How many years did Emperor Human live?
If you tell me about all this,
you will be the best master in the Song House.

Emperor Human was born the third,
and he had eight brothers.
Born in Mount Xingma,
the nine brothers each ran one of the nine regions.
Within each of the regions,
they established the Cardinal Guides for virtuous act and proper human relations,
the beginning of our understanding of the six family relations.
Heavenly, Earthly and Human Emperors,
altogether ruled forty-five thousand and eight hundred years.

The brothers of Emperor Earth ran the imperial sea,
so the five dragons came into being again,
the eldest Huangbo, the second Huangzhong,
the third Huangshu, the fourth Huangji,
altogether five brothers,
with metal, wood, water, fire and earth inside of them.
This was when the five notes of music were formed,
with Gong, Shang, Jue, Zhi and Yu,
and the five dragons and four emperors lived in five regions.

又出五丁氏，气力大得很，
他教百姓挖一坑，
一个坑儿百丈深，
躲水躲雨好安身。
九州九处都太平，
选才德，作用人，
那时才有君臣分。
驾云车，观地象，
东西南北才摸清。
渴有清泉饮，饥摘树叶吞，
寒有木叶遮其身。
燧人氏，有道君，
钻木取火教万民，
春杨夏柘来取火，
秋杏冬檀取火星。
定婚姻，教嫁娶，
男子三十娶下亲，
女子二十嫁出门。
百姓个个喜欢心，
有父有母到如今。
燧人氏，传后人，
传下火种养万民，
万古流传到如今。

四、人祖创世 IV. Human Ancestors' Inventions

Later, there was Emperor Wu Ding, with extraordinary strength.
He taught common people to dig a hole,
a hundred *zhang* deep,
as a shelter from water and rain.
All nine regions were peaceful,
employing and appointing talented and virtuous people.
It was a time when the roles of the king and the ministers were divided.
Mounting clouds, observing geo-phenomena,
people distinguished east, west, south and north.
Drinking from clear springs to quench thirst, eating leaves on the tree to ease hunger,
people also covered their bodies with leaves when it was cold.
Sui Ren Shi, with great wisdom,
made fire and taught millions of people,
to drill poplar in the spring, cudrania in the summer,
apricot in the autumn, sandal wood in the winter.
Formulating marriage rules and teaching about them,
they made men marry by the age of thirty,
and women, by the age of twenty.
Common people all were delighted,
and we have father and mother until now.
Sui Ren Shi passed on to later generations,
how to make fire to give people a good life.
His story has been remembered throughout the ages till today.

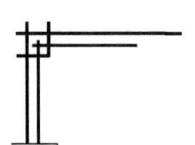

唱起当日有皇氏，
有皇氏，驾元龙，
走遍九州查民情。
又出中皇氏，也是有德君，
生于山东鲁国曲阜城，
有个大庭氏，又出了六粟氏，
后代才出孔圣人。
几个知得这段情？
说得是来道得真，
又把伏羲问一声，
歌师你可记得清？
伏羲怎样来出世？
生于何方何地名？
怎样来把天下治？
怎样作为定乾坤？
怎样来把百姓教，
人伦礼义到如今？

四、人祖创世 IV. Human Ancestors' Inventions

As for You Huang Shi,
he rode dragons,
traveling through the world to survey the situation of the general public.
Afterwards, there was Zhong Huang Shi, also a virtuous emperor,
born in Qufu, State of Lu or today's Shandong Province,
followed by Da Ting Shi and later Liu Su Shi.
Their posterity includes Confucius.
How many people knew about this,
and could tell how it all actually happened?
Also could I ask again about Fuxi:
can the master singer remember his story well?
How was he born?
Where was he born?
How did he rule everything under heaven?
What were his achievements?
How did he teach the common people,
and clarified the proper human relations and etiquette that we still observe today?

金鼓一住又唱起,
歌师又来问伏羲,
听我从头说与你。
他是五帝开首君,
说起太昊他母亲,
华胥地方也不远。
陕西蓝田县地名,
太昊圣母闲游走,
见一大人脚迹形,
圣母忽然春意动,
天上虹霓绕其身,
圣母忽然身有孕,
成纪地方生圣君。
成纪地方在何处?
甘肃巩昌岷州城。

伏羲仁君观天象,
日月星辰山川形,
才画八卦成六爻,
六十四卦达神明。
教人嫁娶治婚姻,
女儿嫁与男为妻。
五帝首君说分明,
可算歌场一能人。

四、人祖创世 IV. Human Ancestors' Inventions

The drum-beating stops, and the master singer resumes.
The master singer asked about Fuxi again,
so let me start from the beginning for you.
He was the first of the Five Emperors.
His mother, Taihao,
lived in Hua Xu, not very far from here.
One day in what's today's Lantian County, Shan'xi Province,
Goddess Taihao going on a walk and,
saw an adult's footprint,
which aroused her desire to make love.
The rainbows in heaven encircled her,
and the goddess became pregnant.
She gave birth to the sage in Chengji.
Where was Chengji?
It is today's Mangzhou City, Gongchang, Gansu Province.

The sage Fuxi observed heavenly bodies,
the sun, the moon, the stars and the mountains.
Only after this did he draw the Eight Diagrams with six yaos①,
in each of the sixty-four diagrams for divination.
He taught and formulated proper ways of marriage,
young women marrying to young men as wives.
Finish the story of the first of the Five Emperors,
you will indeed be the most talented in the Song House.

---

① six yaos refer to the combination of the six Yin-Yang symbols from the bottom up, or the divination method with this combination.

阴人踏了燧人气,
怀孕一十四年春,
才生伏羲一个人。
三十岁上坐龙位,
画出八卦知天文,
唱个地名陕西城,
太昊圣母出山林,
一见神人面前走,
太昊圣母随后跟。

歌师讲得真有趣,
又把伏羲问几句,
不知仁兄喜不喜?
伏羲出世出龙马,
不知出生何地名?
龙马生得什么样?
高有几尺几寸零?
背上又有何物现?
不知是吉还是凶?
他今又把何物治,
修身理性答神明?
伏羲在位年多少?
又有何人治乾坤?
你把根由说我听。

四、人祖创世 IV. Human Ancestors' Inventions

After the woman stepped onto the footprint of Sui Ren,
she was pregnant for fourteen years,
before she gave birth to Fuxi.
He didn't become the emperor until he was thirty,
where he drew the Eight Diagrams and became knowledgeable about astronomy.
It was in a place, which today is a city in Shan'xi,
that Goddess Taihao went for a walk out in the mountains.
As soon as she saw a god walking in front of her,
Goddess Taihao followed him.

How interesting is the way the master singer told the story!
A few more questions about Fuxi,
would it be okay if I ask them of you, my kind brother?
It was said a dragon-horse was born at Fuxi's birth,
but then where was it born?
What did the dragon-horse look like?
How tall was it?
What appeared on its back?
Was it auspicious or not?
What did he create and formulate,
to cultivate people and understand mysteries?
How many years did he reign?
Who followed after him?
Please tell us the stories.

歌师又把伏羲问，
伏羲乃是仁德君，
礼仪人伦从他兴。
孟河一日祥云去，
一匹龙马来出世。
生得满身有甲鳞，
高有八尺五寸零，
背上又有河图现，
天降祥瑞吉兆临。
在位一百一十五年春，
又出共工乱乾坤。

诗曰：节制后天接先天，
全凭指划走云烟，
负图献瑞惟龙马，
呈书宝龟现碧莲。
六十四卦分造化，
剥极而复判天人。
天有三百六十度，
循环往复运期神，
孤阴不生阳难长，
老阴变阳阳变阴。
风云雷电不相射，
水火南北不相侵，
万物陶熔如炉鼎，
按照五行定律音。

四、人祖创世 IV. Human Ancestors' Inventions

You asked more questions about Fuxi.
He was a kind and virtuous man,
the first advocator of etiquettes and proper human relations.
One day when an auspicious cloud rose up in Meng He,
a dragon-horse was born.
With shell scales all over its body,
more than eight *chi* and five *cun* in height,
carrying the Hetu, the Diagrams, on its back,
it was truly a propitious sign.
During the one hundred and fifteen years of his reign,
Gonggong appeared and disrupted the peace.

The Poem says: Reckoning with fiends one after another,
depended all upon his commanding the navigation in the misty clouds,
upon the auspicious dragon-horse who carried the map,
which was presented like a jade lotus by the precious tortoise.
The sixty-four divinatory diagrams show the way of things,
the turn of fortune on reaching the extreme.
The sun rotates three hundred and sixty degrees,
moving in circles magically and endlessly.
Yin alone cannot exist without Yang,
while reaching their extreme Yin and Yang transform into each other.
Although wind, cloud, thunder and lightning are of their own sovereignty,
and water and fire, south and north have their own jurisdiction,
everything is ultimately melting into the nature's furnace,
yet allocated like the musical notes according to the Five Elements.

又将神农问先生。
神农出在什么地？
又是怎样教百姓？
神农山中尝百草，
七十二毒神怎么行？
哪个山中寻五谷？
几种才有稻麦生？
又有何人无道理，
要反神农有道君？
又有什么人不可？
哪个大怒杀何人？
百姓一见心恼恨，
聚集人马诛反臣。
何人力寡不敌众，
百姓杀死命归阴？
神农仁君多有道，
何方归天有道君？
神农在位多少年？
崩于何方什地名？
歌师一一说我听，
我好斟酒待先生。

歌师问得真有趣，
听我一一说与你，
神农治世从此起。

四、人祖创世 IV. Human Ancestors' Inventions

May I ask you now, master singer, about Shennong?
Where was he born?
How did he teach the common people?
How could he be poisoned seventy-two times,
when he tasted hundreds of herbs?
In which mountain did he search for the five grains?
When did rice and wheat come into being?
Who was unreasonable?
Who was to rebel against the wise Shennong,
but was persuaded not to?
Who was so furious that he killed the persuader, and who was the persuader?
Common people on learning about this were so indignant that,
they assembled to condemn the rebelling minister.
But who was outnumbered and then,
killed by the common people?
Shennong, the wise emperor,
where did he pass away?
How many years did he rule?
What is the name of the place where he passed away?
Master singer, please explain to me one by one,
and then I will propose a toast to you.

How interesting are the master singer's questions!
I will indeed explain one by one,
tracing all the way to Shennong's birth.

神农皇帝本姓姜,
指水为姓氏日后为谷皇,
又有神农来出世,
歌师父来老先生,
七言四句念你听。

诗曰：圣人诞生自天工,
首出称帝草昧中,
制作文明开千古,
补天溶日亘苍穹。

南方丙丁火德王,
又号炎帝为皇上。
提起神农有根痕,
他是少典亲所生。
母亲峤氏女贤能,
安登夫人是她名。
配合少典结为婚,
生下两个小娇生。
长子石年次神农,
烈山上面长成人。

唱起神农来出世,
生下三天能说话,
五天之中能走行,
七天牙齿俱长齐,
便问父母名和姓。
神农出世生得丑,
头上长角牛首形。

四、人祖创世 IV. Human Ancestors' Inventions

Emperor Shennong was born with the surname Jiang,
homonymous with river, but was later changed to the Grain Emperor.
As for his birth,
Master singer, senior singer,
let me read the following four lines from the seven-character poem.

The Poem says: The sage's birth was the work of nature,
and he was born in the primitive time to be an emperor,
to build civilization to benefit all ages,
to mend heaven and to inlay in it the moon and the sun.

In the south, there was the virtuous King Bing Ding Fire,
also called Emperor Yan.
This relates to the origin of Shennong,
who was born to Shaodian.
The mother, Qiao Shi, a worthy talent,
was called Mrs An Deng.
After marring Shaodian,
she gave birth to two little children.
Shi Nian, the elder, Shennong, the younger,
both grew up in Mount Lieshan.

Let me sing the song about Shennong's birth.
He could talk three days after he was born,
walk within five days,
grew all his teeth by the seventh day,
so he asked his parents his name.
Though miraculously precocious, Shennong was ugly looking at birth,
having a cow's head with horns on it.

父母一见心不喜，
把他丢在深山里。
山中遇着一白虎，
衔着神农回家门。
父母把他丢水中，
一条黄龙来托起，
救了神农一性命。
父母丢他火中烧，
有一神兽下山林，
遍体透亮像水晶，
扑在火中救神农，
喷出清水灭火星。

神农出世多灾难，
磨难之中长成人，
做了南方一帝君。
当了帝君爱黎民，
可惜天下不太平。
他今教民耕嫁事，
女子采桑蚕吐丝。
当时天下瘟疫广，
村村户户死无人。
神农治病尝百草，
劳心费力进山林。

四、人祖创世 IV. Human Ancestors' Inventions

His parents were so displeased,
that they threw him in the remote mountains.
This was where he met a white tiger,
who carried him in its mouth and sent him home.
His parents then threw him in the water,
where a yellow dragon held him up,
and saved his life.
Afterwards his parents threw him in a burning fire,
but an immortal beast came down the mountains,
who transparently shining like crystal,
rushed into the fire to save Shennong,
spouting sparkling water that extinguished the fire.

Much misfortune after birth,
accompanied Shennong as he grew up,
and became an imperial chiefdom in the south.
As the chiefdom he loved his people,
but the world was far from painless.
He taught people how to farm and to have a family,
and he taught women to pick mulberry leaves for silkworm to produce silk.
But diseases plagued everywhere under heaven,
and families and villages were filled with dead people.
To cure the diseases, Shennong went into the mountains tirelessly,
and tasted hundreds of herbs.

神农尝草遇毒药,
腹中疼痛不安宁,
急速尝服解毒药,
识破七十二毒神。
要害神农有道君,
神农判出众姓名,
三十六毒逃了生,
七十二变还阳草,
神农采回救黎民。
毒神逃进深山林,
至今良药平地广,
毒药平地果然稀。

神农在位百年春,
世间百姓多生病。
出了七十二瘟神,
各种瘟病多流行,
黎民百姓遭灾星。
神农一见心不安,
决心去到大深山,
亲自尝药救难民。

一日来到姜水口,
姜水口上遇怪兽。
身长一丈生双角,
两个耳朵像尖刀,
尾巴足有三尺五。

四、人祖创世 IV.Human Ancestors' Inventions

In tasting the herbs, Shennong was often poisoned,
suffering severe stomachaches,
but then he would hurriedly experiment with the antidotes,
and eventually recognized seventy-two poisonous herbal numina.
Those intending to harm the wise Shennong,
were recognized by him by their names.
Although thirty-six of them escaped,
seventy-two resurrection herbs were recognized,
and collected by Shennong to save the common people.
The poisonous herbal numina fled into the remote mountains,
and to this day the medical herbs are everywhere on the ground,
poisonous ones being quite rare.

During the hundred years Shennong reigned,
people suffered numerous diseases.
The seventy-two numina of plagues,
were ravaging the land,
and were disastrous for the common people.
Heartbroken Shennong,
was determined to go into the remote mountains,
to taste medicines in person to save his tormented people.

One day when he came to the mouth of the Jiang River,
he came across a monster.
It was one *zhang* long with two horns,
with two ears like pointed knives,
a tail three *chi* and five *cun* long.

眼如铜铃生四足，
见了神农不让路，
要与神农争胜负。
神农与他把力斗，
七天七夜分赢输，
方才收服这怪兽。

神农斩下藤一股，
将它拴在大山口，
来了后稷见神农，
神农交于后稷手。
命它犁田种五谷，
此藤取名叫青藤，
怪兽取名为青牛。

神农又往山中走，
一心只奔老林口。
来到深山大老林，
一座巨岩面前横。
神农抬头来观看。
哪有道路上山林？

如若不把山来上，
天下百姓无救星。
当时看见藤一根，
岩上长到岩下面，
藤长总有千丈零。

四、人祖创世 IV. Human Ancestors' Inventions

With four feet and eyes like copper bells,
it didn't make way for Shennong,
but rather challenged him to a duel.
Shennong fought it with a sword,
for seven days and seven nights,
before he finally brought it under control.

Afterwards, Shennong chopped off a strand of vine,
fasten it by a pass in a big mountain,
and later handed it to Houji,
when they two met later.
The monster was given the order to plough for growing the five grains,
and the vine was named Verdant Vine,
while the monster was named Brown Buffalo.

Shennong resumed his undertaking,
unwaveringly going straight to the mouth of the old forest.
When he entered the dense forests in the deep mountain,
he found himself facing a giant rock blocking his way.
Raising his head, Shennont searched around,
Where is the pass up into the mountain?

If he didn't climbed up the mountain,
common people would have no one to save them.
Presently, he saw a vine,
growing from the top of the rock to its bottom,
thousands of *zhang* long.

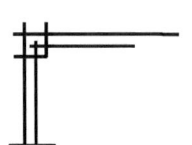

神农抓着这根藤,
顺着藤子往上行。
不觉来到岩头上,
浑身累得汗淋淋。
神农当时喜欢心,
便把此藤取了名。
取的名字叫"红藤"。

神农又往前边走,
肚中饥饿难得行。
耳听乌鸦头上叫,
神农本来知鸟音。
乌鸦叫的神农君,
你今饥渴不要紧。
快快来把大树上,
树上果子多得很。
神农抬头仔细看。
树上牵着一根藤。
藤上结的黑色果,
一串一串好爱人。
神农忙把大树上,
摘了一串一口吞。
甘甜可口真好吃,
能解饥饿长精神。
神农当时心中喜,
连忙给它取了名。
果子名叫"乌鸦子",
藤子就叫"乌鸦藤"。

四、人祖创世 IV. Human Ancestors' Inventions

Grasping the vine firmly,
Shennong rope-climbed up the rock.
Reaching the top quickly,
he was exhausted and drenched in sweat.
Excited,
he named the vine,
the "Red Vine".

Trying to continue his quest,
Shennong now felt the pangs of hunger and could hardly take another step.
Then and there a crow's caws were sounding in his ear,
and Shennong had always understood birds' sounds.
Addressing him respectfully, the crow said:
Do not worry about your hunger and thirst,
but climb up this tree in this instance,
for the many fruits on the tree.
When Shennong looked up to see for himself,
he saw a vine on the tree.
The vine bore black fruits,
which grew in lovely bunches.
Shennong hurried up the tree,
picked a bunch of fruits and put them all in his mouth.
Sweet and tasty, the fruits were delicious,
satisfying his hunger and revitalizing his spirits.
Shennong was elated,
and named both of them immediately,
"Crow Fruit" for the fruit,
and "Crow Vine" for the vine.

解了饥饿往前走,
一心要进大山林。
神农当时不小心,
足下绊住藤一根。
神农一跤摔在地,
浑身疼痛实难忍。
神农心中暗恼怒,
张口封它叫"葛藤"。
受尽千刀与万剐,
火烧棒槌织草绳。
百姓穿起走世界,
叫它永世不翻身。

神农爬起往前行,
过了几山又几岭。
忽然吹来风一阵,
风过走出一畜生。
遍身无毛身发亮,
张口要吃神农君。
神农与兽两相战,
怪兽不明对头人,
趴在神农他面前,
摇头摆尾不做声。
神农将他收伏了,
神农如得贵宝珍,
透明药狮号圣兽,
直到如今医尊敬。

四、人祖创世 IV. Human Ancestors' Inventions

Having satisfied his hunger and thirst, he resumed his expedition,
determined to go into the dense forests.
In his hurry, Shennong,
tripped on a vine,
and fell onto the ground,
aching all over unbearably.
Upset and angry, Shennong,
at once named the vine "Kudzu Vine".
Later the vine suffered countless cuts and was sliced into little pieces,
cured with smoke, hammered by wooden clubs and weaven into straw ropes.
The straw-rope sandals are worn by common people who walk everywhere.
The vine is notorious forever.

Picking himself up, Shennong pressed forward,
tramping over mountain after mountain.
Suddenly, a gust of wind blew across the field,
and following it an animal appeared.
Shining all over without any fur,
the animal opened its mouth to eat Sage Shennong.
The two fought,
and then on realizing whom it was dealing with,
the peculiar-looking animal groveled in front of Shennong,
shaking its head, wagging its tail, and uttering no word.
Shennong subdued it,
regarded it as a treasure,
and named the transparent lion Sage Beast,
which, till today, is the patron sage of medicine.

神农收了药狮子，
命他尝草吃草根。
相伴神农在山林，
尝尽百草品药性。
一日神农找药草，
一座大山高入云。
只见岩上长青草，
一年四季叶子青。
又见岩头生紫气，
万道红光耀眼睛。
神农要把岩来上，
品尝此药才甘心。
当时取出拨云剑，
砍树架梯忙不赢。
大树只有几丈高，
怎能爬上高山顶？
神农便把主意打，
要想办法上山行。
忽然一藤脚下绊，
神农仔细看分明。
只见地下藤一根，
须长牵出千丈零。
神农一见心欢喜，
斩断此藤忙不赢。
便用此藤来捆树，
扎一云梯千丈零。

四、人祖创世 IV. Human Ancestors' Inventions

After subduing the lion of medicine,
Shennong ordered it to taste the herbs.
Accompanying Shennong in the forests,
it tasted all hundreds of herbs to test for their nature and potency.
One day when Shennong was searching for herbs,
he came across a mountain so high that its top was in the clouds.
Green herbs were seen growing from the cliff,
whose leaves were green all year round.
Then he saw purple smoke rising from the top of the cliff,
propagating myriads of dazzling red rays.
Shennong, deciding to climb up the cliff,
and not to stop until he had tasted the herb,
pulled out his cloud-dispelling sword.
Working hard, he filed down the trees and built a ladder,
but how could a tree, only several *zhang* tall,
help him reach the top of the much higher mountain?
Shennong tried to think of a way,
to climb up the mountain.
When he tripped on a vine again,
he examined it closely.
It turned out the vine on the ground,
had tassels extending more than thousands of *zhang* away.
Shennong was rejoiced at the discovery,
busy with chopping the vine,
and then used it to tie the trees together,
to build a ladder that reached thousands of *zhang* up into the clouds.

神农尝百草,
瘟疫得夷平。
又往七十二名山,
去把五谷来找寻。
神农上了羊头山,
仔细找,仔细看,
找到栗子有一粒,
寄到枣树上,
忙去开荒田。
八种才能成栗谷,
后人才有小米饭。

大梁山中寻稻子,
稻子藏在草中间。
神农寄在柳树中,
忙去开水田。
田里下稻种,
七种才有稻谷收,
后人才有白米饭。

朱石山,寻小豆,
一颗寄在李树中,
一种成小豆,
小豆出荒田。
大豆出在维石山,
神农寻来好艰难,
一颗寄在桃树中,
五种成大豆,
大豆出平川。

四、人祖创世　IV. Human Ancestors' Inventions

After tasting hundreds of herbs,
Shennong rid his land of all plagues.
He then went to seventy-two famous mountains,
in search of the five grains.
When Shennong climbed up Mount Sheep-Head,
he looked around and searched carefully.
He found a millet kernel,
and stored it in a date tree,
while he started to till the wasteland.
It took eight seasons for the millet to harvest,
with which we posterities can enjoy cooked millet.

Then he went to Mount Daliang to look for rice,
which hid itself inside the grass.
Storing a grain of it to a willow tree,
Shennong started to till the rice paddies.
He planted the rice,
and it took seven seasons for it to harvest,
with which we posterities can enjoy cooked rice.

On Mount Zhushi, he looked for and found a red bean,
which he stored in the plum tree,
and later red beans were harvested, at the first season,
from the wasteland.
Soybean was found in Mount Weishi,
and to find it Shennong searched painstakingly.
The bean was stored in a peach tree first,
and bore soybean at the fifth season.
Since then soybean has grown on the plains everywhere.

大、小麦在朱石山，
寻得二粒心喜欢，
寄在桃树中，
耕种十二次，
后人才有面食餐。
武石山，寻芝麻，
寄在荆树中，
一种收芝麻，
后来炒菜有油添。

神农初种五谷生，
皆因六树来相伴。
神农教人兴贸易，
物物相换得便宜，
斩木作犁来耕地，
才有农事往后继。

又有夙沙才欺心，
要反神农有道君，
大臣箕文劝不可，
夙沙大怒杀箕文。
百姓群集心大怒，
要杀夙沙这反臣。
夙沙孤寡不敌众，
被百姓杀死命归阴。
神农座位居于陈，
就是河南陈州城，
在位一百四十春，
崩于长沙茶陵城。

四、人祖创世 IV. Human Ancestors' Inventions

Barley and wheat were found in Mount Zhushi,
and Shennong was overjoyed to find two of them.
Stored in a peach tree first,
they later harvested by the twelfth season,
with which we posterities have bread to eat.
On Mount Wushi, he found sesame,
which, stored in a wattle tree first,
harvested the crops at the first season,
with which we posterities have oil with which we make stir fries.

When Shennong began to grow the five grains,
he was accompanied by six trees.
Later, he taught people how to trade,
to exchange articles to live comfortable and affordable lives.
He then filed trees, made ploughs, and furrowed the land,
so agriculture came into being and passed on through ages.

Then came the deceptive Susha,
who defied the authority of the wise Shennong.
When Minister Ji Wen dissuaded him from doing so,
Susha was furious and killed the minister.
The common people were greatly enraging by this,
and wanted to kill the rebellious minister.
Susha was outnumbered,
and was killed by common people.
When Shennong reigned, he lived in Chen,
which is today's Chen Zhou City, Henan Province.
After reigning one hundred and forty years,
he passed away in today's Chaling, Changsha City.

自从神农把驾崩,
又有何人治乾坤?
请你一一说分明。
自从神农皇帝崩,
又有何人治乾坤?
天下有道是无道?
又有何人来兴兵?
哪个与他战不过,
悄悄迁都让反臣?
又有何人来出世,
他与反臣大交兵?
你今一一说我听,
才算歌中一能人。

歌师你且慢消停,
我今本要说你听,
又怕你去传别人。
自从神农皇帝崩,
又有愉罔治乾坤,
只有愉罔多无道,
反臣蚩尤大兴兵。
愉罔惧怕蚩尤凶,
悄悄迁都让反臣,
又有轩辕来出世,
他与蚩尤大交兵。

四、人祖创世 IV.Human Ancestors' Inventions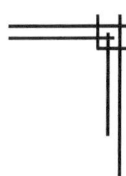

Who was on the throne,
after Shennong passed away?
Could you tell us all about it please?
Who ruled the world,
after Shennong passed away?
Did the *dao* prevail under heaven or not?
Who started wars?
Who was defeated by him,
and then quietly moved the capital conceding to the rebel minister?
Who then volunteered his service,
to fight the rebel minister?
Tell us all these stories,
and you will be the most talented.

Master singer, take your time.
I was going to tell you,
but was just afraid that you would tell others.
After Shennong passed away,
Yuwang began his reign,
but without the *dao* or the principles,
the rebellious minister Chiyou started the war.
Yuwang was afraid of the fierce Chiyou,
so he quietly moved the capital conceding to the rebellious minister.
It was Xuanyuan then who volunteered his service,
and engaged Chiyou in a ferocious fight.

不提轩辕不问你,
提起轩辕问根底,
轩辕他住何方地?
母亲怎样有身孕?
几多月份来降生?
轩辕生于何方地?
龙颜圣德如何论?
他与蚩尤大交兵,
不知谁输是谁赢?
轩辕怎么得吉兆?
要得强力两个人。
怎么访得二人到?
不知才干如何能?
不知设下什么法?
要捉蚩尤这反臣。
不知擒到未擒到?
轩辕怎么为仁君?

你今说与众人听,
才算歌中老先生。
歌师要我讲分明,
说起轩辕有根痕,
要你洗耳来恭听。
轩辕原是有熊君,
如今河南有定城。
附宝名字是他母,
一日出外荒郊行,
见一电光绕北斗,

四、人祖创世 IV. Human Ancestors' Inventions

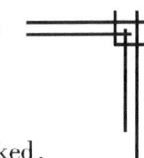

Had you not mentioned Xuanyuan I would not have asked,
but since you did, I have to know all about him, too.
Where did Xuanyuan live?
How did his mother become impregnated with him?
In which month was he born?
Where was he born?
How do people speak about his sagely virtues?
When did he engage Chiyou?
Who lost and who won?
How did he get the good omen
about the two able men?
How did he invite them?
How able were they?
What strategies did they deploy,
to seize the rebellious minister Chiyou?
Did they succeed or fail?
Was Xuanyuan a benevolent ruler?

Tell these to us all today,
and you will be the most learned senior master.
The master singer asked me to tell clearly,
but Xuanyuan has a long story,
Please cock your ears at what I have to say.
Xuanyuan originally belonged to Tribe You Xiong,
in today's Dingcheng, Henan Province.
His mother was Fubao,
who on a walk in a wild countryside one day,
saw a lightning circling the Big Dipper.

不觉有孕在其身,
二十四月怀胎满,
生于开封新郑城。
景里庆云明王德,
四面龙颜天生成。

蚩尤作乱真胆大,
铜头铁额兴人马,
要与轩辕争高下。
上阵就是烟雾起,
层层瘴气遮天地,
白日犹如黑夜里。
黄帝兵败乱如泥,
初立战法用熊罴,
九天玄女立战旗。
九天玄女轩辕母,
造下天书才用武,
千变万化八阵图,
刀枪剑戟戈矛斧,
长有弓,短有弩,
收兵锣,催兵鼓,
云里龙,林中虎,
一声号角排队伍,
大破蚩尤于涿鹿,
才把轩辕立为主,
正安中央戊己土。

四、人祖创世 IV. Human Ancestors' Inventions

Without knowing it, she became pregnant,
and, after twenty-four months of pregnancy,
gave birth in the Town of Xinzheng, Kaifeng City.
With a propitious sign of a wise ruler,
Xuanyuan was born with an imperial appearance.

Chiyou was an audacious rioter,
who, with an army equipped with brass and iron headwear,
was prepared for a showdown with Xuanyuan.
The moment he went into the battle, smoke rose up,
layers and layers of poisonous gas shrouding heaven and earth,
daytime turning as pitch-dark as nighttime.
At first, therefore, the imperial troops were in great confusion and disarray.
Xuanyuan then began to deploy the strategy of using brown bears.
Her highness Xuannv, the mother of Xuangyuan,
set up the banner,
and created the heavenly book of the art of war.
She deployed the Eight Diagrams Battle Formation and changed it often,
with swords, spears, two-edged swords, halberds, dragger-axes and axes,
long bows and short crossbows,
withdrawal gongs and inspiring drums,
dragons in the clouds, tigers in the forests,
——all forming one alliance.
Chiyou was utterly defeated in Zhuolu.
Only then did Xuanyuan begin to ascend the throne,
to govern the land from the center.

风后力牧各显能,
摆下八卦握机阵,
烟雾不得迷大军。
蚩尤困在阵中心,
东撞西冲难脱身,
涿鹿之野丧残生。
蚩尤争位害黎民,
蚩尤兄弟人九个,
困住轩辕难脱身,
轩辕当时慌张了,
即往大泽去搬兵。
风后力牧为大将,
摆下握机八门阵,
打败蚩尤这贼兵,
蚩尤血飞三千里。
至今红土现血痕。
斩了蚩尤天下喜,
小国个个皆畏惧,
并尊轩辕为皇帝。

杀了蚩尤为三节,
三节分尸都有名。
杀了头来为一节,
红口朱雀百利心。
杀了腰来为二节,
腰身化为罗盘形。
杀了三节是他尾,
飞天火星是他身。
魂魄归天化为风,
尸体化为泥巴存。

四、人祖创世 IV. Human Ancestors' Inventions

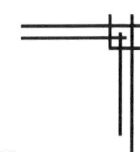

Fenghou and Limu each showed off their special prowess,
deploying the Eight Diagrams Battle Formation,
so that the smog would not confuse the troops.
Chiyou was stranded in the middle of the formation,
tried to break through from the east and west to no avail,
and lost his life in the wild field of Zhuolu.
Vying for power, Chiyou was to bring disaster to people.
Together with his nine brothers,
Chiyou trapped Xuanyuan in the first battle.
Alarmed, Xuanyuan
sent for help.
Coming to the rescue were Fenghou and Limu, appointed as generals,
who deployed the Eight Diagrams Battle Formation,
and defeated traitor Chiyou,
whose blood splashing three thousand *li* afar.
Even today, the red clay testifies to his demise.
Chiyou's death pleased everyone under heaven,
and all the terrified small tribes
now honored Xuanyuan as the Emperor.

Chiyou was cut into three parts,
and each part has left its mark.
The first part was his head,
which became the constellation Zhuque, the symbol of greed.
The second part was his waist,
which gave the shape to the compass.
The third part was his tail,
which changed into the meteors.
His soul turned into the wind,
and corpse crumbled into the dust.

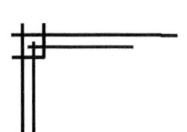

轩辕黄帝坐天下,
河洛之中出龙马,
只因地理无边涯,
山川草木万物华。
轩辕本是仁德君,
无数作为定乾坤,
又命大桡造甲子;
又命隶首作算术;
又命伶伦作律吕;
又命车区制衣襟。
轩辕见民多瘟疫,
又与岐伯做医经。
轩辕将崩有龙迎,
他就骑龙上天座。
在位却有一百载,
少昊接位管乾坤。

不提少昊我不问,
提起少昊问先生,
人不知来尔不愠。
少昊他是哪家子?
哪个母亲把他生?
少昊登基坐天下,
不知吉凶如何论?
那时民间出什么?
百姓安宁不安宁?

四、人祖创世 IV. Human Ancestors' Inventions

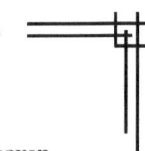

It was when Xuanyuan was governing everything under heaven,
the dragon-horse emerged from the Yellow River in today's Luoyang,
but at the time the boundless land
was all covered by the mountains, rivers and grass.
Xuanyuan was a kind and virtuous sovereign,
and had countless achievements in governing the world:
ordering Darao to develop Jiazi to count the cycle of years;
ordering Lishou to develop math;
ordering Linglun to make Lvlv to adjust musical instrument;
ordering Chequ to design clothing.
When he saw many people suffering from pest,
he and Qibo studied and wrote medical classics.
When Xuanyuan was dying, a dragon came to pick him up,
so he mounted the dragon and went to heaven.
After his one-hundred-year reign,
Shaohao became the emperor to rule the world.

If you didn't mention Shaohao, I would not have asked about him,
but since you did, may I ask the master about him?
Do not be upset when others don't know that you know so much.
Who was Shaohao?
Who was his mother?
After he took office,
was it considered an auspicious or inauspicious period?
What happened to the people?
Was it a time of peace or unrest?

少昊崩驾几多岁？
葬在何方什地名？
什么地方来安葬？
又是何人把位登？
歌师父来老先生。
请你从头说分明。

轩辕二字书上找，
制婚姻，制衣裳。
嫘祖养蚕有绸缎。
公孙轩辕为皇帝，
制下婚姻立纲纪，
百姓开智才化愚。

诗曰：吾初开国号轩辕，
继天立极居人先，
君臣父子吾首定，
兄弟夫妇将道传。

嫘祖又名西陵氏，
衣冠已始养蚕丝，
播种有食用钻火，
不比混沌无人烟。
不意隐世魔王降，
蚩尤倏而生世前，
吞云吐雾来作乱，
吾等造下指南车，
大破蚩尤得安然。

四、人祖创世 IV. Human Ancestors' Inventions

How old was Shaohao when he passed away?
Which city was he buried in?
Which place was he buried in the city?
Who succeeded to the throne after him?
Master singer, the senior master,
do please tell us from the beginning.

According to the history book, during Xuanyuan's reign,
marriage came into being, and people manufactured clothing.
Also, Leizu fed silkworms to produce silk.
When Xuanyuan was the emperor,
he made marriage laws and ethical rules,
so that people became more educated and their ignorance was transformed.

The Poem says: Our country began from Xuanyuan,
succeeding to the throne according to the will of heaven.
The king-minister and father-son relationships were set first,
and brothers, husbands and wives helped to keep the proper relations.

Leizu, also called Xi Ling Shi,
began to make clothing and raise silkworms,
to farm so that there was food to be cooked by using the fire.
It was unlike the chaotic period where there was no trace of man and smoke.
No one realized that quietly a monster was descending upon them:
Once Chiyou was born,
he swallowed clouds, blew fogs and wreaked havoc.
This was when they built the cart equipped with the mechanical compass,
defeated Chiyou utterly and regained peace.

少昊本是轩辕子，
皇帝元配嫘祖生。
少昊登位坐天下，
正是身裹鬼弄人。
民间白日出鬼怪，
龙头金睛怪迷人。
东家也把鬼来讲，
西家也把怪来论。
王母娘娘降凡尘，
教化民间收妖精。
这是少昊福分浅，
他母怀胎有来因，
夜梦天庭众将星，
大星如虹照浑身，
生下少昊曲阜城。
国号金天氏，
掌了锦乾坤，
封了金德王，
江山四十四年春。
少昊驾崩八十四，
葬在兖州曲阜城，
云阳山上来安葬，
又出颛顼把位登。

四、人祖创世 IV. Human Ancestors' Inventions

Shaohao was the son of Xuanyuan,

born to the queen—Leizu.

When Shaohao succeeded to the throne,

it was just the time when ghosts were haunting people everywhere.

They appeared in broad daylight.

With dragon heads, gold eyes, they were bewitchingly charming.

People were talking about the ghosts here,

and people were also talking about the ghosts there.

The Heavenly Queen Mother came down to the world,

to teach people to subdue demons.

This was Shaohao's less fortunate fate.

The story of his birth is like follows:

his mother dreamed of all stars,

a large star shining upon her like a rainbow,

and she gave birth to Shaohao in the Qufu City.

With Jintian Shi as the tile of his reigning period,

he ruled a beautiful country,

and was granted the title of Emperor Jinde.

After reigning for forty-four years,

he passed away at the age of eighty-four,

and was buried on the Yunyang Mountain,

in Qufu City, Yanzhou.

Succeeding the throne next was Zhuanxu.

歌师果然讲得清,
又问颛顼他出身,
你可知道说我听。
颛顼怎么治天下?
百姓清平不清平?
东村人家出么鬼?
怎么治鬼得安宁?
西村人家出么鬼?
何人收服鬼妖精?
颛顼在位多少岁?
葬于何方甚地名?
颛顼高阳崩了驾,
又是何人把位登?

提起颛顼也有名,
也是轩辕后代根,
他是昌意所亲生,
母亲昌意女佳人,
夜得奇梦祥瑞生,
不觉腹中有了孕,
生下颛顼一帝君。
孙接祖业把位登,
国号高阳氏,封为水德君,
七十八年把位登,
葬于濮阳一座城,
原名东昌大府城,
后出帝喾把位登。

四、人祖创世 IV. Human Ancestors' Inventions

Please, master singer, do tell it all clearly.
About the birth of Zhuanxu,
could you tell me?
How did he rule the world?
Were the people honest and peaceful?
What kind of ghost was haunting in certain villages?
How was it subdued?
What kind of ghost was haunting in certain other villages?
Who brought the ghost under control?
How many years did Zhuanxu rule?
Where was he buried?
Who succeed to the throne,
after he passed away in Gaoyang?

Zhuanxu was famous,
and he, too, was Xuanyuan's descendant,
born to Changyi.
His mother, Changyi, a beautiful concubine of Xuanyuan,
dreamed of an auspicious sign,
and was pregnant without her knowing it.
She gave birth to Zhuanxu, the Emperor,
who then succeeded to his grandfather's throne,
with the reigning title of Gaoyang Shi and the name of Emperor Shuide.
After seventy-eight years on the throne,
he was buried in the Puyang City,
originally named Dongchang,
and later Diku succeeded to the throne.

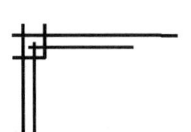

歌师听我讲与你,
把你当做我徒弟,
今天一一传给你。
颛顼高阳把位登,
多少鬼怪乱乾坤。
颛顼人君多善念,
斋戒沐浴祭上神。
东村有个小儿鬼,
每日家家要乳吞,
东村人人用棍打,
打得骨碎丢江心。
次日黑夜又来了,
东村人人着一惊,
将他紧紧来捆绑,
绑住大石丢江心。
次日黑夜又来了,
东村扰乱不太平。
将一大树挖空了,
放在空树里面存,
上面用牛皮来盖紧,
铜钉钉得紧腾腾。
又将酒饭来祭奠,
这时小鬼才安宁。

小鬼有了酒饭吃,
再也不来闹东村。
西村又出一女鬼,
披头散发迷倒人,

四、人祖创世 IV. Human Ancestors' Inventions

Master singer, listen to me,
and, taking you as my pupil,
I will tell you all today.
When Zhuanxu was on the throne,
various demons tried to create chaos in the world.
Zhuanxu was kindhearted,
and he purified himself and offered sacrifices to heaven.
A certain East Village had a small-child ghost,
going to each family everyday to suck mothers' milk,
so all villages beat it with sticks,
and then threw its broken bones to the middle of the river.
But the ghost returned next night,
so the astonished villagers
fastened it tightly,
to a huge stone and then threw it to the middle of the river.
Next night, it returned again,
disrupting the peaceful life of the villagers.
They then hollowed out a big tree,
put the ghost inside the tree,
covered the hole tightly with the cow leather,
and nailed it firmly with copper nails.
They then offered the sacrificial wines and foods,
so finally, the small-child ghost quit.

With wines and food,
the small-child ghost never harassed the East Village again.
But a female ghost appeared in a certain West Village,
fascinating people with her hair straggling over her shoulders.

西村也挖大空树,
女鬼空树躲其身。
忽见一人骑甲马,
身穿黄衣腰戴弓,
一步要走二十丈,
走路如同在腾云。
就把西村人来问,
可见披发女鬼精?
西村人说不知道,
黄衣之人哼一声,
你们不必来瞒我,
她乃是个女妖精。
她有同伙无其数,
八十余万闹西村。
颛顼仁君多善念,
又奉王母旨意行,
捉拿女妖归天界,
西村才得乐太平。
西村听说忙回禀:
空树之中躲其身。
黄衣之人忙起身,
空树之中捉妖精。
一见女鬼腾云起,
黄衣人赶到半天云。
忽然不到一时辰,
鲜血如雨落埃尘。
从此挖树做大鼓,
穿着黄衣驱鬼神。

四、人祖创世 IV. Human Ancestors' Inventions

The villagers there also hollowed out a big tree,
and they let the female ghost stay inside the hollowed tree.
Suddenly, a man riding an armoured horse appeared,
wearing yellow clothes, a bow in the waist,
and, with each of his stride twenty *zhang* long,
he moved like he was riding the clouds.
He asked the villagers:
have you seen the female ghost with her hair dishevelled?
When the villagers answered in negative,
the man in yellow gave a snort of contempt:
You don't have to lie to me!
She is a female demon,
with countless accomplices,
stirring up trouble in a certain West Village.
Emperor Zhuanxu was kind,
but was also acting on the Heavenly Queen Mother's order,
to send for the female ghost and return it to heaven,
so as to bring peace to West Village.
On learning all this, villagers reported quickly:
she was hiding inside the hollowed tree.
The man in yellow hurried to leave,
for the tree to capture the demon.
As soon as the female demon was seen rising up with the clouds,
the man in yellow quickly chased her, also rising up half the sky.
Within an hour,
blood fell like the pouring rain onto the dust.
From then on, people have filed trees to make big drums,
and wear yellow clothing to expel the evil spirit.

这里顺便说一句,
颛顼之时有天梯,
神仙能从天梯下,
人能顺梯上天庭,
人神杂乱鬼出世,
闹得天下不太平。
颛顼砍断上天梯,
从此天下得安宁。

颛顼在位七十八,
崩于濮阳东昌城。
颛顼高阳崩了驾,
帝喾高辛把位登。
讲起帝喾一段文,
他是轩辕四代孙,
父传子,子传孙。
提起帝喾有根痕,
娶妻四个女佳人,
长妻原是邰氏女,
名唤姜嫄女佳人,
生下后稷一条根。
次妻陈锋女钗裙,
名唤庆都小娇生,
夜梦赤龙浑身照,
怀胎二十四月零,
生下尧王在丹陵。

四、人祖创世 IV. Human Ancestors' Inventions

By the way,
there used to be a ladder between heaven and earth during Zhuanxu's reign,
immortals coming down by using it,
and people going up to the heavenly court by climbing it.
Ghosts, taking advantage of the mixing of mortals and immortals,
haunted the world and disturbed the peace.
Zhuanxu cut off that ladder,
and restore peace in the world.

Zhuanxu reigned for seventy-eight years,
and he passed away in Dongchang, Puyang.
After Zhuanxu,
it was Diku Gaoxin who succeeded to the throne.
Diku had his own stories.
He was the fourth generation of Xuanyuan,
with the throne passed down from generation to generation.
Diku himself had
four wives.
the first wife, Tai Shi's daughter,
named Jiangyuan, was very beautiful,
and gave birth to one child, Houji.
The second wife Chenfeng was
nicknamed the little brat of Qingdu.
She dreamed of her entire body being shone upon by an illuminating red dragon,
and after twenty-four months of pregnancy,
she gave birth to Emperor Yao in Danling.

三妻娥氏名简狄，
吞了燕卵祥瑞生，
生下子契一郎君。
四妃诹訾①名常仪，
生下姐挚一条根。
帝喾国号高辛氏，
他是乔极亲所生。

歌师讲得很分明，
又把高辛问先生，
高辛建都什么地？
今是什么县地名？
帝喾高辛治天下，
又有何人作反臣？
高辛要杀反臣子，
何人提头见高辛？
帝喾娶得荣氏女，
其女叫做什么名？
可恨房王作反臣，
有人斩得房王头，
赐他黄金与美人。

高辛有个五色犬，
常跟高辛不离身。
忽然去见房王面，
房王一见喜欢心，

---

① 诹訾（音"邹资"）

四、人祖创世 IV. Human Ancestors' Inventions

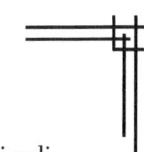

The third wife came from Tribe E Shi and was named Jiandi.
Her auspicious sign came after she swallowed a swallow's egg.
She gave birth to one son—Ziqi.
The fourth, the comcubine, came from Tribe Zouzi Shi and was named Changyi.
She gave birth to one son—Jiezhi.
The title of Diku's reigning was Gaoxin Shi,
and his own mother was Qiaoji.

The master singer has told the stories very clearly.
Could I now ask the master more questions about Gaoxin?
Where did he found the capital?
What is the county's name today?
When Diku Gaoxin ruled under heaven,
which minister rose in rebellion?
When Gaoxin planned to eliminate the rebellious official,
who presented him a head held in the hand?
Diku also married a daughter of Tribe Rong Shi,
what was her name?
When the hateful Fang Wang who revolted,
and then was beheaded,
who was rewarded with gold and a beauty woman.

Gaoxin had a dog of five colors,
which followed Gaoxin wherever he went.
But one day the dog went to Fang Wang's place.
Fang Wang was excited at the sight of the dog,

高辛王犬归顺我,
我的江山坐得成。
当时急忙摆筵席,
赐与王犬好食品。

五色犬见房王睡,
咬下他首级见高辛。
高辛一见心欢喜,
重赐肉包与它吞,
王犬一见伴不寐,
卧睡一日不起身。
莫非我犬要封赠?
会稽王侯来封你,
又赐美女一个人。

又有何样好吉兆?
身怀有孕几月零?
此处叫做什么地?
那时生下有何人?
高辛又娶某时女?
此女叫做什么名?
不觉身怀也有孕,
那时生下什么人?
高辛在位年多少?
又尊何人为天子?
是否是个有道君?
你今一一说我听,
才算有知有识人。

四、人祖创世 IV. Human Ancestors' Inventions

thinking that Gaoxin's dog was pledging allegiance to him,
a sign that the success of his usurpation was now guaranteed.
Right away he held a feast for the dog,
treating the imperial dog with delicious food.

When the five-colored dog saw that Fang Wang was asleep,
it bit his head off and went to see Gaoxin.
Gaoxin was joyous at the sight of Fang Wang's head,
offering the dog steamed meat-stuffed buns,
but the dog pretended it was sleepy,
lying in bed for a whole day.
Does my dog want to be offered other rewards?
I give you the official title of Hui Ji,
and bestow you a beautiful woman.

What was another good omen?
How many months were another pregnancy?
Where was the child born?
Who was born?
Which woman did Gaoxin marry next?
What was her name?
Whom did she give birth to,
after she was pregnant without knowing?
How many years did Gaoxin reign?
Who succeeded him to the throne?
Was he a virtuous emperor?
If you could tell us about all this today,
you will be a truly knowledgeable man.

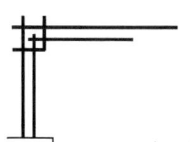

仁兄问得好出奇，
这些故事来问起，
听我一一说根底。
高辛建都名字在，
如今河南偃师城。
高辛仁君治天下，
王犬忙把恩来谢，
领了美女只交情。
后生五男并六女，
人身犬面尾后形，
后来子孙都繁盛，
就是犬戎国的根。

高辛娶得陈年女，
名曰庆都是她身，
庆都年近二十岁，
一日黄云来附身，
身怀有孕十四月，
丹陵之下生尧君。
高辛又娶诹訾女，
名曰常仪是她身，
诹訾常仪生一子，
子挚乃是他的名。
元妃姜嫄生稷子，
次妃简狄生契身，
高辛在位七十载，
顿丘山上葬其身。

四、人祖创世 IV. Human Ancestors' Inventions

My dear friend, you ask good questions,
about these stories,
so let me address them one by one.
The capital Gaoxin founded,
was in today's Yanshi City, Henan.
Gaoxin ruled the country with benevolence,
so his dog thanked him sincerely,
and accepted the beautiful woman with gratitude.
They later had five sons and six daughters,
all having human bodies, dog's faces and tails.
Their offspring were all prosperous,
and were the ancestors of the nationality Quan Rong.

Gaoxin married Chennian's daughter,
who was named Qingdu,
and was almost twenty at the time.
One day, a yellow cloud came upon her,
and afterwards she was pregnant for fourteen months.
She gave birth to Yao in Danling.
Gaoxin also married Zou Zi Shi's daughter,
whose name was Changyi,
who later gave birth to a son,
and they named him Zizhi.
Gaoxin's first wife had Houji,
and his second wife had Qishen.
Gaoxin reigned for seventy years,
and was buried in Mount Dunqiu.

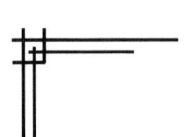

至今大明清平县,
还有遗址看得清。
子挚接位无道君,
九年却被奸臣废,
就立尧帝为仁君。
尧帝为君多有道,
我把根由说你听。

不提尧帝问根底,
不知根底怎样起?
尧帝是个仁德君,
圣泽滔天民感恩。
无奈气数有变改,
又出几样什怪名?
又把民间百姓害,
害得百姓不安宁。
尧帝又令何人治?
不知那人能不能?
何人与他来交战?
怎么收服得太平?
尧帝在位多少载?
帝子几人贤不贤?
帝要交位何人坐?
何人躲于什么山?
何人退病不得闲?

四、人祖创世 IV. Human Ancestors' Inventions

Traces of his rule are still seen clearly,

in today's Qing Ping County, Da Ming.

Later Zizhi succeeded to the throne but ruled without benevolence,

so he was abolished by evil ministers nine years later.

Then the wise Yao became emperor,

who ruled with great virtue.

Let me tell you the whole story.

One must learn from the beginning of Emperor Yao,

for who can be without the beginning?

Emperor Yao was so benevolent,

that people are forever grateful for his sage grace.

Too bad something unpredictable happened,

but what kind of monsters appeared?

They harassed people,

and disrupted their peaceful lives.

Who did Emperor Yao appoint to manage the situation?

Was he capable?

Who came to fight him?

How was peace restored?

How many years did Emperor Yao reign?

Were his sons worthy or not?

To whom did he abdicate his throne?

Who went into seclusion in a mountain? Which mountain was it?

Who asked for a medical leave and yet still kept busy?

当时群臣来商议,
姐挚接位管乾坤。
姐挚坐了帝喾位,
江山九年一旦废,
又荐何人治乾坤?
你今从头说分明,
歌场之中你为尊。

你将尧帝来问我,
我将尧帝对你说,
叫声歌师你听着:
尧帝本是圣明君,
天降灾难于黎民。
他是帝喾次子身,
母亲陈锋亲所生,
生下尧帝丹陵城,
国号陶唐氏,
姓尹名祁是他名,
封为火德王,坐了锦乾坤。
甲辰年间登了位,
癸未之年把驾崩,
十日并出有难星。
禾苗晒得枯焦死,
百姓地穴躲其身。
忽然又是狂风起,
民间屋宇倒干净。
又有大兽大蛇大猪三个怪,
它们到处乱吃人,
尧帝一见后羿到,
忙命后羿拯黎民。

四、人祖创世 IV. Human Ancestors' Inventions

After a discussion among the officials,
Jiezhi succeeded to the throne.
But after only nine years,
Jiezhi was dethroned.
Who was recommended next to succeed to the throne?
Please tell us all about this,
and you will be the most resepctable in the Song House.

Since you asked me about Emperor Yao,
let me tell you about him.
Master singer, please listen to me:
Yao was an enlightened emperor,
during a time when natural disaster happened to his people.
He was the second son of Diku,
bore to his mother—Chenfeng,
and in the Danling City.
The title of his reign was Taotang Shi,
with the name Yinqi.
And he succeeded in the Jia Chen year,
conferred as Emperor Huode, and ruled under heaven.
He passed away in the Gui Wei year.
Disaster befell when ten suns appeared,
scorching all the seedlings,
and forcing the common people to hide in underground shelters.
A fierce gale also sprang up,
flattening all the houses.
Then were the three monsters: big beast, big snake and big pig,
devouring people everywhere.
When Emperor Yao saw Houyi,
he immediately ordered him to save people.

歌师提起神羿等,
我今从头说原因。
神羿生在后羿国,
有穷之地来降生。
母怀一十九月来,
降生之日会说话,
一十二月会飞腾,
要追日月和星斗,
一步能跨百里程。
身高力大无比能,
扶桑大树作弯弓,
撑天竹子做雕翎。
弓开半边月,
箭飞如流星。
弓箭原是他发明,
弯弓射日斩妖星。

后羿当时寻风伯,
他与风伯大战争。
风伯被他射慌了,
即忙收风得太平。
十个日头真可恨,
羿又取箭手中举,
一箭射去一日落,
九箭九日落地坪,
原是乌鸦三足鸟,
九箭九日不见形。
还有一日羿又射,
空中响如洪钟声。

四、人祖创世 IV. Human Ancestors' Inventions

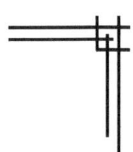

Since the master singer has mentioned the magic Shenyi,
let me tell you about him from the beginning.
He was born in Kingdom Houyi,
and to Tribe Youqiong Shi.
Her mother was pregnant with him for nineteen months,
and he was born able to speak.
He could fly after twelve months,
and he could even chase the sun, the moon and the stars,
with each stride a hundred *li* long.
He was tall and incomparably strong.
A large mulberry tree was made into his bow,
and a sky-tall bamboo was made into his eagle-feather arrow.
When drawn, the bow was as big as half of a moon,
and the arrow flew as fast as a meteoroid.
The inventor of bow and arrow,
he shot down the suns and removed monstrous stars.

Houyi at first was looking for the Wind Spirit,
and soon the two of them were in a war.
The Wind Spirit was so alarmed by his skill of archery,
that he stopped blowing the frightful wind.
Next were the ten dreadful suns.
Pulling out a bow and holding it in hand,
Houyi shot a sun down with the first try.
He shot nine arrows, and nine suns were down from the sky,
with them were falling the feathers of nine three-foot crows.
With the crows dead, the nine suns were no more.
With one sun still in the sky, Yi pulled his bow again,
but instantly came a voice like the peal of a resonant bell.

此是日光真神来说话,
"有劳大羿除妖精,
当年混沌黑暗我出世,
就有许多妖魔与我争。
九个日妖今除尽,
从此民安乐太平。"

后羿当时来跪拜,
拜谢日光太阳君。
九个日妖都射除,
尧帝赏了大功臣。
大海之中生海蛟,
海蛟搅得洪水生。
有一神人把蛟斩,
海蛟化为树一根。
不长叶子高万丈,
花开九个大花苞。
有着一日花开了,
内有人蜂九处飞。
只有此蜂大得很,
尾带利箭放毒水,
毒箭蜇人人命倾。
后羿神箭把蜂射,
从此天下才太平。

四、人祖创世 IV. Human Ancestors' Inventions

It was Immortal Sun speaking,
"Thank you for shooting the monstrous suns.
When I was born during the chaotic times,
many monsters came to fight with me.
Now that nine of them were shot down,
people can live their peaceful lives again."

Houyi went down to his knees to show his respect,
and to thank Immortal Sun.
Since the nine monsters were eliminated,
Emperor Yao rewarded the heroic servant.
There appeared also an enormous dragon in the sea,
surging up waves and causing floods.
A certain immortal killed it,
which then turned into a tree.
Without leaves but thousands of *zhang* in height,
it grew nine giant buds.
When the buds blossomed one day,
out came people-wasps flying in nine directions.
These wasps were extraordinary in size,
and the sharp sting on the tail squirted poison,
that killed people in contact.
Houyi again shot the wasps with his magic arrows,
and the world returned to peace.

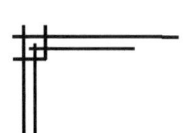

说起后羿有根古,
后羿出世奇得很。
当日有个通天洞,
石洞宽如大龙宫。
有一流水哗哗响,
洞口有石自开门。
有一蟾蜍生洞内,
已在洞中千年整。
一日蟾蜍身有孕,
生一石蛋能自滚。
一日滚滚出洞门,
一只神鹰从此过,
误认自己把蛋生。

口含仙草做下窝,
神鹰坐在窝当中。
有朝一日石蛋破,
产出一子像人形。
一对翅膀背上长,
展翅一飞万里程。
后羿之名天皇取,
天皇封它为将领。
天皇殿上一美女,
美女她叫"嫦娥"名,
原是天皇一使女,
天皇与他作媒证。

四、人祖创世 IV. Human Ancestors' Inventions

About Houyi,
his birth was extraordinary.
There used to be a cave, an access to heaven,
the cave as spacious as a big Dragon Palace.
There was a stream of water gurgling,
and the door of the cave could open automatically.
A toad, born in the hole,
had lived there for a thousand years.
One day, the toad was pregnant,
and later laid a stone egg that could roll by itself.
When it rolled out of the door one day,
an eagle happened to pass by,
and mistook it as its own.

After carrying the magic grass in its mouth and having built a nest,
the magic eagle started to hatch the stone toad-egg in the nest,
When the stone egg broke,
a human-like figure came out.
With a pair of wings on his back,
he could fly ten thousand *li*.
The name Houyi was given by the Heavenly Emperor,
who also conferred on him the title of a general.
There was a gorgeous female in the Heavenly Emperor's Palace,
whose name was "Chang'e".
She used to be a maid of the Heavenly Emperor,
so the Heavenly Emperor helped the two to tie the knot.

后羿、嫦娥结成婚，
不意嫦娥有身孕，
嫦娥又叫常仪名。
一日打开天门看，
后羿一见吃一惊——
大地生烟如火烤，
无数生灵命归阴。
天上地下无滴水，
日后江沽把水生。
这时后羿心烦恼，
拉开天弓不留情，
一箭一日掉下地，
九箭九日命归阴。
神鹰得知遮天来，
护住一日活性命。

此时后羿来找水，
通天洞中来找寻。
找到蟾蜍来言语，
蟾蜍肚里有水存，
吐出清水水又生。
日后叫它到月宫，
夜夜洒露到凡尘。

四、人祖创世 IV. Human Ancestors' Inventions

After Houyi and Chang'e got married,
she soon found herself pregnant.
Chang'e was also named Changyi.
One day when Houyi opened the heavenly door,
he was surprised to see that,
the ground was torched by fire,
and countless lives were killed.
There was not going to be a drop of water in heaven and earth,
until later Jianggu found water.
Houyi was so furious,
that he shot the heavenly bow mercilessly.
One arrow shot down one sun,
and nine arrows ended the lives of nine suns.
Learning about this, the eagle came and cover part of the sky,
saving the last sun.

Later, Houyi went to look for water,
and he came to the cave with access to heaven.
He sought help from the toad,
who stored water in its stomach.
The toad spat clear water, which begot more water.
Later the toad was invited into the Moon Place,
where every night it sprinkled dews into the world.

尧帝在位七十二,
帝子丹朱不肖名,
尧帝要让位许由坐,
许由躲于箕山阴,
又叫子交接父位,
他又退病在其身。
当时群臣来商议,
才荐大舜治乾坤。
不提舜帝犹是可,
提起舜帝治山河,
你把根源对我说。
他父名字叫什么?
他母又叫什么名?
怎么又以姚为姓?
他是何人几代孙?
象是他的亲兄弟?
怎么处处害大舜?

这个根痕你不明,
我今一一说你听:
舜帝父亲名瞽叟,
握登乃是他母亲。
握登生舜姚虚地,
故此以姚为姓名。
黄帝是他八代祖,
他是轩辕后代根。

四、人祖创世 IV. Human Ancestors' Inventions

Emperor Yao reigned seventy-two years,
but his first son Danzhu was not the most talented,
so he arranged to have Xuyou to succeed to the throne.
Xuyou hid himself in Mount Ji.
He then arranged to have his other son Zijiao to succeed,
but Zijiao asked for a medical leave.
All officials gathered together for a consultation,
and this was when Shun was recommended to reign the world.
It would have been alright had you not mentioned Emperor Shun,
but since you have,
please tell me his stories.
What was his father' name?
What was his mother's name?
Why was Yao his surname?
Whose offspring was he?
Was Xiang his brother?
Why did he harm Shun at every turn?

Since you are not clear about these stories,
let me tell them to you one by one.
Emperor Shun's father was named Gusou,
and his mother was named Wodeng.
Wodeng gave birth to Shun in Yaoxu,
this is the reason why his surname was Yao.
Emperor Xuanyuan was his eight-generation ancestor,
so he was Xuanyuan's offspring.

他的亲母早年死，
继母才生象弟身。
继母要把舜害死，
唆使瞽叟变了心。
父亲和弟心一样，
设计要害舜一人。

舜帝犁耕什么山？
市场打鱼何地名？
他又牧羊什么山？
又陶瓦器何地名？
那时尧帝诏书到，
不知所为何事情？
不知舜帝怎回答？
尧帝赐他什么人？
又将何物付与他？
他的父亲怎么行？
如何又要将他害？
怎么设计怎么行？
不知害死未害死？
可有救星无救星？
后又舜继尧帝位，
四海咸服称仁君？

四、人祖创世 IV. Human Ancestors' Inventions

His mother died early,
and his stepmother gave birth to his half brother Xiang.
The stepmother wanted to kill Shun,
and influenced Gusou to think ill of Shun.
The father and the younger brother Xiang now were alike,
setting out to harm Shun.

On which mountain did Emperor Shun plough the field?
Where did Emperor Shun fish and then sell them in the market?
In which mountain was he a shepherd?
Where did he make pottery?
When Emporer Yao's imperial edict came to him,
didn't he know the reason for it?
How did Emperor Shun respond to the edict?
Whom did Emperor Yao grant him?
And what was also bestowed on him?
What did his father do?
How did the father try to harm him?
What was the plan?
Did the plot succeed or fail?
Did someone save him?
Did Shun indeed succeed to the throne after Yao,
and was he called benevolent emperor of the world?

歌师听我说分明,
舜帝当日是明君。
我今一一说你听:
提起舜王根基深,
史记上面说得清,
他是轩辕八代孙。
轩辕长子名昌意,
玄嚣少昊次子名。
昌意后来生颛顼,
颛顼生穷蝉,穷蝉生敬康,
敬康生句望,句望生峤牛,
峤牛生兆牛,兆牛生兆生。
瞽叟出世治人伦,
娶妻握登女钗裙,
生下大舜仁义君。
耕于厉山过光阴,
尧王访贤让大舜,
就将二女配为婚,
二女娥皇与女英,
乃是姑母配玄孙,
哪个知道这根痕?
大舜勤耕于厉山,
雷泽地方做渔人,
草场牧羊燕河地,
又陶瓦器在河滨。

四、人祖创世 IV. Human Ancestors' Inventions

Master singer, listen to me carefully.
Emperor Shun was a benevolent ruler.
Let me then tell you in more detail.
Emperor Shun had his own stories,
which are recorded clearly in history books.
He was the eighth generation of Xuanyuan.
Xuanyuan's first son was Changyi,
and the second was Shaohao.
Later Changyi had a son Zhuanxu,
whose son was Qiongchan, whose son was Jingkang.
Jiangkang's son was Juwang, and Juwang's son was Qiaoniu,
whose son was Zhaoniu, and Zhaoniu's son was Zhaosheng.
Gusou's reign made headway in managing human affairs,
and he married Wodeng,
who gave birth to the kind and wise Shun.
Shun spent his time ploughing in Mount Li.
After Emperor Yao abdicated the throne to Shun,
he also granted his two daughters—
Ehuang and Nvying, to marry Shun.
Those were marriages between aunts and grandson.
Who knows about this story?
Shun worked hard ploughing in Mount Li,
went fishing in Leize,
he was a shepherd in River Yan,
and made pottery in Hebin.

当时尧帝见诏到,
舜帝即忙见尧君。
尧君就问天下事,
对答如流胜于君。
尧帝一听心大喜,
二女与他作妻身,
大者名曰娥皇女,
二者名唤是女英。
舜帝回家见父母,
继母越发起妒心。
象弟当时生一计,
悄悄说与瞽叟听。
父亲叫舜上仓廪,
象帝放火黑良心。
大舜看见一斗笠,
拿起当翅飞出廪,
大舜毫发未损伤。
象弟一计未使成,
又献一计与父亲,
叫他古井去淘水,
上用石头丢井中。

说起他家那古井,
却是狐精一后门。
九尾狐狸早知道,
象弟今要害大舜,

四、人祖创世 IV. Human Ancestors' Inventions

As soon as the imperial edict arrived,
Emperor Shun went to meet with Emperor Yao.
When Emperor Yao asked him about the affairs of the state,
his answers came as smoothly as the running water and better than most.
Emperor Yao was delighted,
and he gave Shun his two daughters to marry.
The elder daughter had the name of Ehuang,
and the younger was named Nvying.
When Emperor Shun returned home to tell his parents about all this,
his stepmother became more jealous than ever.
Seeing this, his brother Xiang set up a scheme,
which he quietly shared with his father Gusou.
The father asked Shun to the granary,
and then the heartless Xiang set fire to it.
Spotting a bamboo hat,
Shun quickly snatched it, used it as a wing to fly away,
and escaped unharmed.
After Xiang failed at his first attempt,
he offered another to his father.
Shun was told to clear out an ancient well,
but while he was doing so, stones were thrown down the well.

About that ancient family well,
it was actually the back door of a Fox Spirit.
The nine-tailed fox knew all along,
that Xiang was to make another attempt on Shun's life,

盼咐小狐忙伺候,
接住大舜出前门,
九尾狐狸来指路,
指条大路往前行。
大舜走至卧房内,
弹琴抚弦散散心。

舜帝长到二十春,
他到厉山把田耕,
后母送饭下毒药,
十拿九稳命归阴。
这时舜帝要用饭,
一只黄狗来走近,
两爪不住来抓挠,
黄狗抓住毒饭泼,
两眼汪汪流下泪,
伸出舌头把饭吞。
舜帝一见心不忍,
让它一气来吃尽,
七窍流血命归阴。
瞽叟见舜害不死,
舜子果然有帝分,
害他念头从此止,
尧帝让位于大舜。
当时黄龙负河图,
未常国献千年龟,
朝中一日有祥瑞,
八元八恺事舜君。

四、人祖创世 IV.Human Ancestors' Inventions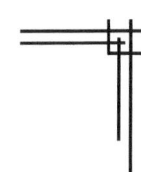

so it made the arrangement for little foxes,
to guide Shun out of the front door,
where the nine-tailed Fox Spirit pointed out a path
for Shun to go home safely.
When Shun returned to his bedroom,
he played banjo to relax.

When Shun was twenty,
he went to Mount Li to plough the field.
His stepmother put poison in his lunch,
which would absolutely kill him.
Just when Emperor Shun was to eat his lunch,
a yellow dog came along.
Scratching with his paws,
the dog finally spilled the poisonous meal on the ground.
The dog was in tears,
but licked the meal from the ground.
Emperor Shun was so moved that,
he let the dog eat all of it.
But, bleeding from all its seven apertures, the dog then died.
Gusou then realized that Shun was not meant to die,
and he was born to have imperial responsibilities.
From then on, he gave up on killing him,
and indeed later Emperor Yao abdicated the throne to Shun.
This was the time when a yellow dragon with the river map on its back,
a one-thousand-year tortoise emerged for the first time.
With this auspicious sign,
eight famous wise talents were willing to serve Emperor Shun.

尧帝在位九十年,
龙归大海升了天,
阳寿一百单八春。
舜帝见尧辞凡尘,
避于河南三年春。
天下百姓感恩深,
趋从如市讴歌声。
天下诸侯来朝拜,
不让丹朱而让舜,
一统山河乐太平。

舜为天子号有虞,
不记象仇封有神,
心不格奸真仁义。
舜流共工于幽州,
放驩兜于崇山,
杀三苗,于三危,
殛鲧于羽山,后来才生禹。
舜因巡猎崩苍梧,
娥皇、女英心中苦,
终日依枕哀哀哭,
泪水涨满洞庭湖:
"我夫在位五十年,
一旦辞世归了天。
丢下商均子不贤,
我们姊妹无靠山,
怎不叫人泪涟涟。"

四、人祖创世 IV. Human Ancestors' Inventions

Yao reigned for ninety year,
and then, like dragons returning to the sea, Emperor Yao returned to heaven,
at the age of one hundred and eight.
When Yao died,
Emperor Shun mourned his death by secluding himself in Henan for three years.
Common people too were deeply grateful for Yao,
and they walked after his hearse and sang high praise of him.
Dukes and princes were also paying respect to him.
Not passing on the throne to Danzhu but rather abdicating it to Shun,
Shun united the world and brought it peace and prosperity.

The title of Shun's reign was Youyu.
Holding no grudges, he granted territory Youshen to Xiang,
so he was truly honorable and just.
Shun sent Gonggong on exile in Youzhou,
Huandou in Chongshan.
He also settled the rebellious Sanmiao Nationality in Sanwei,
and sent Jigun to Mount Yu, who then had the son Great Yu.
Shun passed away while hunting in Cangwu,
which greatly distressed Ehuang and Nvying.
They cried all day and all night lying in bed,
and their tears filled up the Dongting Lake:
"Our husband returned to heaven,
after reigning for fifty years.
He left behind his unworthy son,
and helpless us—the two sisters.
How can we not be sad?"

舜帝过后谁出生？
又有谁来治乾坤？
又请歌师说分明。

舜帝过后出大禹，
夏侯禹王号文明，
受舜天下管万民，
国号有夏治乾坤。
夏朝禹王管乾坤，
他是轩辕后代孙，
受舜天下管万民：
国号夏朝把位登，
他是殛鲧亲所生，
母亲华氏老夫人。
在位二十七年整，
大禹有功为天子。
三过其门而不入，
疏通九河定九州。
九州有名在后头，
再把九州名目数：
东有冀州和青州，
南有扬州共荆州，
西有冀州与梁州，
北有徐州抵雍州，
中间河南有豫州，
又铸九鼎定九州。
从此平安四海滩，

四、人祖创世　IV. Human Ancestors' Inventions

Who was born after Emperor Shun?
Who succeeded him to the throne?
Master singer, please explain it to us.

After Emperor Shun, Great Yu emerged,
whose name was Wen Ming and he was from Tribe Xiahou.
Since Great Yu succeeded to the throne,
he ruled the country with the reigning title Youxia.
Emperor Yu started the Xia Dynasty,
and he was the offspring of Xuanyuan,
and successor of Emperor Shun,
He began to reign as the start of the Xia Dynasty,
and he was Jigun's son,
with his mother from Tribe Hua Shi.
Reigning exactly twenty-seven years,
Great Yu achieved a great deal as a sovereign.
Three times he was passing by his own home without entering it,
devoting himself to dredging the nine rivers and connecting the nine regions.
The names of nine regions,
are as follows:
Jizhou and Qingzhou in the east,
Yangzhou and Jingzhou in the south,
Jizhou and Liangzhou in the west,
Xuzhou and Yongzhou in the north,
Yuzhou, Henan in the center.
He had nine big tripods made to symbolize stability.
Ever since then the four seas were peaceful:

洪波汪汪向东流，
低有湖，高有丘，
造城池，作监囚，
教民稼穑五谷收。

说起大禹他出生，
看我说得真不真？
他的父亲名叫鲧，
以土掩水事不成。
天上盗息壤，
上帝发雷霆，
斩于羽山尸不烂，
后生大禹一个人。

歌师说得果是真，
禹王治水多辛勤，
疏九河来铸九鼎，
从此九州都有名。
三过其门而不入，
决汝汉，疏淮泗，
济漯处处都疏通，
引得水流归海中，
十三年来得成功，
天下无水不朝东。

四、人祖创世 IV. Human Ancestors' Inventions

vast waves flowed eastward;
lakes stayed low, while mounds stayed high;
city walls and prisons were built;
and people farmed and became educated and prosperous.

About Great Yu's birth,
let me tell the story and you tell me if I'm right.
His father's name was Gun,
and he failed to stop the water with dirt.
He then stole from heaven the soil that would grow by itself.
The Heavenly Emperor was so furious,
that he killed Gun in Mount Yu, but his corpse would not rot,
and later Great Yu was born.

The master singer was quite right.
Emperor Yu took great pain to regulate water.
He dredged nine rivers and cast nine tripods,
making the nine regions well-known.
He didn't enter his home even though passing by it three times.
Breaking up Rucha, dredging Huaisi,
he made water run into all parts of Jiluo,
and drain into the sea.
It took him thirteen years and,
in the end, all water was flowing eastward.

禹王告命涂山上,
涂山氏女化石像。
行至茂州遇大江,
黄龙负舟来朝王。
大禹仰面告上天,
黄龙叩首即回还。
渡过黄河到涂山,
天下诸侯都朝见,
黎民都乐太平年。
禹王为君真贤能,
治水疏河定乾坤。
他一饭食其身,
慰劳民间情。
外出见罪人,
下车问原因。
遇事问百姓。
左规矩,右准绳,
不失寸尺待百姓。
禹王在位二十七,
南巡诸侯至会稽,
一旦殂落归天去,
至今江山留胜迹。
禹王分下三支脉,

四、人祖创世 IV. Human Ancestors' Inventions

Emperor Yu worked in Mount Tu,
where a Tushan Shi woman turned into a marble statue.
When he arrived at Maozhou, he met with a huge river,
where a yellow dragon appeared carrying a boat for its back.
Then he looked up to thank heaven,
and the yellow dragon returned after bowing to him.
When he reached Mount Tu after crossing the Yellow River,
dukes and princes from all over the world came to pay homage to him.
Common people were all happy about the peaceful time.
Emperor Yu was truly a wise and worthy sovereign,
bringing all rivers under control.
He ate with common people,
and cared about their everyday experience.
When he saw criminals being paraded in public,
he would stop and ask about their cases.
When he had questions, he would not hesitate to ask common people.
He set up the rules and laws here and there,
and was impartial in applying them to people.
Emperor Yu reigned for twenty-seven years,
and on his way to Kuai ji during his inspection tour of the south,
he passed away.
Even today rivers and mountains bear witness to his monumental achievements.
Emperor Yu had divided the land by three great ranges,

三十六山才有名。
禹疏九河费心情，
定九州，铸九鼎，
阳寿刚刚三十零，
传与帝启掌乾坤。
帝启生太康，太康生帝相，
帝相生仲康，仲康生帝杼，
帝杼生帝槐，帝槐生帝忙。
帝忙生帝泄，帝泄生不降，
不降生帝局，帝局生帝席，
帝席生孔甲，孔甲生帝皋，
帝皋生帝发，帝发生覆发，
父传子，子传孙，
夏朝共传十七君。
禹王丁巳年间把位登，
桀王甲午年间败乾坤，
共有四百八十春。
成汤出来动刀兵，
娶妻扶都女佳人，
白气贯日照浑身，
怀胎生下太乙君，
国号成汤把位登。

四、人祖创世 IV. Human Ancestors' Inventions

and thirty-six famous mountains.
Emperor Yu devoted his life to dredging the nine rivers,
dividing the nine regions, casting the nine tripods.
He died just at the age of thirty,
and the throne was passed onto Diqi.
Diqi gave birth to Taikang, and Taikang to Dixiang.
Dixiang gave birth to Zhongkang, and Zhongkang to Dizhu.
Dizhhu gave birth to Dihuai, and Dihuai to Dimang.
Dimang gave birth to Dixie, and Dixie to Buxiang.
Buxiang gave birth to Diju, and Diju to Dixi.
Dixi gave birth to Kongjia, and Kongjia to Digao.
Digao gave birth to Difa, and Difa to Fufa.
From father to son and from son to grandson,
there were seventeen generations in the Xia Dynasty.
Emperor Yu started the reign in the year of Ding Si,
and Emperor Jie was defeated in the year of Jia Wu,
a total of four hundred and eighty years.
Later Chengtang began to assemble troops.
His father married Fudu—a beauty,
who after her entire body was shone upon by some sunny white light was pregnant,
and gave birth to Taiyi,.
The title of Taiyi's reign was Chengtang, given when he became emperor.

提起成汤出世根,
姓子名履是他名,
他是子契十二代孙。
传至主癸生成汤,
扫灭夏朝定家邦。
乙未年间坐江山,
在位坐了三十年,
阳寿一百染黄泉。
汤亡伊尹摄朝贤,
扶住外丙把位权。
成汤传位与外丙,
外丙传仲壬,
仲壬传位太甲登。
长子金天名少昊,
颛顼高阳氏,
帝喾高辛四代交。
简狄吞燕卵,
生契成汤苗,
伊祁放勋号唐尧,
长子丹朱又不肖,
废子立贤古今少……

四、人祖创世 IV. Human Ancestors' Inventions

About Chengtang,

his name was Zilv,

the twelfth generation of Ziqi.

The lineage reached father Zhugui,

and then he was born to wipe out the Xia Dynasty.

He began to reign in the year of Yi Wei,

reigned for thirty years,

and passed away.

After Chengtang's death, Yiyin acted as the regent,

assisting Waibing to reign.

Chengtang passed the power to Waibing;

Waibing to Zhongren;

Zhongren to Taijia.

The Emperor Xuanyuan's first son was Shaohao,

and he then passed the power to Zhuanxu from Tribe Gaoyang Shi,

and then to Diku Gaoxin, the fourth generation.

After Jiandi swallowed a swallow's egg,

she gave birth to Qi, who was Chengtang's ancestor.

Yiqi's title was Fangxun, Tangyao,

but his first son Zhudan was unworthy.

So he passed the power not to his son but to the worthier, a rare act in history.

诗曰：黑暗混沌无史记，
盘古开天又辟地，
才有日月照九州。
三皇五帝夏商周，
战国归秦及汉流，
司马梁晋隋唐主，
五代宋元大明休。
古今多少兴亡事，
留与后人度春秋。
古今多少英雄事，
争夺江山把名留。
平民百姓讲出口，
拿在歌场唱根由。

四、人祖创世 IV. Human Ancestors' Inventions

The Poem says: Darkness and chaos have no history.
Pangu separated heaven and earth,
and then appeared the sun and the moon to shine upon the world.
Three Sovereigns and Five Emperors preceded the Xia, Shang and Zhou Dynasties,
followed by the Warring States, the Qin Dynasty, and then the Han Dynasty.
There were then Liang, Jin, Sui and Tang Dynasties,
the Five Dynasties and Ten Kingdoms Period, Song, Yuan, and Ming Dynasties.
There was so much rise and fall,
left for later generation to ponder upon.
There were so many heroes,
famous for striving for the throne.
Common people talk about all of these,
and the Song Houses are where they sing about their stories.

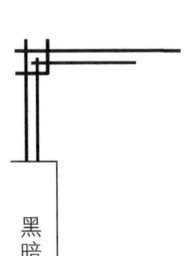

歌　尾

还阳歌（仪式歌舞）
诵词
日吉时良，天地开张，
日出东方，赫赫洋洋！
黑暗混沌，日月开光。
古往今来，厚土之葬。
扫场，扫场，化为吉昌！

锣鼓打出一重门，一重门，
一重门来迎东方。
还阳童子，接引仙女，作鼓乐，
骑青马打青旗，打一把清凉伞，
遮天盖地，奏宫音，撒梅花，
愿主东，家业兴，普降祯祥。

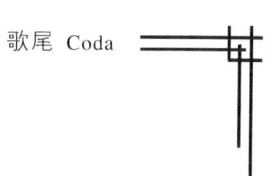

Coda

Song of Returning to Life (Ritual Dance)
Singing-Recite Lyrics
An auspicious time and day are good for activities of heaven and earth.
Rising from the east, the sun is shining brightly.
After the dark chaos, the sun and the moon gave forth light.
Throughout the ages, people have been buried with solemn ceremonies.
Sweep the field and sweep again; good luck is coming!

Hit the gong and the drum out of the first layer of door,
the first layer of door that greet the sun from the east.
Children returning to life and fairies are playing the instruments,
each riding a green horse, lifting a green flag and holding a refreshing umbrella.
Covering up, playing palace music, casting plum blossoms,
wish the host prosperity and propitiousness!